I0773264

Christmas *in* Focus

PRAISE FOR LINDSAY GIBSON

"Gibson's romance is as bright and sparkling as the ruby ring at the center of the painting ... A charming romance that's as warm and cozy as hot chocolate on a winter's day."*–**Kirkus Reviews*** on *The Christmas Promise*

"Lindsay writes the type of stories that will stay with you and have you reaching for your loved ones."*–**USA Today** **Best-selling Author Jenny Hale***

"This new author is automatically a favorite."*–**Page-Turners Reviews***

"...an engaging story and a sweet romance with a dollop of mystery."*–**Book Banter Café*** on *The Christmas Promise*

"A truly lovely story that gently unfolds..."*–**Splashes into Books*** on *The Christmas Promise*

Included in "That Artsy Reader Girl's 2023 Christmas Romances"*–**thatartsyreadergirl.com***

Included in "Over 50 Must Read Kindle Unlimited Christmas Romance Books"*–**everydayeyecandy.com***

"This is a book I 100% recommend to those who are looking for a cute, cozy, small-town Christmas romance novel..."*—**LizNReads*** on *Christmas in Focus*

"I loved everything about this story and I highly recommend it."—***Page-Turners Reviews*** on *Christmas in Focus*

"...a wonderful edition to a reader's Christmas collection of stories."—***Escape to Books*** on *The Christmas Coin*

Christmas *in* Focus

LINDSAY GIBSON

HARPETH ROAD
PRESS
Nashville

HARPETH ROAD PRESS

Published by Harpeth Road Press (USA)
P.O. Box 158184
Nashville, TN 37215

Paperback: 978-1-963483-32-1
eBook: 978-1-963483-31-4
Library of Congress Control Number: 2025947607

Christmas in Focus: An Uplifting Holiday Romance

Copyright © Lindsay Gibson, 2025

All rights reserved. Except for the use of brief quotations in review of this novel, the reproduction of this work in whole or in part in any format by any electronic, mechanical, or other means, now known or hereinafter invented, including photocopying, recording, scanning, and all other formats, or in any information storage or retrieval or distribution system, is forbidden without the written permission of the publisher, Harpeth Road Press, P.O. Box 158184, Nashville, Tennessee 37215, USA.

This is a work of fiction. Names, characters, places, and incidents are the product of the author's imagination or were used fictitiously, and any resemblance to actual persons, living or dead, business establishments, events, or locales is entirely coincidental.

Cover Design by Vanessa Mendozzi
Cover Images © Shutterstock

Harpeth Road Press, October 2025

BOOKS BY LINDSAY GIBSON

The Christmas Promise

Fly Away Summer

The Christmas Coin

Where It All Began

To my mom, who always believed in my writing from the beginning as a little girl—guiding me through the twists and turns of life's mountainous journey as I grew. And still does.

PROLOGUE
ALPINE RIDGE, VERMONT

December 3, 1804
Annie

The December air was crisp, carrying whispers of late autumn's final breath as Annie Foster hauled her basket of squash from the root cellar. The sun had begun its descent, lowering over Alpine Mountain and casting a soft glow over the fields. Annie shivered in the breeze and caught the scent of chestnuts from the smoke drifting lazily from the chimney. Her family would host a joyous celebration the following day, giving thanks for another bountiful harvest and welcoming the winter that would begin any day now—turning the farm into a canvas of white for months.

As Annie walked toward the farmhouse, her husband, Earl, came into view, trotting down the road on his horse. He'd been out most of the day with a few other men from the village on a wild turkey fowling—and he didn't look empty-handed. Turkey stew would be plentiful for the weeks to come.

Annie paused at the door and waited for him to dismount

and settle the horse in the barn. When he reappeared with a proud smile and held up the meat, gratitude filled her for his continued strength to hunt and farm and for the warm hearth inside their house with its large fire to keep them and their four children well-fed.

"A successful hunt I see." Annie beamed up at him.

"Very much so," Earl said, gripping two birds. "I better go dress these and hang them with the others." He retreated to the barn to attend to the birds.

The sound of wagon wheels caught Annie's attention. This time when she turned toward the road, she saw her neighbor, Abigail Martin, approaching, accompanied by townsman Samuel Thayer. Annie slowly drew in some of the cool air before forcing a smile and stepping out to greet them. They pulled up in front of the farmhouse, and Samuel helped Abigail down, a covered basket hanging on her arm.

"Mother?" Annie's oldest son, Leo, appeared behind her, pushing the door open. He had grown tall that summer despite being only seven years of age. "Who is here?"

"It's just our neighbor, Mrs. Martin. Go back inside where it's warm and I'll be right in."

"I hope they aren't here to begin another argument." The boy looked up at her with worry in his gaze.

"Don't you be concerned with that. Now go on inside," Annie said firmly, even though she shared her son's worry.

She and Earl held a troubled history with Abigail Martin and her late husband, John. When their town of Alpine Ridge, Vermont, had been founded a little over ten years earlier, the property line between their parcels of land had been unclear, and tension between the two families had started brewing right from the beginning—that had never fully resolved. The disagreement had quickly escalated into a full debate at a town meeting a couple years back after Earl had begun to replace the old log cabin with their two-story cottage.

He'd been determined to clear out more land going up the mountain for his farm but couldn't until the debate had been settled legally.

For Annie, the new development had turned what had been a tense-but-still-polite situation between neighbors into a deeper breach and tainted the once strong relationship she'd had with Abigail. She'd hoped things would go back to normal once the town settled the two-page map showing the property line that extended the Martin's farm into the mountain, currently marked only by a rock wall near a large stream—an extension Earl hadn't wanted. Annie had urged him to accept the ruling for the sake of peace in the community, but her husband continued to protest that his family rightfully owned the mountain all the way around the stream.

Sadly, there hadn't been a chance to truly mend fences with the Martins. John had fallen gravely ill with dysentery and passed away right before the final hearing the previous spring, leaving Abigail widowed with their firstborn daughter. Despite the rift, Annie had done what she could to be there for mother and child following their loss, but Earl—still resentful—hadn't always made that easy. She'd ignored his bitterness and had managed to somewhat make amends with Abigail. But it was a tentative peace.

Now her husband emerged from the barn with a solemn expression directed at their visitors, and her stomach sank. *Please*, Annie prayed silently, *let their visit be brief.*

"Abigail, good day to you." Earl nodded toward the woman as he approached, eyeing Samuel.

"Earl, how are things?" Samuel walked over and shook Earl's hand.

"Can't complain. Looking forward to our feast tomorrow to usher in a great harvest. How about yourselves?"

"It was a good year for Abigail, and me as well."

Earl slowly studied them. "A harvest together?"

Samuel smiled at Abigail. "That's right." He stood closer to her. "I asked for Abigail's hand, and she has accepted. Reverend Cooper will be conducting the ceremony tomorrow morning. We came to inform you ourselves and to offer this basket of apples to add to your winter food provisions. Let's start the new year on better terms, shall we?"

"Of course, Samuel," Annie said quickly and took the basket from Abigail. She cast a warning glance at her husband before returning her attention to their neighbor. "That is very kind of you. And congratulations on your nuptials."

Abigail smiled at her, seemingly relieved. "Thank you."

"Earl, we also came over so I could address a few things with you. Just some specifics with the land," Samuel said. "Is that alright?"

"I suppose," Earl said.

"I'll be taking over as head of Abigail's farm," Samuel said slowly. "I noticed a few things with the revised map that I'd like to clear up to avoid another public debate."

"Alright." Earl gestured toward the house. "Ladies, carry on inside by the fire while Samuel and I discuss this business." He waved for Samuel to follow him. "Won't you join me in the barn? I'd take you to my study, but I was just getting to this morning's hunt."

"The barn is quite alright."

"Don't be long." The words slipped out before Annie could stop herself.

Earl glanced at her. "Yes, dear . . ." he said, the annoyance on his face clear. "We won't be."

Annie pondered her husband's hesitation, frowning as she watched the men walk away. Why couldn't this issue just be put to rest? She turned back to Abigail who was also staring after them.

"How's that sweet baby of yours doing?" Annie asked.

"She's growing fast and doing well. My mother is keeping her at the moment." Abigail looked at the house.

"Come on now, let's have some tea. Hopefully my little ones won't be too loud while you have this short break." Annie put her arm around Abigail and led her inside. As she closed the door, she peeked at the men walking into the barn and couldn't help but worry about the conversation playing out between them.

———

When Annie finally got her children down for the night, she headed toward the parlor and found her husband leaning over a stack of papers at his writing table.

"Is there anything I can get you, darling?"

Earl popped his head up, a guilty expression on his face. "Annie, I didn't hear you come in."

"Am I disturbing something?

"No, not at all. I was just absorbed in this land deed, reading everything over once more before I store it in the chest up in the attic for safekeeping," he said. He quickly shuffled the papers on his desk, folded them, and stuffed them into an envelope before she could see what they said.

"I trust everything is alright with Samuel then."

"It is."

"I see . . ." She paused against his still contrite expression and short answer. "Well, is there anything I can get you?"

"A hard cider sounds nice."

"Of course, I'll be right back."

He was behaving rather suspiciously, but she didn't dare question her husband. She could only hope that he and Samuel Thayer had settled everything peacefully and everyone could move forward. Nevertheless, she couldn't shake the sudden unease she felt.

"I'll meet you back down here." Earl stood and took the papers upstairs.

When Annie returned with his drink, they sat by the fire and enjoyed their quiet reflections on the blessings of the harvest and the promise of the coming year.

Later, before joining her husband in the chamber above, she thought she could make out snowflakes falling beyond the window. Curious, she stepped outside and, sure enough, the first snow was coming down from the blackened sky. Winter had arrived. Something about the first snow ignited a feeling of comfort as she prepared for the long nights ahead with the people she loved.

Annie picked up the last candle and made her way to the stairs as she thought about Abigail. Knowing Samuel would take care of her neighbor brought some relief, but not from the uncertainty that their property dispute had been fully resolved. Perhaps Earl's nervous response had just been due to the lingering frustration over the years-long land debate that had yielded an unfavorable outcome for him. Regardless, everyone was in good health, and the new year would be a wonderful one for all.

Chapter One

Present Day

"Thanks for seeing me today," Millie Rowan said with a nervous smile as she took a seat in the small conference room, white-knuckling the portfolio in her right hand. "I'm really excited about this opportunity."

Really desperate for this opportunity would be more accurate, she almost said out loud, but pursed her lips shut. She wanted the general manager, Chris, and head of marketing, Hannah, at the Harbor & Marina Resort in Charleston, South Carolina, to think she was put together and professional—not sweaty and anxious over whether this could, at long last, be the job that let her actually make a living as a photographer.

She'd spent years working toward this—building her portfolio, earning a certificate in digital photography online, and working odd jobs to get by. Photography spoke to her in a way nothing else did, and even though her parents had always told her it was nothing more than a pipe dream, she didn't agree. She had been sure it was the right path for her and that she'd be able to land a stable job. But these days, she had started to question herself.

Six years had seemed to slip by since graduating high school and she still hadn't been able to support herself with her passion. Maybe she'd jumped in too quickly without a backup plan, but something had to give . . . and soon. She'd failed to get the job capturing images of food for a restaurant in downtown Charleston and the one assisting a popular photographer of newborns, and she was losing her once confident outlook. No one seemed to want to give her a chance, and she nearly had given up—until this position fell in her lap.

The Harbor & Marina Resort was looking for a new hospitality photographer to showcase the resort's unique atmosphere on their website, at public relations events, and on social media. Her sister, Lila, had pulled some strings to get the interview for her, and Millie had regained her optimism about finding her dream job. Hannah was a friend of Lila's from college, and Millie crossed her fingers that that would give her an edge in the interview. And now, as she handed them the portfolio, here it was: the moment of truth.

While they both looked through it, Millie waited for the questions to begin, expecting them to ask about the images they saw.

"Very nice," Chris, a tall older man with a deep, loud voice said.

Millie smiled, thinking he'd point to a few he liked, but he shut the portfolio and slid it across the table toward her. They hadn't even looked through all the photographs. Her binder was filled with candid photos of people in public, nature, and everyday life around Charleston. Weren't they looking for something similar for the resort?

"I agree," Hannah said. She was a petite woman, similar to Millie's build, making her a little less intimidating. "It's amazing how many different shots you seemed to get around one small city. Have you taken photos anywhere else besides Charleston?"

No, because I haven't been able to afford to travel outside of South Carolina.

Millie's mouth compressed into a tight line as she struggled to contain her intrusive thoughts and shook her head. "Only Charleston, but I would love to have the opportunity to do that someday." Travel photography had always been a dream of hers.

"I see," the woman said, giving Millie a small smile. "And based on your résumé, it appears this would be your first official job as a photographer. Is that right?"

"Yes. I have only freelanced until now, building my portfolio." Millie looked between both managers, her composure beginning to falter. They didn't seem impressed with her.

Chris leaned back in his chair. "This resort is still relatively new. We opened our doors in 2016 and, while we have done well so far, we would like to really kick up our marketing efforts. The hospitality industry is highly competitive, as you can probably imagine."

Millie nodded and waited for him to continue, even though she could already guess where he was going with his statement.

"We are really looking for someone who has more professional experience."

Millie bit back her grimace. There was nothing worse than being told you needed to already *have* experience in order to get a job that was supposed to *give* you experience.

"As you can see," she said, holding on to her calm, "I'm able to produce photos to a professional standard."

"Yes, but without a track record," Hannah slowly said, smiling briefly before continuing, "we can't be certain how you handle deadlines. Whether you're receptive to feedback. Whether you can tailor your work to align with the marketing group's strategy." The woman's tone was gentle—maybe even kind—but the words still felt like a slap in the face. They wanted someone who had already proven themselves professionally . . . and that wasn't her.

"I've listed my teachers in my certification program as references," Millie pointed out weakly.

"But an academic environment isn't quite the same thing, is it?" Chris said. "Besides, hospitality is a highly personal experience for our guests, so we need someone who has worked with others in a setting such as this and is able to bring what we have *to* them, before they even make the reservation. That starts with social media. For example, documenting spontaneous moments with people enjoying their meals in our restaurant. Connection and communication within an environment like this, while capturing those photos, requires experience as well."

"The candid photos I have here display my ability to do that." Millie felt her face heat up with frustration. Just because she hadn't had a photography job within a group setting didn't mean she couldn't connect with people. She had been working as a waitress for years, giving her plenty of experience with customers, but judging by what they'd said so far—that wouldn't help her case. "Or at least, that was my intention."

"Your talent is visible," Hannah quickly said. "Just like Lila informed us. Please keep us on your list to contact. If you gain a little more experience, you can apply again. We could always use more talent on our marketing team with photography."

Millie managed to hold in the tears as she shook their hands and thanked them for their time. She left the office and got on her bike, then headed straight to the beach to collect herself. She pedaled fast, hardly noticing the burning in her thighs against the tears threatening to fall any moment. It was the day before Thanksgiving, yet balmy air still engulfed South

Carolina, causing beads of sweat to build along her brow. The November wind whipped past her, and the breeze under the gray clouds helped keep her breath steady.

Contrasting with the frantic pace of her heart, her long, curly dark brown hair remained secured in a braid down her back while she took a swift turn into the public beach access and slowed. She found a rack to lock her bike on, then kicked off her black flats and walked down to the ocean holding them, letting her toes sink into the sand.

She looked around, and relief poured into her when she saw no one was nearby. She sank onto the sand. A large wave spilled onto the beach, the water rushing closer to her, and Millie finally let herself cry, embarrassment burning all over her face. She had thought they were open to giving her a chance, but it was clear they'd only met with her because of Lila.

Sitting next to the water, buried under a mountain of frustration, she didn't know where to turn. Should she give up this dream? Never mind what her parents would say if they knew she'd received yet another rejection.

A ding from her purse strapped across her chest caught her attention, and through her tears, she read a message from Lila.

> Hey! Stuck at the hospital with lots of babies being born. Must be a full moon coming tonight! I can't wait to hear all about your interview. Jake is doing a shift overnight at the ER in case you're wondering where he is too. There's left over pizza in the fridge if you're hungry.
> Love you!

Millie closed her eyes. *Nope, I can't give up. I can't stay living with Jake and Lila forever.* She had no idea how she'd achieve that without a stable job, but one thing she knew was that she couldn't go on as she had been for the past six years. It wasn't sustainable to keep doing part-time, make-ends-meet jobs in between trying to get her career going. Not if she wanted to earn enough to finally move out on her own. As much as she loved Lila, Millie felt as if she'd never be able to find her true self until she was away from the constant example of her perfect sister with her perfect job as an ob-gyn and her perfect emergency room doctor fiancé.

As Millie tucked her phone back in her bag, she gazed blankly into the distance. The golden glow of the setting sun over the blue Atlantic, a usual harbinger of comfort, was lost on her. She stayed on the beach for a while longer, trying to draw peace and solace from watching the waves roll in. But nothing could lift her mood when her future seemed so bleak. Finally, after a half hour more of self-pity, she stood up and trudged back to her bike to make her way home.

Luckily, the ride to Lila's from the beach was only a few blocks, and after Millie stored her bike in the garage, she stepped inside to instant holiday cheer. The chic Christmas décor matched the fancy apartment, with gold and silver glass trees of various heights placed along the sofa table and small, white-flocked wreaths with tiny gold baubles hanging from the windows. A matching artificial Christmas tree was out of the box and set up just ahead in the living room, its twinkling lights illuminating the darkness. After flicking on the front hall lights, followed by a lamp in the living room, Millie noticed more holiday decorations laid out, not yet put in place. A note was waiting for her on a table.

Millie, as you can see, I started to get this place into Christmas cheer! But then I got called into the delivery room. We can all tackle

*the rest of the decorations tomorrow after
Thanksgiving dinner at Mom and Dad's! XO*

The thought of Thanksgiving with her parents made Millie shudder. It was going to be another excruciating round of Mom and Dad reciting all the ways in which Lila was a success while Millie was, in her parents' eyes, a failure. She knew her sister and Jake worked hard to have all they did, but living in their apartment only brought out a familiar pressure she thought she'd left behind when she'd graduated high school six years prior and moved out of her parents' house—and the suffocating weight of an entire upbringing trying to please them and keep up with Lila.

With a sigh, she headed to the bathroom and turned on the bath, then added some lavender bubble bath. She stared in the mirror at her reflection, noticing wisps of her dark curls had fallen out of her braid and were sticking out in every direction.

"*Millie . . .*" her mother always used to say when she was young, "*since you don't have Lila's nice straight hair, you at least need to comb it better.*" Even her hair was wrong . . .

She pulled out her hair tie, shook the braid loose, then retwisted and secured her curly locks up high and sat with her phone, scrolling through social media while waiting on the large tub to fill. Just before she clicked off her phone, a post from an old friend caught her

*Attention photographers! The ski resort I work for is looking
for a photographer for a special assignment next month. See
the ad below and contact me if you're interested.*

Ashley Fraser, whom Millie had waitressed with at the Wharf House, a restaurant downtown near the water for almost four years, had moved back to her home state, Vermont, the year before, after graduating from the College of Charleston. She'd been offered a marketing position at a resort near the town where she'd grown up. Aside from a few social media interactions and texts, they had mostly lost touch. Curious, Millie clicked on the post and read the details.

Urgently seeking a talented photographer to capture marketing images for us during this holiday season. If you are not local, please still apply! We will accommodate a month of housing, food, and travel expenses if you are the right fit!

Millie couldn't believe it. Just when she had no answers, a possible one had presented itself. It sounded almost too perfect to be real. She started to type a message to Ashley, then hesitated. She thought back to all the rejections she'd gotten—telling her she wasn't experienced enough, wasn't skilled enough, didn't connect with her subjects enough. If she tried for this, would she be setting herself up for another rejection? But if she *didn't* try for it, would that mean she was giving up on her dream?

Maybe she'd have her bath first to think it through. After sliding into the hot bubbles, she leaned back and closed her eyes, hoping to relax. But the interview earlier that day replayed in her mind. Chris and Hannah's facial reactions as they'd hastily looked through her portfolio had initially seemed impressed, but the more she thought it through, the more she interpreted them as annoyed. Sure, they'd complimented her, but had they meant it or had they simply been trying to be polite because of their connection to Lila?

Millie had always been meticulous in her work, but she could see why it appeared to just be a hobby from their perspective. Despite her parents' dismay when she'd traded in a full bachelor's degree in photography for a certificate instead, she'd always thought she would eventually narrow down her specialty in order to start a business in it. She hadn't thought she'd needed a degree to do that. Now, while soaking in a tub in her sister's apartment, she wondered if her parents were right.

As the years passed, the many excuses as to why one area of photography or another wouldn't be successful had kept her at a standstill. All she had wanted was to make her family proud. Waiting too long and trying to carefully plan had only worried them more, and now she was in a panic trying to interview for any and every photography position she could—and living with her sister.

She thought about Ashley's post again and decided to go for it. The worst that could happen would be her friend turning her down, which would be nothing new for her anyway. Sitting up, she reached for the towel on a chair near the tub and dried her hands, then picked up her phone and pulled up Ashley's name.

> Hi! I just saw your post on social media that your ski resort is looking for a photographer. I know it's been a while since we've caught up with each other, but I have been working hard on my skills and portfolio and would be happy to talk about the job. Hope you're doing well up there in Vermont!

Now she just had to wait.

CHAPTER TWO

The overcast sky and cooler temperature the next morning made even Lila's beachy home feel "Thanksgivingy." The apartment was quiet when Millie opened her bedroom door. Lila's door was shut, which meant she and Jake were both back after their long overnight shifts and would sleep until at least noon.

After turning on the coffee pot in the kitchen, Millie leaned over the breakfast bar to wait while it brewed, mentally preparing herself for the day ahead. Their parents lived about an hour away in Moncks Corner in the house where she and Lila had grown up along the bank of Lake Moultrie. They were expecting Millie, Lila, and Jake early this afternoon for Thanksgiving dinner, which would mean a fast dash out the door once her sister and Jake woke. Lila had to be back to see patients in her office on Friday morning, so it would be a quick trip up and back—just what Millie preferred. Neither sister was well-versed in cooking, so they'd picked up a pie from the bakery the day before to take with them.

Millie carried her mug of fresh, hot coffee out to the small balcony off the living room and watched a few birds fly across the marsh below. She hadn't checked her phone yet, but she hoped Ashley would get back to her soon, even with the holiday. Thinking about the job at the ski resort had her wondering if the feeling in her stomach was excitement about the possibility of getting the role or worry it would be another disappointment. She really wanted this break.

The birds made their way through the air again as she sipped the hot liquid that awakened her senses.

"Oystercatchers," a male voice behind said after the sliding door suddenly opened, startling her. Jake waved good morning. "I learned from one of our neighbors that those marsh birds are called oystercatchers. I don't know anything else about them besides that."

Millie smiled. "I would imagine not since most of your time is spent indoors under fluorescent lights saving people's lives."

"True. But it's nice to watch them and whatever else flies around down there. Any coffee left?"

"Yup. Just brewed a full pot."

Jake went back inside and returned with a mug, and they enjoyed the scenery for a minute in silence.

"It finally feels like fall out here. It's been extra warm this season," Jake said.

"Yeah. I'm ready for the heat to die down and for winter to come." Millie turned to him. "You're up early after an overnight shift."

"I got back around five and knocked right out, but it was a crazy night, and I just couldn't sleep much. A family came in from a bad car accident, and when I see kids hurt like that, it's impossible to calm my brain down."

"I can't imagine seeing all you do in that emergency room." Millie brought the mug to her lips. "I saw that Lila started decorating."

"That she did. She didn't want it to happen at the last minute again." Jake chuckled.

"I remember." Millie grinned. Her sister had been determined to watch holiday movies next to twinkling lights, but her patients had seemed to all go into labor at once last December and the decorations hadn't been thrown up until a few days before Christmas. "You two work so hard, though, so give yourselves a break."

"That's what I told her, but she said she wanted to make it feel festive for you all month long this year."

"Well, I'm sure my parents will have their house decorated to the max, so we can all bask in the Christmas spirit today."

Jake nodded. "Yep. It'll be full-on Christmas over there." He hesitated, tapping his mug. "You ready to see them?"

Millie appreciated how sensitive he was to her parents' judgmental ways with her. Early on in his relationship with Lila, he'd come for his first family dinner at their house and later said something to Millie about the difference in their tones with her versus Lila.

"No." Millie exhaled and looked at Jake. "I was waiting for Lila to get up, but I might as well let you know that yesterday's interview was a flop . . . again."

Jake straightened from the railing they were both leaning on and patted her shoulder. "Keep your head up. Something will land for you. You have talent and passion behind that camera, but photography isn't cut-and-dried like other professions. Creatives often have to take a windy road to get where they want to be, but I know you can do it."

"Thanks, Jake. Your support means a lot. I wish my parents saw it that way."

"Saw what?" Lila's voice came from the sliding door.

"You're up early too," Millie said.

"It's Thanksgiving. I dreamed about turkey and mashed

potatoes, and that got me up. I missed all the food last year since I was on call, and now I can't wait."

"Me either," Jake added. "It's rare we're both off call, so I'm going to enjoy the time—and stuff myself with everything your parents serve." He gave Millie another squeeze on her shoulder before heading back inside. "I'm going to go shower."

Lila took his place next to Millie. "I'm assuming y'all were talking about Mom and Dad?"

"Yeah . . ." Millie looked down at her hands gripping her now-empty mug. "And the fact that yesterday's interview didn't go well. They said I'm not qualified because of my lack of experience."

"I see." Lila grew quiet for a moment. "I'm sorry that happened. I was hoping they would see how smart and talented you are and give you a chance."

"Me too. But they did say I could contact them if I gained a little more experience."

"Then the door isn't fully shut, so that's great! Now we just need to figure out how to get you some experience."

"Actually, a new opportunity may have popped up last night." Millie watched the oystercatchers soaring back in the other direction before meeting her sister's stare. "Remember my friend Ashley from the Wharf House?"

"Yes. She moved to Vermont, right?"

"Last year," Millie answered. "She posted yesterday about an immediate opening at the ski resort she works for. They're looking for a photographer to capture some marketing materials for them."

"You mean up in Vermont?"

"That's right. They said they're urgently looking and would pay for accommodations, food, and travel costs for a month."

"Wow. Vermont, huh? Pretty cold up there." Lila turned

around and leaned both her arms on the railing in thought. "But you know what? I think it sounds amazing."

"You do? I mean, I'd be honored to have the opportunity, but I'm trying not to get ahead of myself."

"Yes, I do. It's perfect. And just the right opening to gain some experience. Even though it's temporary, it'll be long enough to gain some valuable skills with a marketing team." Lila's face lit up the more she thought about it. "Did you apply?"

"I reached out to Ashley. Let's see what happens when she gets back to me."

"Crossing my fingers!" Her sister put her arm around her. "Now, let's go eat some Thanksgiving food and deal with Mom and Dad for a few hours. I won't let them tear into you today over yesterday's interview."

Millie shrugged. "They can ask. I'm expecting that. But let's keep this possibility in Vermont quiet unless it becomes a reality."

"Agreed."

The two women went inside to get ready. As Millie clipped back her curls and applied a little makeup, she gave herself a pep talk to keep her patience with her parents. She was in no mood to argue with them about her career again and decided to brush off any negative comments. Since the temperature was lower, she put on her lightweight tan maxi dress with flared sleeves and a belt for the occasion. She was feeling a little stronger since the tears that had overtaken her on the beach the day before.

She was about to slip her phone into her purse when she saw a text from Ashley. A thrill of anticipation surged as she opened the message.

> Millie! So good to hear from you and yes!
> Let's talk! I can't believe I didn't think of you
> before! I know it's Thanksgiving, but we
> need someone to get here by Saturday. I
> hope that would be okay? Would it be
> alright to talk this afternoon around 4:30?

Millie reread the message a few more times. She couldn't believe it. Ashley was talking as if she had a real shot at the job.

> Yes, we can talk then. Travel is no issue for
> me. Talk soon!

Lila was putting on her shoes by the front door, and Millie nearly collided with her as she rushed up.

"Ashley is excited to talk to me about the job later today!" Her heart raced as she thought about the possibility of having her first real professional photography job in two days' time. But, suddenly, reality slammed into her excitement and worry crept in. Could she do this?

Lila drew her brows together. "That's great! Wait, what's wrong? Your face just fell."

"I can't believe this might be a real possibility is all. I've never done something like this before, and it's in Vermont."

"You've always talked about traveling as a photographer one day," Lila reminded her. "Well, here we are."

"Here we are," Millie repeated, staring off.

"Talk to Ashley first and go from there. One step at a time."

"You're right. Okay. It's turkey time."

Millie sat in the back of the car, trying to zone out of the holiday music Lila turned up, her head spinning with ideas about what kinds of images would portray the vibe of a ski resort—besides skiing itself. She'd never been to Vermont and had no idea what kind of scenery she'd be working with, outside of snow, which she'd never seen in real life let alone taken pictures of. She pulled out her phone and found the resort's website, then scrolled through their pictures, taking in the rolling hills blanketed in white, the stunning mountain peaks in the background, and all the smiling faces of people dressed in thick winter gear and ready for a day of skiing fun. It was a whole new world up there. She'd need to get creative since this would be the complete opposite setting from what she was used to in the South.

Relax. She forced herself to put her phone back in her purse, then closed her eyes for the rest of the ride. Lila was right: She just had to take one step at a time.

When they pulled up to her parents' house, Millie's defenses immediately poked at her. Lila squeezed her hand as they walked to the front porch. Staring at the oversized Christmas wreath on the door, Millie paused behind her sister and Jake as they went inside. Getting out of South Carolina might do her some good.

THE LARGE PATIO THAT HELD THE PERFECT VIEW OF Lake Moultrie behind her parents' home displayed the same holiday vibe as inside. The pavilion was wrapped in garland with twinkle lights cascading in all directions. The base of the stone firepit just ahead of Millie had greenery wrapped around it, and each white Adirondack chair held a small red pillow. The outdoor brick gas fireplace even had a wreath secured at the top and two small trees on each side.

"Well, isn't this cozy?" Lila walked up behind her and handed her a glass of wine.

"Yeah, it is, and the patio came out so nice." Last summer, their parents had mentioned the impending remodel, but this was impressive. "I could sit out here for hours watching the lake."

"Then let's sit and watch." Lila put down her glass and went over to turn on the fireplace.

Millie chose a chair closest to the fire and sat before taking a sip of her wine. The twinkling lights sparkled above them under the gray clouds of the late afternoon. Her parents had served a feast for just the five of them, and she could barely take a deep breath she was so full. Luckily, the conversation had been light and easy, with her parents more interested in hearing about Lila's and Jake's work in the hospital, which had opened a whole medical discussion Millie couldn't follow.

"Here you two are," her mom said as she closed the sliding door behind her and joined them with the bottle and an empty wineglass. "The men are discussing golf. Too boring for me."

"The turkey came out perfect, Mom," Millie said, rubbing her stomach. "Everything was so good."

"Thank you. I tried a new herb and butter seasoning this year. Glad it worked out." Mom poured herself some wine and sat back in her chair. "So, Millie, we didn't get to discuss you much at dinner. All that medical talk." She waved her hand with a smile. "But that's to be expected in this family." Millie's father was a retired pediatric surgeon who still loved talking about his field. Her mom, a nurse, still worked part-time at the local elementary school. "How have the interviews been going? Didn't you have one scheduled this week?"

"I did, yes." Her answer danced around what her mom really wanted to know, but Millie had learned that the more information she offered, the more critical her parents became. She picked up her phone and saw it was a few minutes until she was supposed to talk to Ashley. "Actually, if you'll excuse me. I have someone I need to talk to right now."

"Work related?" Her mom raised her brows.

"Yes. I'll be back in a little while." Keeping the details to herself, Millie stood and took her wine with her. Even though she hadn't planned on mentioning her conversation with Ashley, it was a little fun to leave her mom guessing.

She headed upstairs and opened the door to her childhood bedroom, then paused. Her parents had changed hers and Lila's rooms into guest bedrooms, and Millie noticed her mom had changed the décor in the room once again since the last time she'd visited. Looking around, she remembered it had taken them a lot longer to change her sister's room, while her bedroom had transformed only a year after graduation when she'd moved into Lila's apartment—as though they couldn't have waited any longer. Or maybe that was only in her head. She was sensitive about anything to do with her parents.

She walked over to her old desk in the corner of the room and opened the top drawer. Photos of the lake from her senior project sat in an album—along with pictures of all the kids in her class that she'd take from afar. Turning the pages of the album, she saw a picture of her and Lila at her graduation, their arms around each other as they laughed. The determined passion in her eyes instantly reminded Millie of the dreams that had driven her then, now lost in the silence of unfulfilled ambitions. Where had she gone wrong since that photo?

Her phone lit up in front of her on the desk, and she quickly answered. "Hi, Ashley!"

"Millie! My goodness, it has been some time since I heard your voice. It's so great to talk to you."

"Same. I can't believe we let ourselves go months without speaking."

"I guess we're both just busy with our careers."

Millie winced. *Or not so busy* . . . "Yes, that must be it." She chewed her lip, playing along, thankful Ashley couldn't see how embarrassed she felt. She'd probably have no chance at this job if Ashley knew her photography had not amounted to much yet.

"How has your Thanksgiving been?" Ashley asked.

"Good. My parents cooked way too much. How are things going for you?"

"I'm sure it was delicious. And things are good up here. We had a huge snowstorm two days ago, which is a tad early, but it'll make for a great season."

"Season? You mean winter?"

Ashley laughed. "I forgot you're down in low country. I'm kind of jealous since it's so cold up here already. I meant ski season."

"Oh, right, of course." Millie's cheeks burned. Was she flubbing this? "Well, it sounds magical, especially for this time of year."

"Glad you think so. It'll make the temperature shock a little less intense for you."

Millie hesitated. Did that mean she was getting the job? "I'll just have to buy more sweaters before I come," she said slowly, then held her breath.

"You'll need a lot more than sweaters!" Ashley's giggle was infectious, reminding Millie of the nights they'd close the restaurant together and would constantly joke around. "So let me run the assignment by you, the quick version."

"I'm listening."

Millie stayed quiet as Ashley filled her in.

"We're in a rush to replace the photographer we hired since she had to suddenly leave for a family emergency last week," her friend explained. "And we can't wait for her to return because we're meeting with potential buyers soon and need fresh new photos to capture the essence of both the resort and town for the presentation."

"Is the resort privately owned now?"

"Yes. It's been run by the Clarke family since it opened in the winter of 1940. We only found out recently about them wanting to sell. It hasn't even been listed yet."

"And there are already interested buyers?" Millie asked.

"That's right. It's all happening so fast."

"Who are the buyers?"

"A corporation out of Colorado that just purchased Mount Snow and Okemo Mountain. They now have their sights set on acquiring a couple more resorts in the area, including ours. Hopefully. Our mountain is smaller, but I feel they will fall in love with Alpine Ridge if we angle the presentation and photos in the perfect way. That's why your job will be so important."

Millie swallowed against the pressure. The sale would boil down to her photos and how well she could document a town and resort she'd never been to.

"They gave the resort a deadline of a little over two weeks to prepare the pitch," Ashley said.

"This might be too personal, but why would the family want to give up the resort after all this time?"

"That's the part that is hard, but I feel you should know. And once you get to know Alpine Ridge, you'll quickly see how much this town likes to talk . . . a lot. So, you're more than likely going to find out anyway once you're up here."

"Know what?" Millie was curious but had a sudden feeling that selling the resort was more than just a business deal. "If it's personal, you don't need to share."

Ashley sighed. "It's okay. I know you well, otherwise I probably wouldn't say all this in the first conversation. And you're not the first to ask that, because it does seem a bit odd to sell something so valuable. So here it goes . . . Dylan and Joyce Clarke, the owners, had a daughter named Riley."

"Had?"

"Yes." Ashley's voice slowed from the feverish way she'd shared the pitch. "After Riley graduated from college, both she and her parents had high hopes for her to take over the resort—but then the accident happened. Riley got sick with a dangerous bout of the flu two years ago. She was even hospitalized for a while. After she finally started to get better, she was so tired of being cooped up inside that she decided to hit the slopes, but her body wasn't ready for that. Halfway down her first run, she grew weak and lost control. She had a terrible fall that landed her in a coma. She died a couple months later."

"I don't even know what to say. I haven't met the Clarkes yet and feel like I want to give them a hug."

"The whole town did too, but they sort of shut everyone out. The grief of losing their only child, a woman once thriving and full of life, was too much to bear. Not to mention the cost of the hospitalization and funeral sending them into a bigger financial struggle than they were already facing."

"Financial struggle? With the resort? Is it not getting enough customers?"

"The resort has always done well. Some years are better than others, but that's to be expected in any business. It was more of how Mr. Clarke invested his money. All I know is mistakes were made that put them behind. Then Riley was hospitalized."

"Oh, no . . ." Millie sat on the edge of the bed. She couldn't imagine what the Clarkes had gone through. "This story keeps getting worse."

"Because it did. They had just borrowed against their equity on the resort to do some major upgrading, trying to keep up with the larger ski resorts and get the place ready for their daughter to take over." Ashley sighed. "Anyway, we've all tried to be there for them, encouraging them not to give up on it, but they want to sell the resort and all their property so they can retire and leave Alpine Ridge behind."

"In a way I don't blame them, but again, how awful."

"It is. The medical debt on top of the loan is a staggering amount—and I think it's just hard for them to be here now. They're ready to move on. Selling the resort would allow them to pay off the debt and retire someplace else and find some healing. It's been really rough to witness."

Millie empathized for the family and was determined to do her best work for them. "Well, I'd be honored to have this opportunity and get you these pictures for the resort."

"Great! It's yours! Oh, Millie, you have no idea how happy this makes me. I've been having such a tough time the past week trying to find a photographer. The few that our original photographer referred were either unavailable on such short notice or just not a good fit."

And you're sure I am? Millie suppressed her thoughts as a wave of emotion swept over her. She couldn't believe it. She had an actual photography job.

"So it looks like my first stop in Alpine Ridge will be to buy some snow gear," Millie joked.

"The resort can throw in some of those items with your offer since you're willing to travel here on such a short notice. Is it still okay to get here by Saturday?" Ashley asked.

"Just send me flight details, and I'll be there."

"I'll send you those plus the contract. It will have all the details and, of course, when you get here, we will go over more. And just to make sure, you can stay the whole month, right?"

"Yes, that's no problem."

"Perfect! The resort is celebrating its eighty-fifth anniversary at the end of your stay, and I thought you'd like to attend the party. It'll be a lot of fun, and I think it's also the Clarkes' way of saying goodbye to Alpine Ridge."

"What a way to end such a long stint with their business. It sounds fun. I'm glad I'll get to go."

"I cannot wait to see you!" Ashley's voice rose with excitement.

Millie's heart thudded against the mixture of feelings

swarming her, but she kept her composure so Ashley wouldn't pick up on her nerves. "I can't wait either."

Back downstairs, she wiped her sweaty hands against her dress. She wasn't sure if she was anxious about the job or the shock that she finally had an assignment to complete. Everyone was back inside, sitting and chatting in the living room with dessert in their hands, but they went silent when she walked into the room. Lila's eyes were wide, questioning how the conversation went.

"So it looks like"—Millie glanced around the room—"I got my first photography job."

"I knew she'd give it to you!" Lila practically jumped up and ran to hug her.

"Who is 'she'?" their mom asked, shrugging at their dad.

"Ashley, a friend I used to work with at the Wharf," Millie explained. "I'm leaving Saturday to shoot marketing photos for the ski resort she works for . . . in Vermont."

Her parents seemed more confused than pleased, but she ignored their flat response. This was no time to let their judgment affect her. *Vermont, here I come.*

Chapter Three

"Here, I found another one." Lila pulled down a long-sleeved sweater from Millie's closet. "It's lightweight, but at least it'll cover your arms."

"Thanks. I bought a couple thicker sweaters earlier when I was getting toiletries and other things. The offer package Ashley sent specifies that the resort will also buy me a pair of snow pants and a jacket."

Millie was leaving for Vermont the next morning, and as she stuffed her two suitcases, the reality that she was going was surreal. She almost couldn't believe an actual paid photography job was waiting for her there.

"Good. You'll need snow pants for sure." Lila folded the sweater she'd found and put it on top of the others in one of the suitcases. "Maybe you can try your hand at skiing."

"I definitely will." Millie went into the bathroom and came out with her hair diffuser. "Can't forget this. I read that the cold air will make these curls harder to manage."

Her sister walked over and touched her hair. "I've always been jealous of them."

"My curls? Are you kidding? I've always wanted your

straight hair. So much easier to take care of." Millie put the diffuser in a bag for bathroom things and shoved it into a suitcase, then zipped it shut.

"This will be good for you, Millie."

"I sure hope so."

Lila smiled and reached for her arms. "It will. For one, it'll get you out of Charleston and somewhere magical for Christmas. You've always wanted to be around snow during the holidays. And as for your career, this job will be a great professional entry to add to your résumé. Exactly what the resort here was looking for."

"That's the problem." Millie sighed, pulled away from her sister, and sat on a chair next to her suitcase.

"What is?" Lila sat next to her.

"I know I need the experience. But now that the opportunity is here . . . I'm feeling . . ."

"Worried?"

Millie nodded. "A little. But also . . ." She turned to her big sister. "Don't laugh."

"Never." Lila walked over and put her arm around her.

"Just a little scared. Lila, I sat up half the night thinking about the last six years and my career. I thought about Mom and Dad's disappointment when I told them I wasn't going to go to college like they thought I should. And how, since taking that photography course and getting my certification, I haven't grown. I just figured I'd get there and—"

"And you will." Her sister rolled her eyes. "Take our parents out of your worries. You know Dad, so black and white. He thinks there are only three career choices that make sense, and Mom just . . ." Lila nudged her. "Well, you know how she is. If life doesn't progress in perfect order, then it's wrong. You've never done anything 'the right way,' and it drives her nuts."

Millie chuckled and leaned into Lila, but the knot in her

stomach that had been growing all morning didn't cease tightening. She appreciated her sister's encouragement, but she just couldn't shake this feeling of not being good enough. Ashley had offered her this position probably assuming Millie had grown as a photographer since she'd last seen her. But she hadn't.

"I know. I just hope I don't let Ashley down. What if I'm not as good as she assumes?"

"Of course you aren't." Lila turned to her. "You're even better." She tapped Millie's shoulder. "Get some sleep. Big day tomorrow!"

When Lila closed the door, Mille pondered their conversation. For so long, she'd been a silent observer, her camera her confidant. Now that her talent had been recognized and would be thrust into the public eye, she was shaken with anxiety. Her sister would always have her back, but could Millie muster up the same support for herself?

———

"THE CURRENT TEMPERATURE IN RUTLAND IS twenty-nine degrees with partly cloudy skies," the pilot's voice crackled through the speakers.

Did he just say twenty-nine degrees? Millie was already shivering at the thought. When she'd left Charleston early that morning, it'd been in the low fifties, and she'd thought that was chilly.

"Layers and a long, thick coat," the woman next to her said, eyeing Millie's sherpa fleece that had always been enough, until now.

"I guess I should have checked the temperatures before I left. I knew it would be cold, but wow . . . That's cold." Millie gave the woman a sheepish grin. "This trip was only planned a couple of days ago. I didn't have much time to study the weather."

"Don't let the cold scare you too much. It's gorgeous up here this time of year. My husband travels here for work quite often, and we always plan a ski trip during December. The resorts, the towns—it's a holiday dream come true. You'll see."

"I've never been to New England, so that sounds wonderful." The thought of a small-town Christmas with snow brought a tingle of excitement followed by a yawn. "Excuse me." Millie stifled it as best she could. "It's been quite a journey to get here."

They both leaned back as the plane descended and touched down. She'd finally made it.

Over six hours of traveling, with one stop and an hour layover in Boston—not to mention another night of little sleep—but here she was. She'd spent the better half of the morning wondering if she should just turn around and tell Ashley she needed to find someone better suited for the position. Now, after hearing the woman describe what she was about to see, curiosity overran her. She couldn't wait to witness Christmas up north.

With her suitcases, she went to the rental counter to get the car the resort had reserved for her. As she stood in line, she glanced out the window to see snow falling outside. *Didn't the captain say partly cloudy skies?*

"How can I help you?" a man with a warm smile greeted her when she reached the counter.

"I thought it was supposed to be sunny today." Millie looked past him, suddenly worried about driving in the snow.

"That's winter in Vermont for you. Sunny one moment and snow the next." The man got her registered and handed her a ticket to give to the valet in the parking garage.

While she waited for her car, she pulled out her phone and saw a missed call from Ashley. Millie sent a quick message to let her know she had landed and was picking up her rental car. When the valet drove up with it, Ashley's response dinged.

> So glad you arrived! I'll meet you in the lobby in the resort, let me know if you run into any delays with traffic or anything. Valet will park your car when you arrive. Enjoy the scenery! Can't wait to see you!

After tipping the driver, who'd also helped put her luggage in the trunk, Millie got in the car, plugged in the resort's address in the GPS, and then carefully maneuvered out of the parking garage and toward the exit.

"Turn right onto Airport Road," the GPS instructed.

Millie slowed, paying close attention to her surroundings while the snow continued to fall. This was the first time she'd ever traveled on her own, besides a few trips to North Carolina, and she wasn't sure at first if the snow would stick on the roads. Thankfully, they seemed clear.

"Turn right onto VT-103 S."

Heading down the highway, she began to relax and turned up the music, finally taking in her surroundings. A winter wonderland unfolded all around her with tall evergreens on each side of the winding road. The scenery left her speechless. Seeing snow in person was even more beautiful than she'd expected. She cracked the window and the frosty air blew in, sending a shiver down her spine as she caught the faint smell of woodsmoke and pine. After rolling the window back up, she tried to focus while the breathtaking beauty whizzed by.

As she meandered down the route completely mesmerized, she passed a sign for Mount Holly, which she'd remembered Ashley mentioning in her email was her hometown and not too far away from the resort, so she knew she was almost there. She came around a wide bend and that was when she saw it. Okemo

Mountain greeted her with its snowcapped summit and slopes stretching down its sides. The grandeur of the mountain's peaks was just incredible, just like the internet described.

Alpine Ridge was near the larger Okemo resort, according to her conversation with Ashley when she'd called the night before to go over a few last-minute details. Her friend had also explained, when Millie has asked her some marketing questions about the area, that Okemo's guests never hindered theirs. Being so close, many of them learned about Alpine Ridge, a smaller and more intimate option for future trips. Now seeing Okemo in person, she hoped that would stay the same once new buyers took over.

Millie pictured herself on the slopes, twisting and turning her way down, and the thrill of it made her almost forget why she was there. Driving through all the scenery eased her worries a bit as her photographer brain ran through various ideas and techniques she could use to capture the resort's surroundings.

A sign came into view letting her know the turn for Alpine Ridge was approaching, and her anxiety creeped back in. It was time to do what she'd come to do.

"Alpine Ski Resort is on your left," the GPS announced, and she slowed the car.

The sprawling property spread out before her as she turned onto the resort's main road. Millie came to a stop at the entrance and clicked off the music as she looked at the twinkling lights strung across various evergreens. A large, beautifully crafted wooden sign stood nearby with spotlights shining down on bold, cursive script that read: "Alpine Ski Resort." Garland with string lights had been wrapped around the sign, and next to it were two oversized reindeer that appeared to be made of birch trees. The deer wore red plaid scarves around their necks, and a set of extra tall skis were crisscrossed and leaning on them. *Did someone handcraft those?* The aesthetic was charming and cozy all at once.

She texted Ashley that she had arrived, then heard the crunching of snow as she continued driving. To her right, a long wooden bridge crossed over a frozen river, with red Christmas bows on both sides of the railing. The holiday atmosphere had already mesmerized her, and she hadn't even seen the main lodge yet. Anticipation built as she got closer, and when she finally saw it, her mouth dropped open. She parked by the main entrance, then stepped out of her car to get a better look, the warm ambience immediately inviting her in.

More twinkling lights lined the porch railings on what the resort's website described to be a part-Swiss chalet and part-log cabin main lodge. From the large double front doors hung two skillfully shaped oversized wooden wreaths, with soft green garland and red ribbon loosely wrapped around them. The crisp mountain air, with more hints of pine, enveloped her as she admired the tall lit-up evergreens on each side of the porch. The lights reflected off the snow piled alongside the driveway and made the front of the lodge a true winter wonderland.

Two men greeted her and retrieved her suitcases from the trunk. After they took her car to the parking lot, Millie approached the porch steps. Just past the lodge, the setting sun was lowering behind the ski mountain and sending out a cascade of pink, orange, and purple. Clouds streaked the horizon like wispy golden brushstrokes across a canvas. She had never seen anything like it. Before turning back to the steps, she noticed the clock tower to the right with a large red ribbon wrapped down the base. It was like standing in Santa's village.

The front door opened, and Ashley rushed toward her,

gripping the porch rails before she excitedly hurried down the steps to meet Millie at the bottom.

"You're here!" Her friend scooped her into a warm hug.

"I sure am, and this"—Millie waved her hand around—"is incredible."

"Right? It's absolutely magical." Ashley picked up one of the suitcases. "Come on, let's get you inside. You'll be staying here in the main lodge in one of our VIP suites. Just wait until you see it."

"You didn't have to do that. You should leave it open for a paying guest." Millie went up the steps behind Ashley and saw bells that she hadn't noticed before dangling in the centers of the wooden wreaths. They jingled loudly as Ashley pulled the door open. "Are these made of birch, like the reindeer in the front entrance?" She pointed to the wreaths.

Ashley turned and followed her gaze. "Close. These are handmade with Norfolk pine and Cypress greenery."

"So unique. I love it."

"And none of that nonsense about the suite, Millie. The Clarkes wouldn't have you stay anywhere else. Come on, let's get you checked in, and I'll introduce you to Irene."

"Irene?"

"She heads the front desk and pretty much runs the entire office. She's a lifer here in Alpine Ridge, and after retiring from forty-four years of teaching middle school English, she decided to work for the resort as her retirement job. Skiing was always a passion of hers, so she says working by the slopes makes her happy. And we're so glad she's here. She knows everything about this town and is helpful with directing the tourists who come in."

Once inside, the rustic wooden beams of the grand lobby and the central stone fireplace with its warm, crackling flames caused Millie to pause. Evergreen and red holly berries lined the mantel, with a smaller version of the birch reindeer stood beside it, and an oversized basket of firewood sat in front of the hearth. Near the fireplace was the star of the room, a massive Christmas tree, lit from top to bottom. Handblown glass baubles and carved wooden ornaments decorated it and gave it a signature feel. The cozy scene made her want to sit down in front of the fire, but she also couldn't wait to get to her suite and put down her suitcases.

A few guests passed by her, some holding hot drinks and others still in their ski attire from a day on the mountain. Ashley waved at the front desk woman as they approached.

"Hey, Lexi, is Irene back there?"

"Yes, I believe she's still here. Checking in?" The woman glanced at Millie.

"Yes. Millie Rowan."

Lexi typed something and glanced at the monitor, then looked up with a smile. "Powder Ridge Suite. One of our best." After she entered Millie in the system, she picked up the phone to call Irene.

A tall woman with gray-streaked dark blonde hair pulled back in a ponytail came out with a wide smile. She was dressed casually in jeans and a dark green sweater and snow boots Millie saw after she came around the desk.

"Ashley, good to see you!" The women hugged. "I've been so busy back there all week that I haven't seen you."

"But still snuck a few runs in, I see," Ashley said, looking down at the boots.

"You know me, can't stay away."

Ashley playfully rolled her eyes. "No, you can't, which is what worries me."

"She's always fussing over me," the woman said, waving her hand. "I'm Irene. You must be Millie. Ashley has told me all about you." She extended her hand and gave Millie a firm shake.

Millie wasn't sure what Ashley was concerned about. Irene may be older, but she seemed fit and strong.

"Nice to meet you. I'm excited to try those slopes soon myself. It'll be my first time."

"Wonderful! Our ski instructor, Josh, is the best. He will happily give you a lesson or two." She patted Ashley's shoulder. "And your friend here can guide you through it as well. She's pretty good now, although not nearly as good as me."

Ashley chuckled. "Irene has been skiing since she could walk."

"And I will keep skiing until I can't anymore." Irene pointed to the back room. "I have to get back and finish some paperwork before I head home. Ashley will get you settled. I can't wait to talk with you some more, Millie. Welcome to Alpine Ridge!"

Irene left, and Ashley motioned for Millie to follow her down a hallway to the elevators.

"You're on the second floor with a view of the whole mountain. A perfect start to your mornings with a coffee in hand."

"That sounds wonderful. And here I thought I'd be in a tiny room, stuffed away in the back so as not to take one of the nicer rooms away from any guests."

Ashley smiled when they stepped inside, and she pressed the button to the second floor. "You are this year's most important guest. The Clarkes can't wait to see what you put together."

"I'm eager to get started." Millie swallowed and forced a smile so Ashley didn't see the hesitation that gripped her as she followed her out the elevator and to the end of the hall, stopping at the last door. *I hope my skills measure up.*

"Right this way," Ashley said, opening the door and holding it so Millie could go first. "This is the Powder Ridge Suite."

Millie couldn't even move at first. "Are you serious?"

"It's my absolute favorite. It's one of our honeymoon suites, so only one bedroom, which is perfect for you. Plus, there's a washer and dryer in here that I'm sure you'll need since you're staying a month. We're a small resort, with only seven chalets on the property, but they can each fit up to fifteen people, and we have six suites here in the main lodge. We have charm for sure. Go have a look."

Millie walked into the main living area that had a large L-shaped couch and overstuffed loungers next to it with Christmas red-and-white throw pillows and a few matching blankets folded over the backs. A smaller version of the stone fireplace in the lobby was lit and its mantel lined with frosted evergreen.

"Real logs?"

"Not for the suites. Gas. Much easier for our guests."

The suite held charm with a rustic flair and plenty of modern festive touches. A Christmas tree held up by a round wooden crate lit up the corner, with a white linen and lace tree skirt wrapped around the base, resembling snow. Another pair of skis leaned on the wall next to it in a crisscross with more lights around them. Millie walked over to the tree and admired the snowy pinecones, cream snowflake ornaments, gold-sprayed wooden-beaded garland carefully woven from top to bottom, and pops of white berries poking out in various sections.

"The white owl at the top is my favorite," Ashley said.

Millie looked up. "It's all so gorgeous."

"Each suite is decorated with a different theme. This one clearly gives a frosty feel. Well, I'm going to let you get settled for a bit. Would you like to meet for dinner downstairs in our lounge in a couple hours, maybe six thirty?"

"Sounds perfect. See you then."

"There's a folder in the kitchen with a gift certificate to a shop in town where you can buy some snow gear, and I hung one of my extra-thick coats in the closet for you to borrow, but if it doesn't fit, we will happily get another one for you. It's a long, puffy one and will keep you warm. I also put some extra wool gloves of mine in there too on the shelf. Do you have a hat?"

"Yes."

"Good, you'll need it. Especially outside shooting pictures. Don't hesitate to let me know if you need anything else."

After Ashley left, Millie rolled her suitcases into the bedroom. Another miniature tree glowed by the sliding door that led out to a small balcony. Millie stepped outside and held her arms around her waist against the icy breeze. The winter sun was now below the horizon, but it gave a final radiant burst behind the mountain before a purple twilight covered the white landscape. She quickly dashed back inside and grabbed her camera out of one of her suitcases, then snapped a handful of her very first photos of the scenery. Trading in the ocean for this view was almost surreal, but her shivering body reminded her it was actually happening.

Back in the bedroom, she opened her suitcases and began to unpack, getting lost in thoughts of the beauty she'd just witnessed. She hadn't even seen the whole area yet and was already blown away. Keeping her focus on the beauty helped keep her nerves calm and her creativity flowing. It would be any photographer's dream to capture this town and especially that mountain. She was here to prove her skills, and that was what she would do.

Chapter Four
Alpine Ridge, Vermont

November 1927
Evelyn

"Did you get to the house?" nine-year-old Evelyn asked her father as she hurried to meet him at the door.

"Yes, I did." Leroy handed his coat to her mother, Clara, and placed a hand on Evelyn's shoulder. "Everything will be alright, sweetheart."

Flood waters had swept through Alpine Ridge the week before when a storm had dropped over nine inches of rain all over Vermont. The town and much of the state had experienced catastrophic damage. The Fosters were among the luckier ones who had managed to escape to a neighboring farm on higher ground that didn't get swept away by the mudslides. Other families around them were not as fortunate, and from what they'd heard so far, many lives had been lost.

The young couple that had graciously taken in the Fosters was still in town, helping to shovel out the muddy mess in the local businesses. Leroy had headed up to help organize groups to tackle the damage as well, but his own farm would be his biggest hurdle to repair.

"Go on and help keep an eye on your sisters while I talk to your mother." Her father motioned for Clara to follow him into the kitchen.

Evelyn heard her sisters giggling about something upstairs and knew they were alright for the moment. She snuck up to the kitchen door and leaned in close to listen to her parents' conversation.

"And George? Did you check on him?" her mother asked. Evelyn's grandfather, George Foster, had been home with Clara and the girls when the flood waters began to rise. If Leroy hadn't made it back when he had to help George get everyone out, Evelyn wasn't sure they would have survived.

"Yes, he's doing just fine. And before you ask, I told him to come on back with me because he's done enough to help the cleanup. But you know how stubborn he is. He insisted on staying longer."

"I'm nervous to see him work so hard at his age." Evelyn heard a chair pull out. "Okay, I'm sitting. Tell me the damage."

"Clara, the house is in a shambles. It's caved in on one side and most of it is just gone. There was one small section . . ." Leroy sighed. "I shouldn't have gone inside as it was unsafe, but I went in to see what I could salvage."

"Did you find anything?" her mother asked.

"Since the first floor completely flooded, everything was damaged, but the stairs were still there and—"

"Oh, Leroy, thank goodness you made it out before the rest of the house fell on top of you."

"I know. I wasn't thinking. I'm sorry to worry you. But I'm glad I did. The tall clock my grandfather made is still standing, but it no longer works. I still want to retrieve it though."

"That's wonderful. Let's get some men over there to help you move it tomorrow."

"I'll set that up. I also found some of the girls' clothes still dry and brought them back. Up in the attic, a branch must have broken through the small window. It was a mess, but I found a handful of books and photographs and some old papers in a box that my parents stored up there years ago. Some of the papers were wet and destroyed, but I took what I could."

"Are the documents of any value?"

"Yes, there was a deed map and records for the property. The rest, I haven't bothered to look through. When I went back outside, I was looking over our property and saw that the mudslides that came down Alpine Mountain must have been more extreme than we first thought. There's no telling how to claim what's ours now."

"Here we are after the worst flood we've ever witnessed, and you're concerned about the property lines?" Her mother's voice grew louder. "A century-old argument with our neighbors that will never cease. Perhaps we should make sure Bobby and June are alright before you get into it with them. We still haven't seen them."

Evelyn shifted in her stance but kept her focus on the conversation as quietly as she could.

"I'm not going to start an argument with the Thayers. I finally saw Bobby in town today. June, Lawerence, and Kenneth are all safe and, unlike ours, their house was luckily not damaged too much. The water didn't rush inside, but it did knock down their barn. Look"—Leroy's tone became defensive—"I'm just saying that half the mountain was wiped out. It'll be hard to reorganize the boundary line is all. And I'm sorry I couldn't save anything else."

"Don't be. Leroy, our girls are safe and we're all still together. That's what matters."

"I know." His voice softened. "It's just that my family built that cottage in 1802 after replacing the original log cabin, and the structure stood strong for over a century. It's sad to see it destroyed, especially after decades of updates and remodels."

"I know, darling. But we will rebuild." Her mother's footsteps trailed across the kitchen, and Evelyn pushed the door open very slowly to peek in. Her mother embraced her father in a long hug. "And I'm sure you and Bobby will work out the property confusion once again. But Leroy?"

"Yes?" Her father gazed down at his wife.

"Do so with kindness. The people of Alpine Ridge need each other right now."

Evelyn carefully backed away from the door and into the parlor when she heard her sisters coming down the stairs.

"Is Father back?" one of them asked.

"Yes, he and Mother are in the kitchen."

"Good!" her other sister said. "We're hungry! We were going to see if she needed help."

"They are having a conversation, let's not disturb them. Dinner will be prepared soon. Let's go have a walk outside and get some fresh air before dark." Evelyn ushered her sisters toward the door as she thought about what she'd just heard about her home. The last thing she wanted was for her little sisters to overhear it too. They would know soon enough that their house needed to be rebuilt and, being the oldest, Evelyn wanted to shield them as long as she could from the devastating news.

***

Present Day

"I'm so full that once I sit on that sofa chair,

it may be my bed tonight," Millie said, sinking into the over-sized cushions by the fire in the lobby.

She and Ashley had spent nearly two hours eating dinner while catching up and exchanging funny memories from their years together at the restaurant in Charleston. It was good to see Ashley again, and it made Millie realize she'd nearly forgotten how to have fun lately. She rarely made time for her friends, her mind always consumed with the next steps for her photography business, despite it never seeming to move forward.

"Me too! I should have stopped at one bowl of the potato, parsnip, and bacon soup. Free refill nights are dangerous for me." Ashley held her stomach. "But since you passed on the cider donuts . . ."

Millie waved her hands. "No more food."

"Okay, but how about a drink? We have some amazing mulled cider. Since you'll only be here for barely a month, you must try everything." Ashley stood back up before Millie could protest and headed to the bar.

While Millie waited, she watched the fire, its flames pulling her into a trance and keeping her attention as they danced and spat in a mesmerizing rhythm. Just before she rested her eyes shut, a man jogged by and caught her attention as he tried to catch the elevator. He raised his hand to have someone hold the door, but he was too late. Without meaning to, Millie found herself watching him as he pressed the button to wait for the next elevator with his back toward her. His cold weather attire of black snow pants, a dark blue sweater, and a beanie hat suggested he'd spent the day skiing. He pulled off the hat and shook out his dark brown hair just as the elevator door opened again. After he stepped inside, he finally turned and, before she could look away, his gaze found hers. A spark of electricity coursed through her, leaving a tingling in its wake. She kept her gaze on him and, just as the doors shut, the faintest hint of a smile played on his mouth.

"His name is Luke Thayer." Ashley's voice jolted Millie out of her daze. "Quite handsome, isn't he?"

"Oh . . . I was just looking around at the all the festive décor." Millie could still feel the aftershocks of the zing from their connection, which only intensified her warming cheeks.

"Uh-huh." Ashley handed her a glass mug that had orange slices and a cinnamon stick poking out the top. "Don't be embarrassed. Luke's known to turn a few heads around here."

"Is he a friend of yours?" Millie raised the mug to her lips, its spicy scent helping her refocus.

"An acquaintance more like. He's the chairman for Alpine Ridge, so all of us residents know him." Ashley glanced at the elevators. "I wonder who he's going to see upstairs."

"Is a chairman like a mayor?"

"Yes. And his family has a history of being in that position. Many older people around town still remember when his grandfather was chairman and speak fondly of him." Ashley stirred her drink with the cinnamon stick and took a sip. "Yum. This is so good. Try it."

Millie tasted it. The citrusy blend of apple and orange with a hint of clove and cinnamon blended perfectly on her tongue. "Wow, that's tasty. And with the fire going, it's all so relaxing."

"The bartender added a splash of rum for us too."

"Then I'll sleep like a baby tonight." Millie repositioned herself against the chair, the image of Luke fading from her mind.

"Speaking of Luke," Ashley began, immediately clouding Millie's thoughts again, "it just occurred to me that he would be a great person for you to meet with to learn about the town."

"Oh, yeah? Why's that?" Millie tried to maintain a mask of

indifference that belied how intrigued she was at the prospect of meeting the good-looking elevator man.

"Well, for one, he truly loves the town. His family dates back to when it was founded. The Thayer residence is one of the historical homes here in Alpine Ridge. It survived many floods, including the great flood of '27 and the hurricane of '38. It's been restored, updated, and remodeled a lot over the years, but it's a favorite in town."

"I'd love to see it while I'm here." Millie imagined all the photos she could capture of a home that old, but she wasn't sure they would help her project with the resort.

"There's a holiday historical homes tour soon, so you'll definitely have a chance to see it. Homes like the Thayers' would make great photos for the resort's marketing visual," Ashley said, as if she could read Millie's mind. "Tomorrow morning, you'll meet with me and the marketing team to go over more specifics about what we're looking for and to make a plan of action, but I'm thinking we need to add in plenty of images from around Alpine Ridge and highlight the timeless charm of the town. That's bound to have huge appeal for investors."

"Sounds good to me. I'm excited to get started." Millie sipped her drink, not sure if she should keep her curiosity about Luke to herself, but she was intrigued by the little history Ashley had just shared. "Does Luke live in that house now?"

"His parents do, but I've heard rumors they'll be passing it down to Luke soon now that his father is retired."

"Interesting." Millie took the last swig of her cider and put it on the coffee table. "Well, from what I can imagine, the home sounds lovely."

"Wait until you see it. It's stunning. Luke's father was a very successful international investment banker. From what I've heard, he traveled a lot while building his fortune when

Luke was young. When Luke went to college, the house sat empty on and off for years whenever his parents left town. His mom liked to accompany Mr. Thayer on his work trips for weeks or even months at a time. People around Alpine Ridge were a little upset because, as you'll see during the tour, the house is such a big part of the community. Everyone was so happy when Mr. Thayer retired and the house was occupied again year-round. But I hear Mrs. Thayer has her hopes set on traveling again, so Luke will probably take over the property since he's back in town and is now the chairman."

"I love small towns. Y'all know everything about everyone." Millie chuckled.

Ashley smiled. "Oh, yes, we sure do. And by the end of your stay here, you will too." Ashley glanced at her drink, suddenly bothered by something. "Now that I've gossiped enough about the Thayer family, I have something to share about your job here."

"You look a little worried. Should I be too?"

"No, not at all. So . . ." Ashley bit her lip, making Millie grow even more concerned. "You already know about the Clarkes' plans for the sale with this upcoming pitch . . ."

Millie nodded.

"Well, if the town wasn't happy about the Thayers going away for a few years, I'm not really sure how they'll react to the Clarkes selling this place outright," Ashley said with a furrowed brow. "Word about the sale hasn't gotten out yet, but once the whole town finds out, Luke will have to be the one to address the residents with the news alongside the Clarkes after they officially make the announcement."

"Yikes. That's a lot on Luke's shoulders. Why should he be the one to handle the aftermath?"

"If I know one thing about Luke, he not only loves this town, but the people in it too. He doesn't have to become involved, but he will, trying to smooth out the edges. But also, this sale will impact the town in many ways, so he will sort of get thrown in anyway."

"I can see that." Millie pondered what the possible reactions from the residents might be. "Do you think most people will be upset?"

Ashley stared into the fire. "I do. But we're hoping that, in time, everyone will see past the negatives and look at the positives. It'll mean greater expansion for the resort, especially since the corporation we're pitching to recently bought Okemo nearby. Perhaps joint growth opportunities could be in our future, which means an economic boost for the town. But it might be a bumpy road to bring people around to that point of view."

Millie considered what Ashley had said, but after listening to the rich history of the Thayers in Alpine Ridge and how loved just their home was, she could guess how deeply intertwined the rest of the community was to its traditions and ways.

"I can see how that'll be a big change for this small community. I know large corporations have their advantages, especially with the means to expand, but it'll shake this place up . . . or at least I imagine it will. And not all the changes will be good."

"Maybe not," Ashley conceded. "But it's my job to help with the transition, and I have to keep everyone looking ahead and staying positive."

Millie felt abashed. "You're right. I shouldn't have spoken out like that. I'm sure you and the Clarkes are doing what's best for everyone. And I'm here to do what you asked me to do." She gave her friend a confident smile, ignoring the pit growing in her stomach. Once everyone found out what she was there to do, she could be seen as quite a villain. "When are you planning on announcing the news?"

"I was thinking about that the other day. The rest of my

team wants to get it over and done with, like ripping off a Band-Aid, but we haven't secured the sale yet. The Clarkes haven't exactly said when, but they're ready to retire and move on, so I'm assuming soon."

"Do they care about Alpine Ridge and the reactions that will follow the news?"

"Yes and no. It's not that they're uncaring people, but they really are focused on their own situation—their grief and their continued financial struggles since losing their daughter. Mrs. Clarke especially is still so stricken with sadness that she's not thinking about anything except leaving," Ashley explained, shaking her head. "She's doing much better these days than she was when I started a year ago, but I know she still wants to go. Anyway, enough gossip for one night. You must be tired."

A heavy wave of exhaustion struck her. "I definitely am." Millie forced herself up from the chair. "Time to get a good night's rest so I can start bright and early tomorrow."

"Great! Let's meet at the diner in town. You can't miss it. It's the only one. How about around nine?"

"Yes, that works for me. Is meeting on a Sunday okay for your team?"

"We need to get this pitch to the buyers before Christmas, so we're all doing overtime." Ashley stood up. "After the meeting, I'll introduce you to Luke. I know he'd be happy to show you around his beloved town."

Ashley walked her to the elevator door, and Millie pressed the button before giving her friend a hug goodbye. She found herself dizzy with all she'd just heard. Only a day in, and she was already immersed in everything about Alpine Ridge.

Chapter Five

Alpine Mountain stood tall and proud out Millie's bedroom window when she drew back her curtains the following morning. Sunday welcomed her with a chill that hugged the room, and she opened one of the half-unpacked suitcases and pulled out a sweatshirt, then spotted fuzzy slippers she didn't remember owning. Smiling, she picked them up. *Lila.* She slid her feet into them, then grabbed her camera to take some shots of the mountain in the dawning light. She padded into the kitchen to make some coffee and stepped out onto her deck while it dripped. The sun had just emerged from the mountain's crest, and its radiant beams illuminated the slopes, signaling the start of another day of skiers.

She angled her lens toward the sun as it brightened over the snow-covered slopes. Checking the pictures, she felt satisfied and turned off the camera. The icy air didn't stop her from enjoying the view for a minute. When her body started to shiver, she went back inside to get her coffee and noticed the soft lights of the tree twinkling as she shut the sliding door. The holiday décor made the cold come alive in a way she couldn't quite explain. She hadn't been sure how a Vermont winter would be for her, but so far she loved it. Pouring fresh brew into a mug, she took a sip, allowing the hot liquid to awaken her. Her phone rang from her bedroom and she walked in to see an incoming call from Lila. It was just after seven thirty.

"Hey, sis. On your way home from a shift?" Millie answered.

"Yes, a long one too. I was called in for an emergency C-section yesterday afternoon and before I could blink, it was the morning again." She could hear Lila opening her car door, followed by a muffled sound. "Okay, you're on speaker now. How was your first night up there? Is it freezing?"

Millie held her phone out and checked her weather app. "It's twenty-one degrees. So yeah, it's quite crispy here. Thank you for the slippers. They came in handy this morning."

"Oh, wow. That's cold. I hope you can get some warmer gear soon. And you're welcome. I knew you'd need them."

"There was a folder of information on the kitchen counter when I checked in, and inside is a gift certificate to Alpine Gear Exchange. I'll be heading there soon. And Ashley is letting me borrow one of her long winter coats." Millie walked over to the front closet and tried it on. It was slightly small but would do for the few weeks she was there. She'd definitely need some snow pants and whatever other gear skiing entailed.

"That's good. I don't need my baby sister frozen on the mountain up there. I'd have to send Jake to find you."

Millie chuckled. "His upbringing in Georgia would not be a proper fit for a rescue team on the snowy hills of Vermont."

"I know. I'd lose him too. Speaking of peaks, is it as gorgeous as the pictures online?"

"Even more so in person. Lila, I wasn't sure about coming up here, but I absolutely love it. Although, I haven't really spent time out in the cold yet. But the mountains, the crisp air, and the holiday atmosphere with all the festive décor every-where make it even better."

"Well, you are staying in a resort. Of course it'll be extra magical. Hang on a sec." Millie heard Lila order a coffee. "I'm going to need a lot of that today."

"Aren't you going to bed?"

"Ugh. Not right away. I have to make one quick stop at the office and then I will. But I'm so happy to hear you're enjoying yourself. Get out there and take those photos!"

"Will do. Love you."

Millie turned on the shower and went to pick out some clothes. Settling on jeans and a long white sweater, she then rummaged through the bottom of her suitcase where all her socks were and held up a pair.

"I'm going to need thicker socks too." She made a mental note to add those to the list, then got into the shower.

A short while later she was finishing her makeup when her phone lit up again. It was Ashley sending her the address of the diner. Millie responded, then did one last check to made sure her long curls were secured. She'd be wearing a hat, so she had fastened half of her hair back while the rest was loose. In Charleston, the humidity always worried her, and she didn't know what to expect here. She pulled her fleece hat over her head, then put on Ashley's coat and grabbed the soft wool gloves from the closet shelf.

When she reached the lobby downstairs, skiers were already filling up the place. Some guests were checking out, while others wore snow pants and held their skis as they lounged near the fire. The air nipped at her cheeks when she stepped outside and waited for the valet to get her car.

A few minutes later, she was buckled in and cranked up the heat full blast. She typed in the address Ashley had given her and put the car in drive, thankful for a sunny day and no snow falling on the roads. The GPS said she was only six minutes away, which made her smile. Getting anywhere in Charleston in six minutes was impossible. It took that much time just to get to the mailbox in her sister's complex.

As she made her way down the small country road, the sun glittered through the tall trees, causing a glare. She reached for her sunglasses in her purse and tried to pay attention to the directions that kept making her turn.

"There are so many short roads in this town," she said out loud, sliding on her sunglasses.

When she made another left onto what appeared to be the main road in town, she slowed down a bit and glanced around at all the cute storefronts. The first one was an antique shop that had sprayed frost on its front window with snowflakes clinging across it. To her right, Green Mountain Books had a tall stack of books, shaped like a Christmas tree with lights wrapped around the sides, displayed in their front window. People were walking down the sidewalk, bundled up and not letting the temperatures stop them. She'd need to do the same if she was going to get her job done.

"Your destination is on the left."

Crestview Diner was so small Millie almost drove right past it, despite the GPS saying she had arrived. She pulled into the parking lot behind the building. The top of Alpine Mountain was directly in front of her, making her pause. She wasn't sure she'd ever get tired of seeing it.

Inside, the diner had about five booths lining the windows and only a handful of small tables set up in the center, making it easy to spot Ashley waving at her from one of the corner booths. A man and woman were with her and greeted Millie when she reached the table, both shaking her hand.

"I'm Cassidy, the marketing assistant, and I also handle our social media."

"Hi, Cassidy. I'm Millie." She sat down next to Ashley, across from the two others.

The man smiled next. "And I'm Danny. I'm the digital strategist, and I handle getting traffic for our online content and new marketing strategies."

"Nice to meet you both. I'm so pleased to be here." Millie looked up as a waitress approached the table with a wide smile.

"You must be the fourth person they were waiting on. Welcome! What would you like to drink?" she asked Millie.

"Coffee and a glass of water, please."

"Coming up. I'll be right back to take everyone's order."

Ashley slid a menu toward her. "Their apple cheddar omelet is a favorite."

"Apples in eggs?" Millie asked.

"Better get used to apples in everything," Danny said, picking up his orange juice to take a sip. "And maple syrup."

"Well, if it's a favorite I'll give it a try." Millie looked around the table. "And maple syrup on anything sounds good to me."

When the waitress returned, they placed their orders and then Ashley pulled out some paperwork. "I brought our latest notes for the pitch plan for Peak Holdings—the prospective buyer. How about we start there and run through it for Millie?" she said with a glance at her team.

Millie read over the bullet points, which mainly laid out details regarding their client base, successful marketing campaigns from the past, and general market trends for the area.

"As you can probably see from what you're reading, we want to show them how profitable this mountain can be. They already own some larger establishments, so we're pushing the idea of a more specialized, boutique experience for honeymooners and people looking for weekend getaways —things like that," Cassidy explained.

"We'd like to expand to more families, but with the Clarkes—" Danny stopped, quickly turning to Ashley.

"She knows what happened," Ashley told him. She turned to Millie. "They just haven't been able to move forward with new ideas since losing their daughter. All those strategies are good for helping Peak Holdings understand the area, but we want you to use your skills and tell a story with your photos."

Danny nodded. "Yes, and highlight the history and charm of the town, angling it in a way that will work best in the pitch. The Clarkes have a long history in this town, dating back to Mr. Clarke's ancestors, who at the time were named Foster. They settled here back in colonial days. The family history sets our resort apart and makes it more attractive to a new buyer because we haven't gone so commercialized . . . yet. The place has a lot of individualized character, hopefully making it more appealing for Peak Holdings to invest in."

Yet. Millie repeated the word in her mind. She had no doubt the larger resorts in Vermont were a huge success, but it was sad to think the atmosphere of this quaint little town would probably change with new owners of the cornerstone business.

"Do the Clarkes have any input in this plan?" Millie was curious when she'd get to meet them. "Of course I can also hear it from them too. Which is hopefully soon?"

"Yes, they've gone over everything with us and are excited to meet you tomorrow. They're out of town until then," Cassidy said.

"Sorry, I forgot to mention where they were yesterday and that they planned on meeting you Monday." Ashley gave her an apologetic look. "But until then, I recommend getting a feel for the area. Get out there and work your photography skills. I know you can help us create the most visualized pitch possible. Just wait until you get to know this town. Its essence will light up everything you capture in its unique way."

The waitress returned with their breakfasts, and the team spent the rest of the meeting recommending spots for Millie to visit and photograph. Ashley handed her a list of all the upcoming local holiday events, including a gingerbread house-making contest.

"I just think that will be fun to go to, but take photos everywhere you go," Ashley said, laughing at how intrigued Millie looked as she read over the list.

By the end of the meeting, she felt much more prepared and was looking forward to getting started. When the others left, Ashley turned to her as she slipped on her coat.

"I managed to get ahold of Luke just before you got here and, as I expected, he said he'd be delighted to meet you and show you around. He said to meet him at his office, which is just down the street at the town hall." Ashley zipped up her coat. "Want to brave the cold and walk?"

"Now that I have this wonderful long coat, I think I can handle it."

"Glad it fits." Ashley put on her gloves. "It's a short walk, and it'll give you a chance to see the main street a little more."

Outside, their breaths came out like smoke against the chilly air. After Millie grabbed her camera from her car, she followed Ashley down the street. The bare trees that lined the road had twinkle lights in them and Millie slowed down to take a couple long-view shots of the trees and light posts. Some of the photos would be for the pitch, but the rest would be for her family to see the beauty of this town. Flakes drifted down from the sky and a small passing cloud sparkled in the sun that came back out once it moved.

"I feel like I'm in a holiday movie." Millie held up her camera and angled toward the dark cloud contrasting with the deep blue sky next to it.

"I remember thinking the same thing when I first arrived. That cozy feel is here year-round too, just like in Mount Holly, my hometown, which you passed on the way in yesterday."

Millie couldn't wait to show Lila these pictures. Maybe

she'd email her a few later to give her a taste of where she was. Passing by storefronts with garlands of evergreen swagged across the front windows and wrapped in crimson ribbon, Millie was instantly engulfed in a sense of nostalgia at the vintage appeal.

She glanced ahead and saw an old red wagon with large wheels sitting in front of the town hall.

"Look at that old wagon," Millie said, holding up her camera. "I have to get that."

"That's Alpine Ridge's famous Christmas wagon," Ashley explained. "They set it up every year, and lots of tourists and local families love to take holiday photos in front of it. It dates back almost two hundred years, but is still sturdy enough to be hooked to a horse during our annual parade."

Millie went across the street and began to take pictures. Greenery lined the whole wagon, with poinsettias inset throughout. She stepped closer and snapped a few shots of the driver's seat that held large burlap drawstring bags with the words "Don't open until Christmas" and "Ho Ho Ho" on them in bright red writing. Millie began to make her way around the wagon with her camera to capture the Christmas presents filling the back.

"I see a plaque here," she said, lowering her camera and inching closer, not paying attention to her footing. She tripped and plopped into the snow.

"You okay?" Ashley called from the sidewalk.

"Careful, the shoveling around the wagon isn't all that great this morning," a male voice said near Ashley.

"Luke, I didn't see you walk up. I was just escorting Millie to your office," Ashley said.

Luke hurried across the snow and helped Millie up.

"Clumsy me," Millie said, trying not to get herself fixed on his eyes that matched the blue skies above.

"Is the camera damaged?" he asked, looking at her hands.

"Nope, it's all good. I managed to hold it up above the snow." Millie pointed to the plaque. "I was trying to get closer to read that."

"It says: 'Municipal Town Clerk, Earl Foster, 1804,'" Luke said, extending his hand to lead her back to the sidewalk. His strong grip drew her focus, nearly making her stumble again. "This was his wagon."

"Foster?" Millie looked at Ashley.

"You know, in the year I've lived here, I've never read that plaque. But, yes, that is the same Foster family we just told you about." Ashley turned to Luke. "I didn't know that was their wagon."

"Sure was," he said and glanced at Millie. "Luke Thayer." He held out his hand again and squinted at her, taking a closer look. "I think I saw you at the resort last night."

"Oh, right." Millie's cheeks flushed against the fib, as she tried to play along. "I knew I recognized you. You were the one rushing to the elevators." She noticed Ashley smiling at her before turning to Luke.

"What brought you to the resort?" Ashley asked.

"I was on my way to say goodbye to my cousin who was in town for the weekend with his wife on a ski trip for their anniversary." Luke cast his eyes on Millie again.

"Oh! Sorry. This is Millie Rowan." Ashley pointed to her.

"Nice to meet you, Luke." Millie took his hand again, suddenly caught off guard by the extra-long stare he gave her. "Thank you for taking time out of your Sunday to show me around Alpine Ridge."

"It's my pleasure. I love showing off my hometown. Ashley says you're taking some pictures for the resort."

"Yes, and I'm already inspired with everything I've seen so far and can't wait to dive in some more."

"She flew here from South Carolina. We knew each other back when I was living there for college," Ashley explained.

"And no one knows this place better than Luke, so this is a real treat for you, Millie."

"Thanks for the compliment." Luke grinned and turned to Millie. "Let's take a walk and maybe we can grab some hot chocolate at the coffee shop across the street to warm up before we get going?"

Suddenly powerless against his charming smile, she forced herself to look away. "Sounds like a plan." She looked at Ashley who was now beaming at their exchange.

"Well, you two seem good to go. Millie, I'll call you a little later."

Ashley headed back toward the diner to get her car, leaving Millie alone with Luke. The man was even more striking close up, and his eyes hinted at untold stories about Alpine Ridge, filled with a rich history he seemed eager to share. And she couldn't wait to hear them all.

CHAPTER SIX

"President Coolidge's father, John, wanted to figure out how to extend the life of his milk, so thus began his cheese company," Luke said as Millie walked around the old building with her camera held up.

They'd been walking through town and had even taken a short drive to see some notable spots on the outskirts over the past few hours. She had guessed Luke would be knowledgeable while taking her around, but it still surprised her just how much history he knew, and not just of Alpine Ridge, but all of Vermont. For such a quiet state, it was packed with culture.

"President Coolidge grew up here?" she asked, clicking a few pictures of the sign on the factory.

"Yes, he did." Luke watched her as she bent herself in a strange way to get a better angle. "You're quite good at that. I'd never be able to get into all the positions I've seen you do since we started the tour."

"It's all about the lighting and the angle." She pointed up to the sky. "Now that a few more clouds have covered the sun, it'll make for better pictures. You'll see."

"I'm looking forward to it, and I'm sure the Clarkes will

love what you put together." He eyed her, a sudden curiosity on his face. "Would you like to tell me about the job you're doing for them, perhaps over some lunch? The café in town makes delicious soup. Unless, of course, you need to get back to the resort."

The hopeful glint in his eyes would have made it impossible to say no even if she wanted to.

"Nope, I'm free. I'd love to try some." She reminded herself to be careful with what she said about the resort and the project she was hired for. As per her discussion with Ashley, she couldn't tell Luke about the Clarkes' plans to sell. She'd have to think fast.

They got back in his car and she was relieved when he turned up the radio instead of chatting, giving her time to think. Lying felt wrong, but what else could she do?

Within minutes they were standing in front of Alpine Café looking for a free table. They found one, and she slid out of her coat and hung it on the back of her chair before taking her seat. Soon they placed their soup orders for that day's special, Vermont cheddar cheese soup. Luke added an order of the café's freshly baked apple loaf to go with it.

"I insist you try the loaf too. It'll be warmed up and drizzled with butter when they hand it to us."

"Sounds delicious. Can't wait."

"There are so many great restaurants here. The food is what got me to come back," he quipped.

"Just the food?"

"Well, that and maybe a few other reasons." He winked and then turned his ear toward the lady calling his name for their order. "Ours is ready. I'll go get it."

When he returned with two bowls and two slices of apple loaf on a tray, a sweet smell with a note of nutmeg wafted toward her. The bread was so soft it melted in her mouth as soon as she took a bite.

"Okay." She took another bite. "I can see why you came back for the food," she mumbled.

"Told you." His eyes lit up with enthusiasm as he picked up his spoon.

"So where were you coming back from?" she asked.

"I went to college in Baltimore." Luke swirled the soup with his spoon. "Lived there for a while afterward, but this is home. I've been back for a couple years now. We're a small but mighty community. And there's nowhere like it."

"This town is small, but after everything you've shared with me today, it seems so much larger with all the tourists that come in to ski and its rich history."

"You don't need to be a big city to be interesting," he said with playful smirk. As he reached for his water, his piercing blue gaze met hers, mirroring the serenity of a wide open sea, holding her spellbound. "Go on." He nodded toward her bowl, making her blink.

She looked down at the creamy soup. "Okay, here I go." She picked up her spoon and sharp, tangy cheddar cheese hit her tongue, balanced by the sweetness from the milk, which made it a perfect blend. "I've never tasted cheddar so good."

"I bet you can find some Vermont cheddar down there in South Carolina."

"I'll have to look when I get home."

"How are you liking Alpine Ridge so far?" he asked, taking a spoonful of his soup.

"Well, it's only been a day." She looked around the bustling café. It was mostly full of skiers taking a break from the mountain and still wearing their ski pants as they walked in and out. "But I'm really enjoying it so far. This place has such a different vibe from what I'm used to, but it's a good one."

"That's great to hear. So tell me about the job for the Clarkes. What are these photos for? Marketing?"

"Sort of." She still wasn't sure what to say and wanted to avoid any further discussion about marketing, so she shifted tracks. "The resort is celebrating its eighty-fifth anniversary this year, as I'm sure you know. They'll be using the pictures to market the celebration and to share. It's a special time."

"I bet it is. We've been talking about the celebration in town for months. I can't wait for that party." Luke took a bite of his loaf, then glanced past her in thought while he chewed. "You know, the Clarkes and my family haven't always had the closest relationship over the years, which is a shame since they're our neighbors. But in spite of that, we've always supported the resort and all they've done."

Millie grew curious. The town seemed close-knit, so this hint at some kind of long-standing feud was strange to hear. "Are they just not the friendly neighbor type?"

"They're friendly enough . . . for their standards, but not Alpine Ridge standards." He shrugged.

"I see. . ." She picked up her water and took a sip, trying not to pry. "Well, that must make it hard for y'all to establish a friendship."

"Yes, it does. But the rift is mostly because of a dispute over some boundary line between their property and ours that started over two hundred years ago."

Millie quickly swallowed her water. "Did you just say, two *hundred*?"

"Yup. Isn't that wild? And as much as I like history, as you've witnessed from the tour today, I can't pretend I know that much about it. My grandparents were pretty indifferent on the subject and never offered much information."

"Interesting." Millie put her hands around her glass and leaned forward. "The story about their daughter, Riley, is so sad."

"Ashley told you about that?"

"Yes. I hope it's okay that she did." Luke looked so serious

Millie started wondering if it was a town secret outsiders shouldn't know. "It's just that I haven't met them yet, but I am here to do a job for them so I wanted to learn more about them."

His hesitant posture made her shift in her seat.

"That makes sense," he finally said. "I'd want to know about the people who hired me too."

"Did you know Riley?"

"I did, somewhat . . ." He fiddled with a napkin.

"We don't have to talk about her." The last thing Millie wanted was to upset him. They had been getting along well so far and his knowledge of the town was useful in helping her put together a plan for how she wanted to handle her assignment. Ashley had asked her to tell a story, and that was what she intended to do, but maybe this particular part of Alpine Ridge's story was too deep and too sad to get into.

Luke smiled, waving his hand. "Sorry. I just haven't talked about Riley in a while."

"*I'm* so sorry. I shouldn't have brought her up."

"No, no . . . It's okay. Like I said, I only knew her a little bit." He paused and she followed his gaze toward an elderly couple that had finished eating and was heading for their table.

"Good afternoon, Luke," the man said once he was next to them. He leaned on his walker and offered his hand.

"Mr. and Mrs. Jones. How are things?" Luke shook the man's hand.

"Can't complain. I'm up and alive for another beautiful day," Mr. Jones said, looking at Millie with a warm smile. "Hello there."

"Hi, I'm Millie," she said, sticking out her hand.

"Nice to meet you, dear," the man said before introducing himself and his wife and waggling his eyebrows at Luke.

"Enjoy your day," Luke said as they headed to the exit, then chuckled under his breath before turning back to Millie.

"Sweetest couple ever. They both grew up here in Alpine Ridge and have been together since they were teenagers. If Mr. Jones was able to get around easier, I'd have *him* give you a tour. He knows more than me. But being in his late eighties, I don't see that happening."

"Wow . . . late eighties? He's moving around pretty well, in my opinion." She stared after the couple as they exited the café. "Listen, I really hope I didn't stir anything up for you by bringing up Riley. What happened to her is just so tragic, so I understand it's not a good topic."

"You didn't stir anything up. Riley was a good woman and, yes, it was really tragic. It's just that . . . You know how I just said there were tensions between my family and hers?"

Millie nodded.

"Just before Riley got sick, we met to talk about some stuff she had dug up about our families."

"Was it anything important?"

"Well, we only met once and planned to meet again, but then she got hurt. I didn't have enough details to continue the work on my own once she was gone."

"Details?"

"Yeah . . . about Alpine Mountain." Luke smiled. "I don't want to bore you."

"I'm not bored. I'm intrigued."

"Well, all she told me was that she didn't think the mountain belonged entirely to her family, according to a diary of her great-grandmother's and an old, faded part of a surveyor's report. She had just moved back home, and I guess she stumbled across this diary in the attic that even her parents didn't know about."

"Sounds like something I'd be curious about if I were you."

Luke shrugged. "Yes and no. I mean, who knows what

report she was referring to. There were so many over the decades."

"Doesn't the town have deeds and records?" Millie asked.

"Of course we do, so I brushed off her concern, which resulted in a heated discussion. Although, the old rumor is exactly that—something about a land dispute that had started in the early nineteenth century, just after the town was chartered. I don't blame her for being curious about what her great-grandmother wrote."

"Now there's a pitch for a mystery movie."

"I'll say." Luke sat back. "But like you said, we have the records and there's nothing to argue over anymore. I wasn't about to restart that war over her great-grandmother's diary. Things have settled down over the years. Although, from what she said, it sounds like the feud was still running hot back in her great-grandmother's day."

"What did the diary say?"

"Apparently, her great-grandmother, whose name was Evelyn, was secretly dating my great-uncle Lawrence, and they were worried about what their families would say if they found out. But they were set to marry each other regardless after Lawrence returned from the war . . . but unfortunately he died while serving. She also mentioned something about a rock wall on the deed map and settling the dispute once and for all."

"That's interesting."

"Yeah, it did grab my attention, but like I said, I don't see how there could be any new information. All the deeds are public records. I think it was just a misunderstanding back then. Besides, I never got to meet with Riley again, so it's neither here nor there."

"True."

"Ready to head out?" Luke asked, checking the time on

his watch. "We've been here quite a while. The staff may kick us out soon."

Millie grinned. "I hadn't noticed. But, yes, I'm ready."

"Let me pay up front, then I'll meet you on the sidewalk."

Millie headed outside and Luke soon joined her, rubbing his hands together. "The cold sure hits you after sitting in a warm café." His eyes were now a sharp blue against the backdrop of the gray clouds.

"It's definitely a shock to my Southern bones."

Luke smiled. "I'll bet. Where you parked?"

"My car is parked behind the diner," Millie said. "You don't have to come with me—I can walk back to the diner from here since I see the sign." When she returned her gaze to him, he was watching her, which sent a subtle tremor beneath the thick layers of her coat. "Thank you for the hot chocolate and lunch—and for taking me on a tour."

"You're welcome. I—"

"Luke!" A slightly older woman with big black sunglasses waved as she walked toward them.

"Mom? I thought you were still in Boston."

"There's only so much shopping one can do for the Black Friday weekend." She took off her sunglasses, revealing the same deep blue shade as Luke's eyes, and smiled warmly at Millie. "Hello, I'm Deborah Thayer."

"Hi Mrs. Thayer. I'm Millie."

"Nice to meet you. Please, call me Debbie." The woman looked at the café. "I was just grabbing some coffee and heading to the grocery store. Did you two just come from the café?"

"We did," Luke said, gesturing to Millie. "I took Millie on a tour of the town, and we ended with some their famous soup."

"A tour? Did you just move to Alpine Ridge?" Debbie asked.

"No, I'm only a visitor—I'm here to take pictures of the ski resort for the Clarkes. I'm a photographer." Millie smiled at Luke. "And your son was kind enough to show me around so I could get a good feel for the town when taking photos."

Debbie smiled. "He's the best for that sort of thing. Say, would you like to come over to our house tonight for dinner? We love having a nice Sunday evening feast when we're in town, so there will be plenty."

"I would love to. Thank you."

"Great! Luke can give you our address. Would five work?"

"Works for me. See you then," Millie said, and Debbie ducked inside the café.

"Well, I guess I will see you tonight then." Luke stared into her eyes, making it increasingly difficult for her to tear her gaze away from him.

"See you then."

After he gave her his address, she forced herself to look at the sidewalk and headed for the diner to get her car. It was kind of his mother to invite her to dinner—just the kind of small-town welcome she'd heard about and watched in movies. By the time she reached her car, she wasn't sure if it was the home-cooked meal she was looking forward to or seeing Luke again. Both sounded great, but would either be available to her if they knew why she was really in town?

Chapter Seven

The last rays of sunset surrendered to the cold night ahead as Millie stood outside the Thayer home in awe. Its rugged beauty was illuminated by soft electric candles in each window, and a front porch light cast a warm glow across the snow-covered lawn. When she looked up at the clear night sky, she admired the scattered stars twinkling above her.

She continued to the front door and paused to take in the large fresh Christmas wreath filled with pinecones and winterberries, accented with a red-and-white bow. It wasn't lit up like most wreaths, making it the perfect natural fit for the age of the home. Glancing one more time around her, she wondered what the house would look like in the daylight.

Her purse vibrated and Ashley's name appeared on her phone screen on an incoming message.

Hey! I just spoke with the Clarkes. They're back in town and excited to meet you. They invited us to breakfast tomorrow at their house before you get going with your day. Can I pick you up at eight?

Millie replied with a yes and then clicked off her phone. She rang the bell and heard a faint "Coming!" behind the door. When it swung open, Debbie greeted her with a big smile. She was wearing a green plaid apron and holding a pair of oven mitts.

"Welcome to our home! Come on in. I hope you like glazed ham. I just pulled it out of the oven."

"Thank you for inviting me and, yes, I do like ham," Millie said, inhaling something savory and sweet from the kitchen while noticing the large chandelier next to a winding staircase. "Smells like you're cooking a delicious meal back there."

Debbie led her to the living room where Luke and another man were sitting. "I wanted to give you some traditional Vermont food. Ever had corn fritters?"

"I have not, but I love all kinds of food. I look forward to trying them."

Luke turned, catching her eye just before Debbie leaned closer. "I don't want to brag, but I'm using my grandmother's recipe instead of my mother-in-law's because it's better," she said, whispering so the men wouldn't hear her.

Millie chuckled. "I won't tell."

Debbie looked at the men sitting on the couch. "Brandon, this is Millie." She held her hand out toward Millie, looking back at her. "Millie, this is my husband, Brandon Thayer."

Brandon stood and came over to shake her hand. "We're happy you're here with us tonight. Luke was just telling me about the photography job you're doing for the resort and how you traveled from Charleston. How are you liking the cold and Vermont so far?"

"Surprisingly, I really like the weather. I wasn't sure how I would fare with the temperatures, but it's not bothering me as I much as I anticipated."

"Millie, have a seat while I finish up in the kitchen. Dinner will be ready very shortly. What would you like to drink? Wine? Beer?"

"Actually, I have to be up early tomorrow to have breakfast with the Clarkes, so I better pass on the wine or beer."

"How about some hot cider? Non-alcoholic, of course."

"Sounds perfect." Millie sat down next to Luke, who casually threw his arm across the back of the couch.

Debbie dashed to the kitchen and returned with a mug. "Here you go. Fresh hot cider."

Luke eyed her mug after his mom went back to finish cooking. "You're going to be sick of apple cider once you leave here."

"I'm not sure about that. So far, I love it."

"So, Millie, tell us about the job," Brandon said, leaning back with his beer. "I grew up with that resort, so I can't wait to see what you capture. Are the Clarkes just preparing for their anniversary party and need fresh marketing material, or are you shooting for something else?"

The way Brandon talked about the resort suddenly made her stomach twist. This family cared so much about the town, and they had no idea the Clarkes were planning to sell the resort. She had a feeling they'd be crushed when they heard the news, more so than Ashley had first let on.

"Yes, they need new marketing material." That wasn't exactly a lie. The pictures *would* be used for marketing purposes. "And I'm sure they'll use my photos for anything else they need in the future." Sort of a lie. The future of the resort wouldn't involve the Clarkes, but the new owners could certainly use the images.

"That's great. Getting out there and taking pictures will really give you a feel for Alpine Ridge," Brandon said.

"I started to share the town with her today," Luke said, peeking at her out of the corner of his eye. "We had a full tour all morning. I showed her as much as I could."

"And I'm sure there's still so much she will discover." Brandon turned to the entry of the living room when Debbie appeared.

"Dinner is ready, everyone. Luke, take your friend to the dining room, and we'll be right there."

Luke stood and reached his hand down to help Millie up. "Right this way."

The gesture made her blush, especially when he gazed at her for an extra beat.

The pocket doors in the living room slid open, and Luke brought her into a large dining room with another chandelier hanging above the rectangular table, which was set for dinner.

"Wow, how elegant." Millie looked at the old built-in hutch featuring china pieces displayed on all five shelves and small lights to showcase them. Crown molding hugged the ceiling. She glanced at Luke. "You'll need to show me the rest of this house after dinner."

"Or you can come back for the annual holiday historical homes tour. It's this Wednesday night, and our home is part of it."

"So I've heard." She grinned at him. "And that's now two invites to your house? I'm in. This place is gorgeous."

Luke pulled out one of the chairs for her. "My parents have worked hard over the last twenty years remodeling this place and making it what it is today. The entryway was originally built in the Victorian age, and the original home started out as one story. There's been a lot of expansion over the decades."

Brandon came in holding two glass bowls, followed by Debbie who was carrying the ham. They placed the dishes in the middle of the table.

"I just need to get the dinner rolls and the fritters, and we'll be all set. Start digging in!"

Debbie went back to the kitchen, and Millie saw baked beans in one bowl and a salad in another.

"Maple baked beans. You'll be addicted to them with your first bite." Brandon handed her the bowl.

Millie filled her plate, and even though she'd just met the Thayers, she felt at ease as they began to eat.

———

"How about some coffee outside?" Luke suggested after dinner as he watched Millie wrap her arms around her waist. "Don't worry, we have a firepit." Outdoor firepits in Charleston were always comfortable, but Millie wasn't sure about experiencing one in the icy night air.

"I hope it's a big one," she said.

"Very big. Dad installed it last year, and we have soft couches and thick blankets out there too." Luke nodded toward the back door when she didn't answer right away. "Come on, you won't be cold, you'll see."

Outside, he led her down a lit-up walkway, and when they reached a large patio, the first thing she saw was a pool closed up for the winter. Next to it stood a trellis with covered furniture. She could imagine summer days enjoying that pool or having a drink under the pergola.

"It's Mom's favorite part of the house." Luke paused and followed her gaze. "In the spring, summer, and even early fall, she plants an abundance of flowers around it. I know you can't see well in the dark, but just to the side is a path that leads to her garden beds."

"I bet it's beautiful then." Millie glanced up at him. "Any gardening skills?"

"Me?" He laughed. "Not at all, but I suppose I'll have to learn soon. My parents are going to move out and travel for a while. I believe Mom wants to live down South somewhere afterward, leaving all this to me."

"My mom is a gardener and has taught me a lot. Too bad I won't be here in the spring to give you a hand with that." Millie waited, but he remained silent. Did she say something wrong?

"Or," he finally said, "I'll just have to fly you back up here to take photos of my attempt at matching what my mom does out here. The historical society would get a kick out of whatever I come up with."

He was joking, but when he mentioned flying her back up, Millie was surprised by her instant hope to come back. Keeping her tone flat to hide her enthusiasm, she put her attention back on the darkened patio. "I'd love to see Vermont in the warmer months. I read in one of the brochures at the resort about the lakes and waterfalls." But by spring, the sale would likely be complete. Would she still be welcome then, once Luke learned of the part she'd played in it?

They started walking again. "People don't often think about Vermont as a place to come during the summer, but we have a lot to do, like kayaking, visiting lakes and waterfalls, hiking, horseback riding on the trails, and enjoying some great food at our festivals. It gets hot here, but it's not an intense hot like where you're from."

"I'll have to plan a visit then."

He turned to her, making her nerves tingle. She moved her focus ahead again.

"So where is this firepit?"

"Right over here. Dad wanted to make room for more seating, so he had the patio expanded in this area where there are fewer trees and we can see the stars."

Luke led her past some more bushes and the walkway suddenly opened. He was right, they were under the clear night sky. Millie looked up and the stars she'd seen when she first arrived sparkled brighter now that she was farther from the house lights.

"I see what you mean. What a perfect spot."

"Have a seat. I brought out the blankets earlier. I'll get the fire going."

Millie chose a couch and sat down before pulling a thick wool blanket across her knees, then watched as Luke turned on twinkle lights that cascaded over her, instantly creating a warm ambience. He picked up a few pieces of cut wood from a basin and stacked them in the pit.

"A real wood firepit. My parents have a gas fireplace on their back patio."

"I love the smell of real wood fires." He pulled out a lighter from his vest coat and, within seconds, small flames jumped across the starter shavings.

The flames began to blend into each other and grew taller until the larger wood caught, crackling and sending off heat. As the round brick pit filled with a steady fire, Millie held her hand up against the hot flames. Luke was right—she wasn't cold at all.

"Sit tight. I'm going to get our drinks. Mom said she would brew some coffee after we finished eating, so I bet it's ready."

When he left, Millie pulled the blanket up higher, leaned back, and watched the flames dance on top of each other. Dinner had been delicious, with pleasant conversation. Brandon had asked her about Charleston and her family, then shared about the time he'd taken Debbie there for a visit. Millie had laughed, listening to how lost they'd gotten in the many quaint avenues and side streets as they'd tried to find where they'd parked the car. She'd asked them about living in Alpine Ridge, and Luke had chimed in with some of his memories from childhood.

Everything had gone well until the last couple questions

when Debbie had asked Millie where she had gone to school and how her photography business had got started. Neither question had a clear answer, and Millie wanted them to see her as a true professional, but to keep the conversation flowing, she had said she'd taken some classes in digital photography and that she was still growing her business. To her relief, the Thayers had encouraged her to keep working at it and said they couldn't wait to see her photos from her time in Alpine Ridge, never once hesitating in their responses.

It wasn't until after they were done talking that Millie had realized she'd been bracing herself, somehow convinced the Thayers would be as dismissive and disapproving as her parents. But that hadn't been the case at all. She wasn't sure how she felt about getting such ready acceptance from near strangers when her own parents still hadn't given it to her.

Tangled in her feelings, relief had washed over her when Luke had mentioned he was stuffed, closing the dinner discussion. Now in the silence under the stars, her thoughts turned back to her parents. For years she had told herself it didn't matter what they thought. When she'd graduated from high school, doing the exact opposite of what they had spent years drilling her to do had felt good, rebellious in a way, as if she were being brave and bold by asserting her right to choose her future. Yet she still found herself dwelling on it now, drawing up old hurts and annoyances.

"I'm a grown woman," she whispered to herself and inhaled the crisp air. Rolling her shoulders, the tension slowly unraveled, and the crunching of leaves caught her attention.

"Okay, two coffees, nice and hot." Luke appeared holding a tray and handed her one of the mugs.

"Thank you, waiter," she teased, eyeing the plate also on the tray.

"Mom insisted I bring these cookies out. She just made them this afternoon. Cranberry and white chocolate chip."

"That sounds good." She reached for one after he set the tray between them on the couch while he pulled another blanket out for himself. The tart flavor balanced the creamy white chocolate just right. "I could eat all of those."

"Me too." Luke picked one up and shifted so he faced her. "I had a nice time learning about you at dinner. I've never been to Charleston. In fact, I've never been to South Carolina. I might have to take a trip to see you before you come back here." Shadows of the flames moved across his face, their rhythmic motion mirrored in his steady gaze.

That's two visits he's mentioned now. Maybe he hadn't been joking before. Millie crossed her legs against the shiver that shot through her. It was beginning to become obvious that something was brewing between them, but she worried it might be on false premises. Not just because she was helping the Clarkes sell the resort but because Luke believed she was a professional who had her life as together as he did. He was a college graduate, as well as Alpine Ridge's youngest chairman, while she was an amateur on her first paid job. The embarrassment stung in her cheeks as she looked at him.

"You'd . . . love it there," was all she managed to say.

For the next hour, Millie switched the conversation to more about the town. It was all she could think of to keep the spotlight off her. She recalled what he'd told her about Riley and the property lines on Alpine Mountain.

"I don't want to overstep my boundaries, but I can't help being curious about what Riley wanted to share with you before her accident. What if she was correct that there was some kind of mistake in the deed—that the property lines are wrong somehow? That would mean the resort is on your land too."

Luke glanced at the firepit and took a sip of his coffee. "Yeah. It's definitely something I have thought about a few times, but it seems like a stretch. Surely if that was the case, someone would have figured it out years ago. If I tried to bring it up now, I can't imagine anyone would take it seriously. Not even my parents."

"They don't know about your conversation with her?"

He hesitated then shook his head. "No, I left it alone, especially after she got hurt. It was more important to support the Clarkes as best we could through that time."

Millie didn't say anything for a moment but then agreed with him. "True."

"Besides, the Clarkes are running a wonderful resort that the town and all our yearly guests absolutely love. It isn't the largest resort in the state, but it and the town offer a more personalized touch with a great reputation. Alpine Ridge is able to serve the needs of the ski community, which is our biggest source of income. Why would I want to pick a fight with the family that's keeping this town thriving?"

"Yes, I can see that," she said, forcing a smile while her stomach churned and she tried to swallow a sick feeling. His innocent expression as he watched her only made it worse—she felt as if she was the bad guy in disguise. She almost blurted out the truth, but Ashley's face flashed across her mind. It wasn't her business to tell Luke what the Clarkes were planning on doing. It was the resort's job to break the news when they were ready.

She needed to leave so she could think this through. Maybe she'd ask Ashley to talk to the Clarkes about making the announcement sooner. The sale could upset the towns-people, but after getting to know Luke and his family a little more, she was beginning to care about Alpine Ridge and what it represented. She thought the locals had a right to know what was coming.

"As cozy as this firepit is"—she glanced at him—"and the company, I better get going. I have an early start tomorrow, but this has been wonderful." Millie stood, steadying herself against the cool breeze once she took off the blanket. When he reached his hand out to help support her wobbly legs, she trembled even more. He'd been so nice and polite . . . and had no idea what was about to occur.

"You're welcome. I know my parents enjoyed meeting you, and so did I."

He paused as if to say more, but she took a step toward the house, making him follow. He picked up the tray and walked down the path next to her in silence. When they reached the house, he brought everything to the kitchen and met her back outside with his parents, who stood in the doorway.

"Thank you for dinner and for a good evening!" Millie called over to them.

"You're very welcome. We'd love to have you back soon!" Debbie said and they both waved before going back inside.

"Thank you again for the tour, the soup earlier—everything. It was a great day, and I feel like I'm part of this town already," Millie said to Luke.

He escorted her to her car. "You are. Alpine Ridge loves our guests. Just wait until the upcoming holiday events, starting with the historical homes tour. Will I see you back here for that?"

Luke's hopeful eyes made her nearly melt on top of the snowbank piled behind her.

"The resort gave me the list of events. They'd like me to shoot at as many as I can, and the historical homes tour is on there so, yes, I'll be here."

Luke stepped closer, and she quickly opened the car door, then ducked inside and turned on the ignition.

"See you soon!" After waving, she maneuvered the car to turn around so she didn't have to back out of the dark driveway.

As she passed him, his puzzled expression followed her fast exit. But she was certain it was for the best, saving him from disappointment once he found out about the job she'd come to do.

Chapter Eight

October 15, 1940
Evelyn

As Lawrence Thayer walked toward her, Evelyn placed her hand over her stomach to calm herself. He was a man now, tall with slicked-back brown hair, and not the young boy who'd chased her in the schoolyard. She'd always had her eye on him, and when he'd finally taken her behind a maple tree by her house and kissed her one evening in July under a humid night sky, she'd realized he felt the same way.

While she'd studied American literature at Middlebury College, Lawrence had pursued a bachelor's degree in civil engineering at the University of Vermont. They'd gone long stretches without seeing each other, but she'd thought of him often. Her younger sisters had suspected how Evelyn felt, but she'd never wanted to talk about it, fearing their parents would find out.

The Thayer family had been their neighbors her entire life, yet in a way they were strangers. A long history of ups and downs, most of which she didn't understand, had left a lingering awkwardness that only grew stronger between their fathers, Leroy Foster and Bobby Thayer.

Mr. Thayer was always talking about the property lines. He argued that they hadn't been properly recorded to begin with back in 1804 and that after Alpine Mountain had experienced mudslides in the flood of 1927, the Fosters demanded more than their due. Mr. Thayer didn't have the paperwork to prove his claims, though, since the flood had destroyed some of the documents. As a result, no one gave his claims much credence—but he'd never given up. He'd been determined to reestablish the deed map as far back as Evelyn could remember.

Her father, Leroy, was just as stubborn about it, keeping a century-old fight between the families ongoing. Evelyn had been young when the flood had happened, but she remembered enough to know that the town had been so damaged that trying to sort through the records had been a nightmare.

Surveyors were brought in after the flood to make the best of what was left of Alpine Mountain, but none of it was done perfectly. Evelyn knew the fight had never been fully resolved since then, and the town mostly chose to stay well out of it—leaving the neighboring families to their feuding over what the surveyors tried to conclude.

As Lawrence approached her with an adoring smile and holding a box, she didn't care one bit whose land crossed which part of the mountain.

"Evelyn." He pushed the box under one arm and took her hands. "Sorry I'm late meeting you."

"It's quite alright," she said. "I laid out a blanket for us and brought a picnic—ham sandwiches, apples, baked beans, and chocolate cake I got from the bakery to celebrate with you in this stunning autumn landscape." She waved her hand around, showing off Vermont's fiery hues of orange and red that had replaced the once-verdant mountain. She had waited by one of their new favorite spots in an open area on the mountain that overlooked the scenery. "A lovely lunch for the birthday boy."

"Sounds delicious," he said, taking her hand and guiding her down on the blanket next to him.

Lawrence was twenty-two today and excited about his planned career as a certified engineer, an option made possible in Vermont thanks to a law passed the year prior that now licensed their engineers. It would open more opportunities and financial rewards for him—and their future together. Evelyn's goals as a librarian were much simpler, but it was the perfect job for her, surrounded by literature and history. Together, they were positive about their path forward and had begun to discuss finally telling her parents about their relationship.

The Fosters had spent the past two years clearing trees for new ski slopes and building a small resort, with plans to open that December. It would feature nine new trails and a rope pull. The town was greatly looking forward to the new business, hoping to relieve some of the tension that had been building with the progress of World War II overseas. Germany was pushing through with more invasions, the most recent in the Soviet Union, and it felt as though America was on pins and needles waiting to see what President Roosevelt would do now that Congress had approved the nation's first peacetime military draft. Not to mention that the next day was R-Day: Registration Day. Was the United States anticipating its involvement in the war?

Evelyn wasn't sure, but as she looked into Lawrence's brown eyes, she feared what it would mean for him—and for the whole town. A lot of young men might end up getting sent overseas if their country joined the fighting. What would happen to those of them who were left behind? And her family's ski resort . . . Would they be able to continue running it?

"What were you busy doing?" she asked.

"I was late because my father just gifted me this." He opened the box and pulled out a black camera, proudly holding it up. "It's the Kodak 35 with a *range finder*."

Evelyn chuckled. "I don't know what that means, but you look delighted, so I am too!"

"It means it has a focusing mechanism that allows me to measure the distance when I'm aiming toward something to capture and put it in focus. I can't wait to try it out." Lawrence pointed the camera to the fall foliage and twisted one of the knobs at the top. "Especially on these trees."

Seeing him with his new camera was like watching a child on Christmas morning. Photography had been a hobby of his for the last few years. During college, taking pictures became a form of stress relief.

"I can't wait to see how your pictures come out with that." She watched him take a few more shots. "Lawrence, I overheard my father earlier, talking about the registration tomorrow. I'm so worried."

He lowered the camera, and his tense body language told her he wasn't surprised by the statement. He must have been just as concerned. The news from overseas was growing more frightening by the day.

Lawrence turned to her, set his camera down, and took her hands. "I am too, but we have to stay calm. Just because I register doesn't mean I'll get picked right away. Or even qualify for service."

Right away. Evelyn swallowed, trying to keep her composure. The last thing she wanted was to upset him on his birthday, but his words only made her feel worse. Of course he qualified. He was healthy, not married, and already finished with college—all perfect requirements for the military.

"So that means eventually you will likely be drafted."

"Maybe," he said, trying to assure her with a smile. "The

United States hasn't officially entered the war yet. The president just wants to start training more men is all. Come on, let's eat and drop this war talk."

"Good idea," she said, but she still felt uneasy. The United States may not be in the war yet, but she wasn't sure how long they could hold out. "Then I'll accompany you while you take pictures and teach me more about the camera."

Lawrence kept his gaze on hers. "Evelyn . . ."

"Yes?" A gentle warmth surged through her chest as he caressed the palm of her hand.

"I love you," he said, nearly whispering, as though their parents were nearby.

"I love you too," she said, her eyes stinging with joy. "So very much."

"Whatever our parents say or however they react, it doesn't matter. I want to marry you, Evelyn Foster. And perhaps together we can end this nonsense between our families. All the land will become ours anyway after we wed. We will fix this. I promise." Lawrence being the oldest of the two Thayer sons, his father had allotted the house and property to go to him one day. Regardless, his brother, Kenneth, was also ready for the constant arguing to end.

"I can't wait," she said as he drew her close and sealed his promise with a soft kiss.

"And don't you worry about the state of our world right now," he said. "Or the draft. I'm not going anywhere."

———

Present Day

"Irene?" Millie said when she entered the resort lobby. "I'm surprised to see you still here." Her head was consumed with her evening with the Thayers—mainly the way Luke had looked at her when he'd mentioned visiting Charleston—and she'd almost walked right past Irene without seeing her.

The woman glanced up from the computer. "Our overnight front desk person is sick, and I'm covering the first shift before someone else comes in around midnight. It's all good, though, because it gives me a chance to catch up on paperwork when it's quieter like this. And anyway, tomorrow is my day off." Irene narrowed her eyes. "Where are you coming back from looking so flushed? Did you take a walk?"

"Oh, no. I was just at the Thayers' house for dinner," she said.

Irene stood up and came around the desk. "Really? How'd that go?"

"Debbie Thayer made a nice dinner and we had good conversation. They are such kind people."

"Yes, they are. Very gracious and a big part of this town, contributing to just about every cause and new development to improve Alpine Ridge. Did Luke invite you to dinner?"

"His mom did actually, but that was because we bumped into her after he gave me a tour of the town this morning, and then we had some delicious soup at the café on main street." Millie studied the woman's odd expression. "Why do you ask?"

Irene quickly shook herself out of the trance she appeared to be in. "Oh, no reason. Well." She chewed her bottom lip before continuing. "Actually, can you sit for a moment?"

"Yeah, I can, but only for a little while. I have an early start tomorrow. I'm meeting the Clarkes for breakfast." Millie followed Irene to the couches by the fire.

"I'm glad you'll finally meet them. They are also good people, even if they're still working their way through a tough two years since . . ." Irene shifted in her stance. "Do you know about their daughter, Riley?"

Millie nodded. "Yes, Ashley told me what happened."

"So tragic." Irene sat next to her. "So the only reason I asked is because Luke has . . . Well, I don't know how to say it without giving away his entire life's story. But he isn't as social as you might think."

"Really? He opened up easily with me and told me all about the town."

"That makes me happy. Luke is like a son to me. I remember holding him as a newborn." Irene paused, crossing and uncrossing her legs, clearly trying to find the right words. "You see, growing up, he was such an active young boy and always had lots of friends. He was outspoken and even the star hockey player for the high school team. He loves Alpine Ridge, and I always used to joke that one day he'd be the chair on the board of selectmen, and I was right."

That all sounded like what Millie would have expected from her interactions with Luke so far.

"So what happened?" she asked. "He still seems open and pleasant."

"Oh, he is . . . very much so, but he's not the Luke we all remember. After college, he came back home and introduced us all to his college sweetheart who . . ." Irene stopped and looked at her hands for a moment.

"It's okay." Millie could tell Irene was struggling with whether to share this information. "You don't have to tell me. It's not like I'm dating him, and, besides, he may not want me to know this."

"You'll find out, especially in this town while you're spending time with him. People are watching, believe me. Because . . ." She smiled at Millie. "I already knew you two were at the café earlier. A few women from town came to ski today and said they saw you there together."

Millie grinned. "Wow. I'm not used to such small-town gossip."

Irene leaned over and patted her knee. "Well, get used to it. Luke is so loved around here that anywhere he goes, there are eyes on him. The women who told me were happy to report the news because we're all waiting on him to get back out there and maybe start dating." She raised a brow.

"No, no. That wasn't a date," Millie said, waving her hands. "He was just being polite after giving me a tour, and then his mom happened to see us when we left. Like I said, she was the one who invited me to dinner."

"Uh-huh." Irene didn't look convinced. "Anyway, all I wanted to say is that it turned out his college girlfriend was trying to use him for the wealth the Thayers have. Brandon Thayer was very successful in his career."

"Yeah, I heard about that too and how they traveled a lot." Millie shook her head. "And how awful about Luke's ex-girlfriend."

"It was. He had proposed to her, and shortly after he found out she wasn't faithful either." She sat back against the couch. "The woman almost convinced him to marry her without a prenup and nearly took him to the cleaners." A loud pop from the fireplace caught Irene's attention, and she watched the flames. "Since then, he's kept to himself for the last year, which has been hard to see at only twenty-seven years old. He should be out dating and having fun. Needless to say, the women I spoke to—and myself—were happy to see him spending time with you today."

Millie's heart went out to Luke. She'd never gone through anything like that, but she was familiar with solitude and loneliness. Outside of one man she'd casually dated on and off for a year and sporadically seeing her friends, her anxiety over her career had kept her isolated for the most part. It was ironic how she'd put so much thought into photography, yet she'd been stagnant with her success.

"Then I'm happy he appeared to be enjoying himself with

me. We did have a good time, both at the café and his parents' house."

"Good! I hope it continues." Irene stood and Millie followed. "You better go get some rest."

"You're right. Goodnight." Millie headed for the elevators, her mind circling the new information about Luke. He seemed like such a great guy and had a lot to offer a woman one day, but she didn't want to get Irene's or anyone else's hopes up that the woman would be her—especially after the Clarkes made the announcement about the sale.

———

THE ROOM WAS DARK WHEN MILLIE'S ALARM startled her awake Monday morning. She tossed off the covers and found a somber gray sky that looked as if it was about to unleash a snowstorm any minute. She picked up her phone and, sure enough, her weather app had alerted her of a snow advisory of one to two inches coming, plus a missed call from Lila.

Millie padded into the bathroom and turned on the shower, then tapped her sister's number.

"Hey, sis!" Lila answered, sounding extra awake.

Millie smiled. "How much coffee have you had already?"

"Not enough to get me going this morning. You caught me just as I've parked at the office. I called before to check in. How's everything going?"

"It's going well so far. I had a nice tour of the town yesterday, followed by a wonderful home-cooked meal at a resident's home. I could get used to this small-town life."

"Sounds like you're enjoying yourself then," her sister said.

"Very much so." The bathroom began to steam. "Today will be my first snowstorm too."

"I hope you won't be driving in it. The locals don't need

to have to dig you out from the side of the road." Lila's laugh echoed through the phone.

"I definitely won't be. Ashley is driving me around today. She's picking me up for breakfast with the resort owners soon, so I better get ready. But Lila?" Millie paused, not sure if she should even bother asking, but she couldn't help herself. "Have Mom and Dad asked about me? Mom texted the first day to make sure I made it up here, but when I responded that I had, she didn't say anything else."

A car door shut and Lila's breathing became a little heavier as she started walking. "You know them," she said. As the background traffic noise faded she lowered her voice. "Never ones to bother anyone. I just got inside the office, so I need to go too. I'll talk to you again soon. Love you!"

Millie ended the call and stepped into the shower, letting the hot water wake her up. Her sister's words rang through her mind. *Never ones to bother anyone.* Except for Lila. They were in constant contact with her sister, wanting to know all about what was happening in her job and life. They bragged to everyone in Charleston about how great an obstetrician Lila was, and while Millie agreed about her sister's skills and success, Millie had always hoped they would someday be just as proud of her.

Finished in the shower, she turned off the water and pushed her parents out of her mind. It was time to meet the Clarkes.

CHAPTER NINE

The snow was falling fast and thick as Millie hurried to Ashley's SUV when her friend pulled up to the front of the resort.

Ashley smiled at her when she got in. "Hi! This is one of those cold snowstorms."

"Aren't all snowstorms cold?" Millie asked, her arms crossed as she tried to warm up.

Ashley chuckled and carefully drove down the driveway toward the road. "No. Some are the fun kind where kids can go outside and play in it for hours without turning into icicles. But today it's only sixteen degrees. I think this winter will be a rough one."

Millie glanced at the falling snow outside her window. "It's beautiful though."

"Yeah, except not while we drive in it. But, thankfully, this SUV does well in the snow." Ashley turned up the music and Christmas tunes played as Millie continued to watch the white scenery pass by. She had seen snow in movies and TV shows her whole life, but as the flakes danced in a whirlwind through the air—it was clear the videos did no justice to the real thing.

"I feel like a kid witnessing this. It's so exciting. I'm really loving this more than I thought I would." She turned to Ashley. "And a fresh new layer for the slopes, which I can't wait to experience."

"Then maybe by the end of your stay, I can convince you to move here." A smile played at her friend's mouth.

Millie considered the statement and realized it didn't overwhelm her to hear the idea. Perhaps she was meant to settle down in the north. There was a resort back home she had a chance to reapply to, but something about Vermont was grabbing hold of her.

"Not sure you'll have to do much to convince me." Millie looked out the window again when Ashley slowed at a stoplight. The snowflakes flipped in circles when the car fully stopped. "I'm already being sold on that possibility."

"You know you're always welcome here." The light changed and Ashley turned onto a side road that Millie recognized.

"Ah, this is the road, right? I recognize it from last night when I went to the Thayers'."

"You were at Luke's parents' house last night?" Ashley glanced at her wide-eyed.

"His mom invited me for dinner after Luke and I ran into her outside the café."

"A café date yesterday too?" Ashley's mouth dropped open. "And here I was excited about the hot chocolate he offered to get before I left. Sounds like it was quite a day."

"It was, but it wasn't a date." Millie snorted. "We just got some soup after walking around outside all morning. Anyway, his mom is so nice. She invited me over for a home-cooked meal."

"Debbie is the sweetest person, and you're right—this is the road. The Clarkes are just next door. But let's go back to your date at the café—"

"It wasn't a date!" Millie said again, louder, and laughed when Ashley gave her a funny face.

They turned into a long driveway and Millie looked ahead, but didn't see the house yet.

"How did Luke seem when you were at the café?" Ashley asked.

"He was fine. Easy to talk to and polite." Millie remembered what Irene had shared with her. "I saw Irene at the front desk last night when I got back, and she pretty much asked me the same thing."

"I'm sure she did. She will gossip about anyone at any time, and she knows *everything* about this town. Give her a week, and she'll figure out where you live in Charleston and all about your family."

"I don't doubt that. She offered me a lot of information about Luke. And she seemed happy he spent time with me yesterday."

They slowly made their way around a bend, which finally revealed the house.

"Wow. Look at that."

A gorgeous redbrick home stood in the distance.

"It's a beauty alright."

Millie peeked over at Ashley, not sure if she should bring up this part, but her friend seemed to know a lot about Luke, too, despite what she'd originally said. "I know Alpine Ridge isn't the town you grew up in, but you're pretty up to date on Luke's life for only being 'acquaintances.' The small-town gossip must trickle over to you too," she teased.

Ashley laughed. "You got that right. But Mount Holly is just as small as here, so listening to local chatter in a tiny community is all I know. Why, what's up?"

"Well, Irene shared how worried she has been about him. So I'm wondering if you knew about that."

Ashley nodded. "I did know, and I wouldn't be surprised

if she told you about his ex. That story has really bothered her. Luke is like a son to Irene."

"Yes, she mentioned that. It sounds like it was terrible."

"It was. And Irene is like the whole town's second mom and really cares, so I know she's been sincerely worried about him. Personally, I've only heard about how he used to be prior to that relationship, and since I didn't know him back then, I have nothing to compare. But the times I've crossed paths with him, he's had this look to him."

"A look?" Millie prompted.

"I can't describe it. He's always pleasant, but if you happen to catch him by himself, you can see this sadness on his face, even though he clearly tries hard to cover it up. Unlike Irene, though, I happen to think he's started moving on lately. Taking over as the town's chairman has really absorbed him. When I look at him now versus a year ago when I first arrived, I see him as just a laid-back, hardworking man."

"I see that too." Millie didn't say anything else as she stared in amazement at the large, brick house with black shutters that was now right in front of them. Small Christmas wreaths hung on every window and twinkle lights cascaded in the bushes along the front of the home. More greenery lined the black front door, and the small square, covered front porch extended out with white pillars.

"Here we are." Ashley parked and turned off the ignition.

"It's so classical looking," Millie said, then stepped out of the car, staring at the home. "Do you know when it was built?"

"This is the family's second house on the property. They built this one after the 1927 flood wiped out the earlier farmhouse. The brick is much sturdier in case we ever flood that bad again."

They walked up onto the porch and knocked. A faint

"Come on in!" reached them from inside and Ashley opened the door.

"Hello?" she called.

A woman appeared at the top of a large winding staircase and made her way down to greet them.

"Ashley! Good to see you," the woman said, then pulled her in for a hug and glanced at Millie. "And you must be the famous Millie she's been bragging about. I'm Joyce Clarke."

"Nice to finally meet you," Millie said and extended her hand.

But Joyce waved it off. "Can I hug you instead?" Before Millie could answer, the woman embraced her. "You have no idea how happy I am that you're here and were available for this job."

"I'm happy to be here too." *It's not like there were any offers holding me back in Charleston.* Millie scrunched her nose against the thought and smiled at Joyce.

"Ashley said you were beautiful, but my goodness, look at you! Those curls are amazing." Joyce stepped back to admire her. "Remind me of Riley's," she added under her breath.

"Joyce," Ashley cut in to distract the woman still staring at Millie with such sadness in her eyes. "Where should we put our coats and purses?"

Joyce blinked before turning toward Ashley. "You can leave them here in the front hall on the chair right there. I'm going to find Dylan. Breakfast is already done, so go have a seat in the sunroom. You know where that is, right?"

"Yes," Ashley said and gestured toward the hallway. "Come on, Millie. You can see the rest of the original part of the house before we get there. The sunroom was added only a few years ago."

Joyce headed in another direction and Millie walked behind Ashley, looking up at the old sconces that now held electric antique-styled bulbs. "I love that they kept the sconces intact."

Ashley followed her gaze. "Yeah, I've always loved that about these old homes."

They passed a living room with posts and beams across the ceiling that looked to be in the middle of getting redone. "Are they remodeling?"

"Yes. They've updated a bunch of things over the years, but the beams that were in that living room needed to be replaced before they list the home." Ashley pointed to the boxes around them. "Watch your step. They're getting the place ready for an estate sale."

"I get the resort, but I can't believe they're selling this place too," Millie said in a low voice in case Joyce or her husband was nearby.

Ashley leaned toward her. "Me either. But none of us at the resort would dare say that to them."

They reached the bright sunroom, equipped for all seasons with nine-pane windows that looked similar to the ones in the front of the house and an arched ceiling with a large fan. A small woodstove fireplace sat in the corner, warming the room nicely. The wide-open room gave them a good view of the property and the snow still falling outside. A round table was set for breakfast, and they each took a seat.

Millie took a closer look around her. "I absolutely love this room."

"I do too. Last year Joyce had the whole house decorated to the max for the historical homes tour and the resort's holiday staff party. She put a large Christmas tree in here with added twinkle lights above. It was so pretty that I sat in here most of the night."

"Hi, Ashley." A man appeared in the doorway holding a steaming mug.

"Dylan, how are you?" Ashley stood again to shake his free hand.

"Doing well. How were things at the resort while we were away?" he asked as he sat down across from Millie and flashed her a wide grin.

"Everything ran smoothly, and Millie here arrived and is ready for the job."

"I see that," he said, holding his hand out across the table. "Dylan Clarke."

"Thank you for having me for breakfast. You have a wonderful resort," she said as she shook his hand. "And a lovely home. I'm in awe with how beautiful it all is."

"That's very kind of you. Joyce and I sure do love this home. It's been in my family for generations, and we have many memories here." His expression turned wistful.

Millie sensed he was thinking about his daughter and glanced at her friend who gave her a knowing look.

"Ashley has been so helpful," she said quickly to capture his attention again. "She got me settled in the resort and has really painted the picture of what you need for the pitch, but I'm looking forward to hearing from you and Joyce too."

"Ashley is our best employee," Dylan said, his face relaxing into a smile.

"He tells everyone that," Joyce teased as she came into the room holding a pot of coffee. "Would anyone like some?"

"Yes, please." Millie raised her mug.

"But he's not wrong," Joyce said, winking at Ashley. "We couldn't do half of what we do at the resort without her."

"And Irene!" Ashley held up her finger. "Let's not forget her."

"Of course," Dylan said. "Irene has been taking care of me since I was a child." He looked at Millie. "She used to babysit me when she was barely a teenager herself."

"I love how tight-knit this town is. My mind has been

flowing with ideas for ways to display that." Millie took a sip of her coffee, the strong roast instantly giving her a buzz.

"I'll be right back with the food, but carry on with your conversation." Joyce finished filling the mugs and dashed out of the room.

Dylan leaned back in his chair with his coffee. "I'm glad you have ideas already because marketing is not my area of expertise. Joyce has some thoughts that she'll share, but I'm okay with whatever you come up with. I'm sure it'll turn out great. Ashley wouldn't bring just anyone to do the job."

Millie's heart thudded against her chest. Little did Mr. Clarke know it was her first professional assignment. It took everything in her to muster up a confident smile.

"No, I wouldn't." Ashley grinned in her direction. "I worked with Millie for several years down in Charleston at a restaurant and saw her work ethic and talent firsthand whenever she'd take pictures while we were out together, so I know she will do a great job."

Joyce returned with a tray holding a bowl of scrambled eggs, stacks of toast, and bacon, and placed it down in front of them. "I also have maple sugar pancakes coming right up!"

"Dig in, everyone," Dylan said and picked up the plate of bacon.

While the three of them filled their plates, Joyce came back with the pancakes and a jug of orange juice. "I can get you some water too, but this is fresh-squeezed."

"Everything looks delicious. Thank you, Joyce." Millie picked up her fork. "I've never had maple sugar pancakes, but then again, I've never really had much maple anything until coming here."

"They're a Vermont classic and a special treat." Joyce put food on her own plate and sat down. "That's why I made them, for you to enjoy."

For the next hour, the group chatted casually about

Millie's upbringing in the South and about her family. She could see why her parents loved to talk about Lila. It was easy to brag about her accomplishments and being a doctor and bringing babies into the world. Then Joyce surprised her with her next question.

"Your family sounds very successful. But I think what you do is special. Being a creative takes hard work and talent that not many of us have. What are your favorite photos that you've taken to date?"

Millie's mind spun as she replayed all the times when it was just her and the camera over the years. How could she pinpoint any favorites? They all meant something to her, something she couldn't quite explain at the breakfast table. After years of living under Lila's shadow, she'd picked up her first camera in a high school photography class. It was also where she felt the most comfortable in those years—using it to cope with the lingering sense of inadequacy she'd had her entire life under the crushing weight of her parents' favoritism for her older sister.

"It's hard to say which ones one would be my favorite. When I look at each photo I've taken, I remember where I was at the time and what I was observing and feeling," Millie began, watching Joyce lean toward her. "Each picture I take has a different meaning and is special in its own way."

"Interesting. So it sounds like you not only take pictures of the world through the lens of your camera, but also capture how *you* personally viewed the people and places at the time. Is that correct?" Joyce asked.

"Exactly." While looking at Joyce's supportive eyes, something in Millie stirred. Her initial fear of not having enough experience as a photographer momentarily eased. "I've taken so many candid pictures of strangers on my own time, capturing unguarded moments of joy, sorrow, and every emotion in between."

Joyce drew her hands together with a wide smile. "I knew Ashley would bring us the right person, and that's definitely you, Millie. Your passion is exactly what we need for this pitch."

Dylan cleared his throat. "I think what my wife is trying to say, and please correct me if I'm wrong, dear, but we want you to bring those emotions to life through the pictures you take of this town, the resort, and the people here. You see, the corporation we're talking to—Peak Holdings—has invested in the largest mountains here in Vermont. We are very small in comparison."

"That's right." Joyce beamed at Millie. "And we want to show them how size doesn't matter. It's Alpine Ridge and what it represents that make the purchase a good investment. Hearing you describe your work I'm convinced your photos will do just that."

"This will be a fun project to put together," Millie said, feeling a lot more relaxed about her abilities after seeing how happy her response made the Clarkes.

"We will knock this pitch out of the park for you two. But . . ." Ashley paused, appearing suddenly flustered. "There's an issue Millie brought up at the diner the other morning."

Millie shifted in her seat, not knowing what Ashley was about to say. "I'm sure whatever it was isn't relevant to the goals we just discussed." She looked nervously at her friend, wanting to avoid any potential upset.

"It is, though." Ashley ignored her pleading stare and focused on the Clarkes. "When are we planning on telling the town about this potential sale?"

Dylan crumbled a napkin in his hand and looked at Joyce. "We talked about that while we were away."

Joyce looked at both women. "Yes, we did, and we agreed that, while the town needs to know our plans, we don't want that knowledge to disrupt the feel of Millie's pictures. I'm not sure she could capture what we just discussed if everyone knew what we were planning to do with the photos. It just won't be the same vibe."

Because the townspeople would be too upset to let me photograph them if they knew about the sale. Mille twisted her mouth against her thoughts, trying to maintain a professional composure. This shouldn't be bothering her, especially because she wasn't a resident, but the thought of Luke's face after hearing the truth about her job sat heavy on her mind. He loved the resort. The town loved it—just the way it was.

"Soon," Dylan chimed in. "We will share this soon."

When Millie and Ashley returned to the car, the radio was the only thing filling the silence for a few minutes. The guilt of being the one to create this pitch for the Clarkes only grew heavier on Millie's chest.

"I know they don't want to ruin my chance of getting good images around town and the essence of Alpine Ridge, but, Ashley, don't you feel bad not telling people?" Millie asked.

Ashley immediately drew her brows together. "Sometimes, but I have a job to do. And so do you." Ashley kept her eyes on the road. The snow was slowing down, and the plows were already cleaning up the roads, making for a smooth drive back to the resort. "Don't worry about the drama of the sale. Keep your focus through that camera lens and create some magic."

Luke jumped into Millie's thoughts again, but she tried to push him aside. She just needed to do what she did best and keep to herself and out of the gossip. Though something told her that would be easier said than done.

Chapter Ten

Ashley waved and drove off after dropping Millie back at the resort, saying she had to head to an appointment that was off the property. Millie decided to go over the schedule for the week back in her room before taking a walk around. She couldn't wait to hit some spots on the town's holiday events list. She was sure to capture many happy smiling faces at all the Christmas fun.

By the time she finished sorting through the list and putting a schedule together, it was well past noon. She was still full from breakfast but went down to the lobby to get something hot to drink at the café inside the resort. After scanning the specials on the board outside the door, she settled for a chai. Inside, Millie was welcomed with holiday cheer. A Christmas tree in the corner was decorated in a simple buffalo-red plaid ribbon with large wooden snowflakes, pinecones, red holly berries, and flashing white lights, continuing the rustic theme of the resort. Under the tree, presents were wrapped in brown paper, with red ribbons and vintage bells tied on top and dangling off the sides.

To her right, evergreen garland with more twinkle lights

adorned the large windows, giving her a perfect view of Alpine Mountain. Skiers were sliding down the slopes, enjoying the fresh snowfall. As she watched the lift take more people up, she was drawn in to the wintery scene, only looking away when a tap on her shoulder told her it was her turn to order.

A few minutes later, with her tea and camera in hand, she began to explore. She'd only been in the restaurant, lobby, and her suite so far and was ready to check out the other public areas of the resort building. As she walked down a hallway, she was surprised at how big the space was.

A small sign caught her attention: "Library." *A library in a resort?* Curious, Millie pushed open the door and found herself in a square room where two walls were lined with shelves and filled with books. An electric fireplace was already turned on and sat adjacent to the shelves and a couch. Two armchairs were beside it with lamps on the side tables for extra lighting. A few other chairs were scattered around the room for more seating.

Stepping back, she held up her camera and took a few shots. The library was traditional in its design, which she found interesting. Was this room built when the resort first opened? If not, when? Questions started to pour through her mind as she picked up one of the books off the shelves: *The History of Vermont's Forestry.* She opened the book, then leafed through the old pictures showing men clearing the state's thick forests. After putting it back on the shelf, she browsed some other titles, all about Vermont's history. Glancing down, she counted seven large photo albums sticking out on the bottom shelf where they didn't quite fit. She picked up one and sat on the couch to look through it. It was full of old black-and-white photos. The title at the top of the first page was handwritten in pen: *Alpine Ski Resort's First Christmas Post WWII,*

December 1945

Tracing her finger along the pictures, Millie leaned closer, admiring the fashion of the time, the old Christmas décor, and what the resort had looked like then.

"These are fantastic," she mumbled to herself.

For the next hour, Millie combed through all seven albums, looking at photographs from when the resort was built in the summer of 1940, before the war, and then seeing the women of Alpine Ridge doing their best to run it while many men were away fighting. The pictures showed how the resort had progressed through nearly a century. As she continued browsing the albums, she gained a clear picture of how the resort had started and operated over the years, complete with visuals. Some of the people in the photos had probably passed away by now, but she couldn't help wondering who they were and about their life stories. She also saw the Clarke family's original farmhouse and the current home right after it was built in 1927.

When she got to the more recent albums, she recognized Dylan and Joyce in their earlier years together. The first picture was of them toasting inside the resort's restaurant in 1992. It was neat to see how everything was decorated then versus what she'd seen when she was there with Ashley the other night. Seeing the Clarkes' smiling faces on the next page, out on the mountain and ready to hit the slopes, made her a little sad. She'd just met them, but their life together as a couple had been centered around this resort—more so for Dylan, whose family had started it in 1940. He had spent his entire upbringing there. And they were selling it all.

The last album had pictures from the winter of 1998. Maybe there were more albums kept somewhere else? Millie hoped so because she was totally invested in the resort's history. When she flipped to the final page, she caught her breath as she read its title: *Riley's First Alpine Christmas*. There were only five pictures, and Millie's eyes suddenly stung as she looked at the photo of Joyce holding baby Riley, who was bundled up so much that all Millie could see was her little face. Behind them was Alpine Mountain with skiers all over it —where Riley's fall had changed everything for the Clarkes only two years ago.

After closing the album, Millie picked up her cold chai and took the last sip. *Pictures really do tell stories*. She thought about the sales pitch the Clarkes wanted her to take photographs for, and as she felt the emotions from flipping through these albums bubbling to the surface, she became eager to put the pitch together. If these photos could draw her in, then surely Peak Holdings would feel the same about her images. That had been her entire goal all these years with her work. Sure, she'd taken practice shots here and there at friends' birthday parties over the years or at family gatherings, but it was the photos she'd taken in public that spoke volumes. Her entire portfolio told stories, and like these old albums had done for her, her portfolio had the same effect on everyone who had browsed through it . . . even if it hadn't quite landed her the job she'd needed. Until now.

Something suddenly shifted in Millie, and she felt a profound sense of self-assurance emerging within her for the first time since she'd arrived, pushing her out of the cloud of doubt that had gripped her for so long. She was about to get in front of the action and the residents of Alpine Ridge and tell their stories in real time. She was more ready than ever.

———

Millie set down her bags and camera in the living room of her suite on Wednesday afternoon, feeling as if she'd run a marathon after carrying in everything. When she woke up that morning, she knew it was time to take the gift card the resort had provided and go get some ski pants, which she perhaps should have done before stepping out in the snow the day before. She'd spent most of the previous day standing out near the slopes capturing pictures and—a last-minute idea—B-roll video of the skiers on the mountain from afar.

The staff near the ski lift had agreed to be included in close-up photos, as did the parents of the children she'd photographed, and she had fun making them laugh as they tried to look casual for the camera. It was her first run working directly with people while she took pictures and so far everything was running smoothly. She also met Josh, the resort's lead ski instructor. While watching him give some preschool-aged children a lesson, she carefully maneuvered her camera around him and the kids to get that perfect angle. It pleased her how emotive he was as he went through his lesson, which would make the pictures even better. Not to mention, he was a natural at teaching, and she couldn't wait to get herself out there for a lesson.

The day had been a productive but cold one. Even though she wasn't flying down the slopes, she struggled to stand in the icy breeze, so a visit to Alpine Gear was needed. The sales associate was helpful and showed her what she needed. When she tried on the snow pants in the dressing room, she'd grown sweaty almost immediately, so she knew they would keep her legs toasty out on the mountain.

Now back at the resort, it was time to get ready for the holiday historical homes tour.

Her phone buzzed from her purse and when she pulled it out she saw that it was Lila.

"Well hello there, stranger!" Millie answered, still catching her breath.

"Were you just running or something?" Lila said.

"I just dragged in two heavy bags from my car to my suite, and one of the bags included new snow boots." Millie picked up the bag with the boots and took them out of the box, storing them in the front closet.

"It's official." Lila chuckled. "I've lost you to Vermont's snowy landscape."

"I was out there yesterday taking pictures of the slopes, and even with the jacket that Ashley lent me, I came back in and couldn't feel my legs. These new snow pants will be great out there."

"Have you tried skiing yet?"

"Not yet, but I met the head ski instructor yesterday. He's really good at teaching, which I'll need. But I'm excited to try soon."

"Good! How's everything else with the job going?"

"So far, it's been going well. I experienced a first yesterday working directly with subjects in a professional setting out on that mountain. It was so much fun." Millie smiled, remembering how the staff had kept laughing every time she'd held up the camera, but eventually they'd gotten in the groove, and she was looking forward to scrolling through the pictures she'd taken.

"See? You're a natural. This job is just as perfect for you as I knew it would be. Getting away from South Carolina and trying something new was the best thing you could have done."

"Thanks."

Her sister was right. Despite how supportive Lila had always been of her career, it really made a difference to get away to a place where people saw her just as herself, not as Lila's little—and perhaps, unsuccessful—sister. Or maybe that had only been in her head since that was how her parents always seemed to view her. The camera had always been a crutch for Millie, a tool to vent for so long, and yesterday—taking those pictures as a hired expert—had begun to free her from that emotional burden.

As soon as her parents came to mind, she had to ask. "How are Mom and Dad?"

"You know, I haven't spoken to them in a few days. I've been so busy at work, but last I heard they were spending the weekend in North Carolina visiting some of Dad's old college friends. But . . ." Lila grew quiet. "Before they left, I told them how great everything seemed to be going up there for you. Dad asked a couple questions about the job, mainly about the town and resort, but I didn't have many answers for him. Maybe you should call them."

"Yeah, I will soon." Millie sighed, not wanting to tell Lila that was the last thing she wanted to do. Being on her own, doing what she loved, was exactly what she'd told her parents she would do after high school, and even though Alpine Ski Resort had hired her to do just that—she didn't want to get caught in a conversation where they tried to convince her that making a living with photography after only one job would be impossible. "I just don't feel like putting up my defenses with that conversation right now. I'm really having a nice time here."

"Millie . . ." Lila's frustration was evident in her tone. "You have nothing to prove to them. I just think observing how you sound and learning about what you're doing will help them see how wonderful being a photographer is for you."

"Okay. I'll give them a call." Millie would rather not argue. Lila just wanted their family to grow closer, and she wanted that too. Perhaps her sister was right. Maybe checking in with them without putting up a wall of arguments would start that process of reconciliation. "I have to get going. There's an event in town—a holiday historical homes tour."

"I wish I was there to see those old New England houses, particularly with all the snow. Have fun!"

When she hung up, Millie changed out of her black leggings and into jeans over a white body suit and then slipped on a long dark red boho sweater. It was always easier to take pictures with her hair out of her face, so she pinned back some of her curls and let the rest fall down her back. After adding a little makeup, she was ready to go. Ashley was meeting her in the lobby, and they were going to get a quick bite to eat in town before the tour. She pulled on her tall brown boots, grabbed her camera and purse, and headed downstairs.

"How do you feel about some pub food?" Ashley asked once Millie found her by the front desk holding a piece of paper.

"Anything sounds good. I haven't eaten since this morning." Millie had only grabbed a quick breakfast wrap at the resort's café before shopping. "What's that you're holding?"

"The addresses and schedule for tonight. Our front desk hands this out along with a map for our guests every year. I know where most of the houses are, but sometimes there's a family who can't participate, so I wanted to check the list to know for sure where to go. This year looks pretty full of participants, minus the Clarkes' home."

"Well, I'm glad I got to see their house at breakfast Monday."

"Me too, plus you can check out the estate sale and see more of the house then. Come on, let's go to the tavern in town. They have good craft beer and wings. Not to mention their mac and cheddar cheese is the absolute best in the state. Well, according to us here in Alpine Ridge, that is."

"I have nothing to compare it to, so it'll be delicious to me!" Millie grinned and followed Ashley outside. "This'll be a fun night. I'm looking forward to seeing all the houses."

"And taking lots of pictures," Ashley added as they stepped outside into the chilly December air.

CHAPTER ELEVEN

A quick meal at the tavern ended up being a productive hour in the noisy establishment as Ashley introduced Millie to many residents while they were seated at the bar observing the lively atmosphere.

"What a perfect place to take some pictures." Millie stood up when Ashley immediately nodded. "Let me grab my camera out of the car. Be right back."

When she returned, Ashley pointed to a woman in the front, talking to one of the hostesses. "That's the manager, and I just got the okay from her to take photos."

"We can ask each table and—"

"Or . . ." Ashley got up and faced the dining area, cupping her hands. "Attention, everyone!" Her voice boomed across the restaurant and all the diners grew quiet. "As many of you know, my name is Ashley, and I'm Alpine Ski Resort's director of marketing. Millie and I"—she pointed to her—"are putting together some marketing materials about Alpine Ridge. She's our photographer, and we'd love to take some pictures of the tavern's customers, so please let me know if you are willing to be photographed, and I'll have you sign an agreement saying we can use these photos. It would help us out a lot. Thank you!"

Millie laughed at her friend's boldness. "Well, that'll speed things up."

As hands around the bar went up, Ashley had people e-sign the document she'd prepared on her iPad, while the bartender, Mack, offered Millie a lesson on how they crafted their brew and the history of the tavern. An idea occurred to her, and with Mack's agreement she propped up her camera on a small table tripod she always carried in her photography bag and faced it toward the bartender to record him while he gave her the information. She used her phone to take notes as she listened. Perhaps she could put together dialogue for the pitch and explain what she was capturing through *her* eyes as an outsider looking in. She'd need to run it by Ashley, but figured it would be a bonus when she submitted her final files for the project. The resort hadn't expected B-roll, but she'd already filmed the skiers and was ready to do more. A mixture of still shots and videos could really amp up the pitch.

A short while later, Millie finished recording Mack just as Ashley came back, pointing across the restaurant. "All set. Every table but that party of ten over there in the back agreed."

Millie glanced at Ashley's iPad. "Try having people fill that out while standing by the slopes in the freezing cold."

Ashley grinned. "It's the hardship of this job I suppose."

Millie slowly walked around the bar, taking as many candid shots as possible and even some posed ones, such as another one of Mack holding up a large pint glass and pouring the beer. The excitement of photographing and meeting so many great people had nearly made her forget how hungry she was, until their food arrived at the bar.

She found Ashley chatting with a couple she knew who had just been seated. "Our food is at the bar." Millie nearly ran to it, her stomach now screaming at her with Ashley right behind her.

They'd ordered all the tavern favorites: wings, mac and cheese to share, and Mack's specialty that he'd insisted they try —Vermont farm tacos with short-rib beef, specialty slaw, and a mixture of sauces.

Millie was silent as she tasted everything, and when she looked up, Ashley was beaming.

"Good, huh?"

"I can't get over the food since I've been here," Millie said as Mack finished drying a glass and came over with a grin. "What is this recipe? It's so good."

"I'll never tell! Enjoy, ladies!" He went farther down the bar to serve his other customers.

The women finished their food and Millie got up to take a last quick round of photos of a few more tables before they paid the bill.

Ashley glanced at her phone. "Time to go see the houses," she said and picked up her coat.

"I could eat that mac and cheese every day," Millie said, barely able to draw in a breath as they walked out of the tavern.

"It's that good Vermont cheddar."

"Must be," Millie said and got in the car. She turned on her camera and scrolled through some of the shots she'd taken. "I haven't edited any pictures yet, but these look perfect. I can't wait to see them on the computer."

"Me too." Ashley backed up the car and they were off to start the tour.

They arrived at the first house only a few minutes later. Millie opened the car door and saw people walking inside another home next door and into a couple other houses close by.

"These homes are closer together than I would have thought, considering how old they are."

"This is the original colony square, or rather, the town common from when Alpine Ridge was first chartered in 1794," Ashley explained. She extended a finger. "Just down there, where the lit-up steeple is, is the original meeting house, otherwise known as the congregational church. Every square in New England had a meeting house constructed first and the town common was then built around it. The families that own these historical homes will talk a lot about the town too. You'll learn a lot. And the best part is, they will be dressed in character from an earlier period."

"Wait, before we go in, I can take pictures, right? I don't want to disturb them while they're in their roles."

"Yes, everyone in these homes is ready for you and already signed the agreement."

Millie prepped her camera and they walked up to the first door. A festive wreath hung on it with simple evergreen branches and crimson holly berries similar to the one on the Thayers' front door. It was a cheerful welcome to the flow of guests.

The women stepped into the inviting foyer and were instantly transported back in time. The year 1818 was written on a small plaque just outside the front door, but inside the owners had chosen to portray the year 1860 according to a small sign that was in the entryway and had information for guests to read. The aroma of freshly baked cookies and roasting meat wafted through the air, mingling with the scents of pine and woodsmoke. A sense of wonder filled Millie, just like when she'd walked into the Thayer and Clarke homes. She took a few shots of the old staircase and other elements that served as a testament to the town's rich history and the architectural heritage of the structure.

A vast fireplace was fully blazing when Millie followed

Ashley into the living room where a woman tended to a large black pot that hung in its center. Millie squeezed her way to an open spot near the woman and angled the camera just right to capture the scene.

"The stewed beef is nearly simmered enough." The woman turned from the pot. "Let me help you, Abby." She went to the table where a teenage girl was rolling out dough.

"Thank you, Mother. I have this dough nearly ready to be shaped for the next loaf," the girl said. "This year's harvest was plentiful and will make for a wonderful holiday celebration."

"It sure was." The woman picked up the dough and began to shape it. "And I made plum pudding this year to indulge in."

"How delightful," the young girl said.

Millie inched closer and crouched to get a good picture from below of both women leaned over the table. When she straightened back up, Ashley was by her side.

"This is so cool," Millie whispered.

"Yeah, it's my favorite holiday tradition. Let's keep going."

By the time they finished the first house, Millie was hooked. "This is so fascinating," she said as they walked back to the next home in the square. "But I noticed the plaque on the front of the house wasn't the same year the actors were portraying."

"The year on the plaque is when the house was built." Ashley turned up the heat when the car was on. "Every year the homeowners get to choose a different decade to act out. I believe the next house, based on the schedule, will be the late 1700s when Christmas wasn't even widely celebrated in America yet."

"Wow! Okay." Millie held up her camera. "I'm ready."

An hour went by and the women finished with the fourth house on the colony square. This one had decided to showcase Christmas in 1900, with more recognizable traditions, such as a tree with presents under it. Millie had taken an abundance of pictures and was ready for more.

"How about we head to the Thayers' house now? Wait until you see Luke all dressed up," Ashley said waggling her brows.

"Stop it." Millie playfully nudged her. "Why are you and Irene so invested in what happens between Luke and me?"

"Didn't Irene explain the man well enough for you? He sat in the café with you on a date. That's a first for him in years."

"Okay, now you're stretching the truth a bit. And—again —it wasn't a date!"

"Sitting at a table in a restaurant with a woman then. It was the first time anyone around here has seen him do that since his awful ex." Ashley held up her hand when they reached her car. "And don't try to say he was just being polite."

"Well, he was," Millie mumbled as she got in.

"No, he wasn't. I asked him to show you around Alpine Ridge, explain a little of our history, and that's it. The café date was all him and, besides, I saw the way he looked at you when he first found us by that wagon."

"You mean when he laughed at me falling in the snow?" Millie blushed again thinking about it.

"He was intrigued. I saw it all over his face." Ashley drove down the quiet curves of the country road that led to the Thayer farmhouse, and Millie stayed silent. Luke was handsome alright, but whatever attraction Ashley thought he'd had for her was on a ticking clock with the sale looming over them. As she pictured all the smiling faces she'd got on camera the past few days, she felt a pang of guilt knowing they'd be dealing with the same tough reality.

———

After they parked a little ways down the Thayers' driveway in line with the other cars, Ashley and Millie made their way to the front door. The Thayers had added some more modern lighting to the driveway, which Millie was thankful for as she tried not to slip on the snowy surface.

"Just wait until you see Luke," Ashley said again. "His acting skills are always the talk of the town."

"Oh, yeah? Why's that?"

"Let's just say he and his parents get really into their roles . . . a bit too much." Ashley giggled. "And they always portray ancestors of theirs who were living in the home at the time they choose to reenact."

"I can't wait to see."

Millie got behind Ashley as they approached the front door that suddenly swung open to reveal Luke, brilliantly dressed in what appeared to be early-twentieth-century attire of a brown, three-piece wool suit and a flat newsboy hat.

"Bobby, you dashing young gent," Brandon said from behind Luke, who stood in the doorway rubbing his fake bushy mustache. "Allow these ladies through."

Luke took off his hat and nodded toward the women. "Ah, welcome to our humble abode, Miss—"

He glanced at Ashley who couldn't help but smile.

"Ashley."

"Miss Ashley! And you are?" When his sharp blue eyes, which stood out against the brown suit, found Millie's, she struggled to find her voice.

"Mi-Millie," she finally said, biting her lip against the laughter.

Luke took her hand and drew it to his lips, pausing just before he kissed it, his mischievous eyes on her while she regained her composure.

"Come on in, Miss Millie," he said, making her whole body heat up.

Behind him, Ashley smirked before she mouthed, "*I told you so,*" which Millie tried to ignore.

"My name is Bobby Thayer," Luke continued. "And this is my father, Andrew. My wife, June, must be in the kitchen finishing up with our meal, and our two lads, Lawrence and Kenneth, are around here somewhere."

"Nice to meet you." Millie smiled, glancing at Ashley. She was right—the Thayers really got into this.

Jazz music played in the distance and Debbie came around the corner wearing a fitted green velvet dress that hugged her waistline, with matching long gloves. Her hair was swooped back with finger rolls along her brow, accessorized with a short, see-through veil that hung slightly over the side of her face.

"Come on in, ladies! I'm Andrew's wife, Elizabeth Thayer." Debbie beamed at them, playing her role well. "We have all kinds of hors d'oeuvres in the other room. Dinner will be brought out soon."

When they entered the next room, the formal dining room, Millie immediately drew up her camera toward the table. A small evergreen on the side table atop a white tablecloth caught her eye, and she snapped a few test shots, then quickly adjusted her lens. On the long dining table, oranges and pomegranates intertwined in the greenery amid place settings of nice china. The air was thick with the scents of cinnamon and cloves, and the room was aglow with soft, warm light from candles all around. Moving toward the windows, she got some pictures of them adorned in festive swags of holly and mistletoe.

More people entered the dining room and Brandon came in behind them. "We're so glad you could join us for our holiday soiree," he said, holding up a glass with what appeared to be bourbon. Millie neared him with her camera and Brandon stayed in character. Unlike the other homes that acted out scenes as if the guests weren't there, the Thayers included everyone, which was a fun mix-up.

Luke and Debbie appeared again and regaled everyone with tales of Christmases past in their home. Luke's extravagant acting entertained everyone, making the room roar with laughter at his antics. Millie clicked away with her camera at the joyous scene. Ashley tapped her a few times when she caught Luke's gaze in Millie's direction, but she kept her focus on the pictures they needed.

"It's been hard rebuilding the town after the great flood last year, but a new year is on the horizon. To a healthy and prosperous 1929!" Brandon held up his glass and put his hand next to his mouth as he leaned toward Luke. "And perhaps to getting our property line sorted again with the Fosters," he said, pretending to make a snide comment only to Luke, but loud enough for all to hear.

Millie scanned the room when she heard the subtle snickers among the guests and wondered if they understood the joke. She remembered what Luke had shared with her at the café about Riley's great-grandmother—Foster must have been her maiden name. Were disputes over the property line still lingering today? She hadn't thought so, especially considering how easily Luke had brushed off Riley when she'd tried to open the discussion, so perhaps Brandon's comment was intended as humor.

Brushing it aside, she and Ashley continued through the rest of the house, and when they started to make their way back down the long staircase from the second floor, Luke emerged at the bottom.

"I hope you had a simply marvelous time," he said, winking at Millie and making her blush all over again.

"I did; thank you for having us, Bobby. You and your

parents are the most delightful hosts. And the decorations? Absolutely spectacular!" Millie gamely played along with the theme of the house.

Luke grinned, his eyes twinkling against the soft lighting. "Ah, yes. We like to think we're a bit of a festive bunch. Perhaps next year I can even convince you to join us for a Christmas dance."

Millie's heart skipped a beat as he took her hands and shuffled his feet.

"Then I'll need to invite her back up for a visit," Ashley said with a wide smile as she opened the door. "Goodnight, Bobby."

"I bid you both farewell, ladies, and Merry Christmas." Luke closed the door behind them and Millie was nearly breathless from being totally swept up from the 1920s Christmas the Thayers had presented so perfectly—or was it the way Luke had taken her hand, twice?

They walked back down the driveway toward the car, and Millie could feel Ashley's eyes on her.

"Don't even start," Millie said, despite the smile she still wore.

"I won't. In fact, I don't need to. I can see it all over your face, even in the dark."

Millie didn't know what had just happened in there. She'd seen how Luke behaved with the other guests, still playing his role, but much more reserved than he was with her—and he didn't take anyone else's hand.

Shaking her head, she got into Ashley's car and looked down at her camera. *Stay focused on your job, Millie. Not on the handsome Luke Thayer.*

Chapter Twelve
October 16, 1940

He couldn't stop staring at the number on the draft card. Lawrence stood outside the US military registration center in Burlington in awe, trying to process what had just happened. After being asked numerous questions, interviewed about his specialties, and undergoing a medical examination, he was presented with a card. Now what?

He knew this day would be one America would always remember, but he had so many mixed feelings. On one hand, he was proud to stand up and serve his country, but on the other he was nervous about the unknown. Would he be called up? For how long? And was the country about to enter the war?

To help settle his nerves, he took out his new camera and decided to walk around the city. Raising the Kodak 35, he focused on the dozens of people around him. Many men held the same confused expression he had worn once they were done registering. Women were wiping their eyes or walking with their heads held high next to their men. It was a very emotional time for everyone.

He clicked shots of the mountains in the distance and the streets that were littered in fallen leaves as they surrendered to the impending winter. Before heading back to Alpine Ridge, he stopped in the tavern in the new Hotel Vermont for a drink.

"Pale ale, please," Lawrence told the man behind the bar, then sat down just as someone pulled out the seat next to him. After he was handed his pint, he nearly swallowed it all in one gulp.

"I second that," a male voice next to him said. When he turned, he saw a man holding up his mug. "Today brought a lot of uncertainty."

"It sure did," Lawrence said.

The two men drank in silence, the tensions of the war circling in their minds.

"Name's Ron." The man stuck out his hand.

"Lawrence." He gave him a firm handshake. "Where's home for you?"

"Rutland. You?" Ron took a swig of his brew.

"I'm not too far from there. Alpine Ridge."

They grew quiet again, finishing their drinks.

"I better start the long drive back." Ron stood and picked up his coat.

"Same here." Lawrence eyed him. "Say, may I ask you something?"

"Sure."

"What do you know?"

"About the draft?" Ron paused in thought. "Probably not much more than you. But I did hear that they'll begin to draw numbers soon and we'll serve for a year."

Lawrence nodded. "Thanks." *A year?* That felt like an eternity. "Safe travels."

"Same to you." Ron glanced at him one more time. "And let's hope our numbers won't be called—and that our country will stay out of the war."

"Let's hope." Lawrence watched the man walk toward the door. A part of him wanted to stand strong for his country and didn't mind being called to serve, but he'd just finished college. He wanted to start his career and get a ring on Evelyn's finger. Marrying her was his biggest ambition. But first he needed to get her father's blessing. Compared to that battle, fighting a war might seem easy.

———

"The Christmas season is coming in fast," Evelyn's father, Leroy, said to one of his loggers as Lawrence approached him the next morning in the crisp October air. "I'd like to see the last of the lumber shipped off in four weeks' time. That will take us up to mid-November before the holidays. And before the ground freezes."

The lumberjack team was getting the next haul off the mountain. Nearby, the log cabin that would be the main building of the resort was framed and standing, but there was still so much to be done.

"Yes, sir," the logger said to Leroy, then cast his attention toward Lawrence before walking up the mountain.

"Lawrence," was all he said before he started walking.

"Hello, Mr. Foster."

"How's your family keeping?"

"Very well, thank you. And yours?"

"All healthy, and for that I'm grateful."

"Good to hear." Lawrence moved his gaze down to the crunching snow under their boots. He knew how Evelyn was, but Leroy wasn't aware of that—and was about to get a surprise. A sudden gust of wind caught him off guard, and his anxiety began to take hold. Asking her father for her hand was going to be harder than he anticipated.

"I'm making my way up the mountain to the last clearing area. Is there something you need before I go?" Leroy asked, already looking irritated by Lawrence interrupting his workday.

Lawrence looked up toward the freshly cleared paths for the slopes. "It's looking like a ski mountain now. It'll be wonderful for the town once you open."

"Yes, it will be." Leroy's attention shifted behind him and when Lawrence turned around, his father was walking toward them, causing them to stop.

"Lawrence, there you are," Bobby said, exhaling a cloud of hot air as he hurried over and glared at Leroy. "Hello. Just needed to find my son."

"Then I'll leave you to him," Leroy said.

"Wait a moment." Lawrence held up his hand. "Father, I came here to talk to Mr. Foster. Can whatever you need wait?"

"I really need to get to one of the rock walls up at the clearing site, so I don't have time to linger. Good day, gentlemen." Leroy started to walk away, but Bobby nearly lurched at him.

"Hold on, which clearing site?"

"Why is that your concern?"

"Is it on the west side of the mountain?"

"Oh, here we go," Leroy said, shaking his head with a hand on his hip. "Bobby, like I just said, I really don't have time for this."

"A rock wall that shows up in that location means you better make time for it. May I come see it?"

"No, you cannot. Again, I'm very busy and this is not the time or place for an argument over a pile of rocks."

"It is when those rocks might be part of my property!" Bobby's voice rose.

"Father!" Lawrence jumped between them when the two men grew closer. "Let the man get back to work, and we can discuss the rock wall another time." He took his father's arm, gently tugging him.

Leroy stormed off, and Lawrence watched his opportunity slip away.

"Why were you here talking to that man anyway?" Bobby asked.

"I . . ." Lawrence tried to think of an excuse. This was not the time to tell his father he and Evelyn wanted to get married. Besides, the conversation had to start with Leroy. "I needed to tell him that one of his loggers was lost on our land. Must be a new worker. I didn't want him to get in trouble for showing up late." It was a pathetic excuse, but it was all he could think of.

His father narrowed his eyes, clearly not convinced. "I need you back at the barn to start winterizing it. Snow is coming, I can feel it. An early winter is heading our way."

Lawrence followed his father back to their property, trying to put aside the exchange. The tension between their families was troubling, but he clung to the hope that perhaps one day, after he and Evelyn wed, the land could finally be combined and settled.

———

Present Day

"READY?" MILLIE SHOUTED UP THE HILL, HOLDING her hand up. "One . . . two . . . three . . . *Go!*" The kids hopped on their sleds and giggled with delight as they slid down the hill on Thursday afternoon. She got pictures from as many angles as she could and even managed to click at the right moment as snow flew up over one of the little boys as he used his boots to slow himself, grinning with excitement.

Josh, the ski instructor, had found her in the café earlier and told her where all the children of the town went sledding, which was behind the public library. According to him, there were people there all winter long after school. He thought it would be a perfect activity to photograph, especially with all the parents standing by to give her permission. Since she had nothing else planned besides starting to edit what she'd taken so far, she decided to get some fresh air and go. Once she'd arrived, everyone agreed it would make some great marketing shots, showing the happy smiling faces of kids enjoying a winter activity.

Large bulb outdoor lights hung from the evergreens near the hill, connecting to the library for power and illuminating the sledding run. Librarians had come out twice with hot chocolate for the kids, and she was able to get a few pictures of that as well, highlighting how connected the community was no matter what they were doing.

"It's Millie, right?" one of the mothers asked, holding a sled as she walked over to her.

"Yes, that's right." Millie lowered her camera and faced the woman.

"I'm Brandy. Two of mine are out there," she said, gesturing behind her. "Would you like to give it a try?" Brandy held out her sled. "I can hold your camera."

"Hmm. Well, I did put my snow pants on." It took only one glance up the hill for her to pull the strap to her camera over her head and hand it to Brandy. "Yes! I'd love to!"

When she started trudging through the snow to the top, a few kids pointed to her.

"Look! The photographer is coming!"

"Bet you can't go as fast as me!" one of the boys shouted.

Millie picked up her pace. "I bet I can!" She reached the

top and planted herself on the sled right next to him. "Wanna race?"

The boy's face lit up. "You're on!"

A girl near them came over. "I'll do the countdown."

Millie shifted on the sled with her feet holding her in place. The boy got on his sled and gave her a challenging smirk.

"One . . . two . . . three . . . *Go!*" the girl called out, and Millie lifted her feet and used her hands with all her power to get herself going, but the boy—far more experienced at the art of sledding—was already flying down in front of her. The kids at the top were cheering them on, and Millie burst out laughing when she started to spin in circles. It was the first time she'd ever sledded and she wanted to go a hundred more times!

When she reached the bottom, she used her foot as she saw the boy do and tried to stop herself, but she was too late and collided into a man.

"I win!" The boy was already jogging toward her with his arms up in victory.

"Yes, you sure did!" Millie smiled at him before looking up to see who she nearly knocked over. "I'm sorry, I—" Her words were lost when she saw him.

"Getting into your job, I see?" Luke grinned. He was holding a cup of coffee, but he reached out his free hand to help her up.

"Participating gives me the right vibes for the pictures," she said, brushing off her pants that were caked in chunks of snow. "But that was a blast! I could do that all day."

"First time?"

Millie nodded, looking him up and down. He was wearing a thick coat and jeans. "I think I might do it one more time. Too bad you aren't dressed to join me."

The corners of his mouth twitched as he turned to a man

near them and held out his cup. "Do you mind?" The man took his coffee. "May I borrow your sled too?"

"Absolutely. Go for it."

Luke picked up the sled and looked at Millie. "I'm a Vermonter. A little snow on the jeans won't bother me."

"Race?"

"You're on!"

Luke and Millie went back up the hill and all the kids clapped excitedly.

"Mr. Thayer will definitely beat you, miss!" one girl said.

"I don't know about that," Millie said, holding her sled to her chest. "I think I can take him."

When Luke positioned himself on top of his sled, he glanced up. "Are you going to sit?"

"I will. On the count of three."

The same girl who counted before held up her hand. "One . . . two . . . three . . . *Go!*"

Millie ran a few steps then hopped on her sled headfirst, going down full speed on her belly and brushing right by Luke. The kids cheered louder when she passed him. At the bottom, she spun once before rolling off, just as Luke bumped his sled into hers.

"You cheated!" he said, trying to contain his smile as he got up.

"I didn't start before the count, and I sledded down the hill just like you. So I didn't cheat." Millie grinned. "I got clever."

Luke jogged over to the man holding his coffee and swapped the sled for his drink. "Thank you."

"A first-timer got you, man," he said to Luke.

Luke chuckled. "That she did. It's a good thing she's so pretty—makes it hard to get mad at her." He winked at Millie, who took a step backward, trying not to overreact to the compliment. "Get enough pictures here?"

"I-I did," she said as he got closer and the warm hues of the setting sun behind him lit up the features on his face. Parents began to gather their things and take their children home. "Looks like it'll be dark soon."

"I bet you're hungry after all that fun out here."

He began to walk toward the parking lot and she fell into step with him.

"I am." A shiver ran down her against a cool breeze. "And cold."

"How about I take you to one of my favorite restaurants? It's a steak house, but they also have delicious seafood."

"*He was intrigued. I saw it all over his face.*" Ashley's words echoed in her thoughts. "You sure? Were you planning on doing something else this evening?"

"I'm always busy doing something, but eating dinner was on the list," he joked, easing her nerves.

"I was planning on doing that too," she teased back, glancing up at him. "How did you know I was here sledding?"

"I didn't," he said, pausing by her car. "I was at the library talking to the staff about the upcoming gingerbread house contest, and when I heard all the kids, I came out to watch. This was my favorite sledding hill growing up. And then I found you."

When he turned to Millie, his expression was calm as their eyes locked, sending her heart racing.

"How about you text me the address to the steak house. I'm going to go change out of these wet snow pants and can meet you there. Would an hour from now work?"

"Perfect," he said, opening her car door for her. She rattled off her phone number and got in as he held the door. "Glad to have your number now so I don't have to wander around, hoping to randomly run into you."

Millie fought to keep her expression even. "Yeah, that'll be much more convenient. See you in an hour." She shut the door and after he walked away, she blew out her breath. Maybe Ashley and Irene were right, and he *was* interested in her. He had certainly caught her attention.

Her mind raced as she drove back to the resort, thinking about the sale and dinner with Luke. She decided that tomorrow she'd bring it up with Ashley again. She wanted to clear the air with Luke. There was no reason that at least he couldn't know. The rest of the residents of Alpine Ridge were a different story, and she understood the Clarkes' position on wanting to keep them in the dark a little longer so Millie's interactions with them would remain warm and friendly for the photos. But that wasn't needed for Luke. And especially not now as she was starting to get to know him. The way he stared at her with curiosity made her stomach flutter. The Clarkes' plans for the resort weren't her fault, nor would it be entirely bad for the town. He'd come around . . . she hoped.

———

A couple hours later, Millie sat in the steak house by a blazing fire with a large Christmas wreath hung above the mantle, while the waitstaff buzzed by wearing Santa hats. Millie barely noticed them. She was so absorbed in conversation with Luke. The restaurant was a little empty when they'd first arrived, but quickly filled up shortly after they sat down and tried not to pay attention to all the heads turning to steal glances at them. As soon as they placed their orders with the waitress, the conversation flowed, and they were hooked on each other.

Millie grinned while Luke waved his arms, telling her a story about how he'd created his own ski resort when he was ten years old, digging tracks in the woods behind his house, ultimately getting himself lost. While he went through the events of that day, she found herself enraptured as she listened.

The way his face scrunched up when he laughed at his young self's antics sent a flutter through her chest—with a sense she'd never experienced before. She leaned forward, listening to every part of the story, but his voice seemed miles away. What had begun to brew between them before was gaining momentum.

"The police had to get their canine unit out there to help find me." They both erupted in laughter. "All because I wanted to compete with the Clarkes and make our own resort." He picked up his water glass, shaking his head at the memory. "But nothing else could compare to what they've made. They created something so special for our town and so unique just for us."

"Yes." Millie swallowed, keeping her composure. "They sure did."

"Needless to say, my mom didn't let me venture outside to play in the snow by myself for quite some time after the search team finally found me."

"I don't blame her. You got lucky they did find you." Millie stifled a yawn. "Excuse me. All that sledding must be catching up with me."

"I'll get the waitress." He looked around the room and spotted her, then held up his hand. "But speaking of the Clarkes, did you know they're holding an estate sale? I think it starts tomorrow."

"Oh." She wasn't quite sure how to respond. "You heard about that?"

Luke hesitated, drawing his brows together. "Why wouldn't I?"

"No reason," she quickly said. "I just wasn't sure if you knew they were moving."

"There have been whispers of them wanting to pack up and move away from the mountain for the past year." The waitress came over. "We'd like to pay the bill." He gave her his credit card and turned back to Millie. "I don't blame them for wanting to move. It must be hard staying here after everything that's happened. I hear they just want to sell as much as they can and downsize."

"It's just them, so that sounds like a good idea."

Luke nodded. "It is, but it's also a shame to see them sell a home that has been in their family for so long. But, anyway, they have a great team at the resort who can conduct the day-to-day operations. I think a little time away from Alpine Mountain and even the town may help them heal easier."

"Yeah, it probably will." It was all she could think to say.

"I don't think they're looking to move far," he continued. "And with your talent to help them see the important place the resort has in the town, everything will be fine."

"The resort holds a lot of history, that's for sure." The photo albums from the library flashed through her mind and she remembered how absorbed she had been while paging through decades of the resort's past.

"Yeah, and their home does too. Are you going to check out their sale?"

"I think I might. I love browsing through old furniture and things from the past. It's like walking back in time."

"I agree. I may even have a look myself."

After the waitress returned with his card, they stood up.

"Thank you for dinner," Millie said. "It was so good. All the food I've had here has been delicious."

"Yep. The farm-to-table ingredients and talented chefs we've been blessed with have our visitors coming back just for the food."

"I believe it."

When they got outside, Luke gently grasped her hand. Normally, the touch would have sent a thrill through her, but all she could think about was what he'd just shared. He was so proud of the resort the way it was, and it was clear he didn't want it any other way for his town. She felt like a traitor while he held her hand and quickly pulled hers away as they reached her car. Avoiding his eyes, she unlocked the door and opened it, then held it between them. "I better get to bed. Another busy day of pictures is ahead of me tomorrow."

"Yeah." Luke's face fell at yet another abrupt ending to a wonderful evening together.

Millie slid into the car and closed the door, then waved and turned away so she didn't have to watch him stand there in confusion. What a mess she was in.

Chapter Thirteen

Friday morning welcomed Millie with beautiful blue skies filtering the dawn's early light through the curtains. The soft glow gently roused her from a hard slumber. After tossing and turning for hours trying to settle herself to sleep the night before, she had finally fallen into vivid dreams. She'd dreamed of Luke standing before her with the residents of Alpine Ridge behind him, wanting to know what was happening with the resort, demanding that she give them answers, staring at her with accusation on their faces as if it were all her fault.

She sat up in bed, rubbing her eyes against the brightening room, and everything from the day before slammed into her thoughts. If she wasn't thinking about the job at hand for the resort, she was thinking about Luke and the town. It was beginning to tire her out.

"I need coffee," she said out loud and tossed off the covers.

While the coffee brewed, she pushed her mind onto another topic—the conversation with Lila the other morning about their parents. Outside of the heaviness surrounding everything about the resort's sale, there was something that had lifted—all the pressures she'd felt back home in Charleston. She'd been in Alpine Ridge almost a week, but it felt much longer. The food, the friendly residents, the staff at the resort, catching up with Ashley, and spending time with Luke—it felt was as if she was part of this community. And she was in a groove with her photography. Why couldn't she just pick up the phone and share her joy with her parents? *Because there was always an element of uncertainty with them.* She never knew what they would say that might be hurtful.

She poured the fresh coffee into her mug and sipped. A weakness that still gripped her prevented her, once again, from calling them, and she instead slid her feet into her slippers, pulled a sweatshirt over her pajamas, and went out on the balcony to catch the last of the sunrise.

The air was frigid, but it was exactly what she needed to clear her head after thinking about her parents. She stood on the porch, slowly drawing in her breath, allowing the cold air to revitalize her, and switched her thoughts to the day ahead. The sun was now fully peeking out from behind the mountain, its orange hues turned a brilliant yellow, sparkling against the snowy slopes. It was a gorgeous day.

Back inside, she went to shower and get dressed, planning the day's events in her mind. It was the first day of the Clarkes' estate sale and while they would be opening their home for the whole week, she decided to head over to see everything the first day, before the pieces were taken away, leaving the house empty. After seeing the old pictures in the library, she figured it would be nice to have some updated images of the home as it stood today. She didn't have an exact plan for how she'd incorporate the shots in the sales pitch, but something was pulling her to do it and, as a creative, she always opted to follow her intuition. Even if she didn't use the images for marketing purposes, perhaps the Clarkes would like to have them for keepsakes.

After a quick shower, she changed into her last pair of clean leggings and an oversized sweater. She needed to do some laundry and was grateful her suite came with the ability to do that. She started the washer and checked the time. It was too early for the estate sale and there were still plenty of images she could edit while waiting, but first, breakfast. Standing in front of an empty fridge, she switched tracks. She still hadn't picked up any groceries after a busy first week and got her coat on to go to the store. There was a stove to cook on in her small kitchen so she could stock up on some basics.

The valet drove her car around, and she asked one of the men where the grocery store was. He gave her the name of their local market, and a short drive later she pulled into the small parking lot. Outside the front door was a stack of fresh, pre-cut Christmas trees, plain cedar sprig wreaths, and other handmade greenery décor. She grabbed a basket and made her way inside.

A coffee station to the left displayed a sign that said "Enjoy some holiday cheer on us! Free cup of our very own peppermint mocha coffee." How could she not? She poured herself a cup, then added a little whipped cream on top and noticed the bags of coffee for sale, all wrapped in red bows. She was barely through the front door and already impressed.

The sweet and minty flavor of the coffee went down smooth, warming her right up as she continued inside. The store only had five aisles, but they were well stocked and had what she needed. She filled her cart with milk, eggs, bread, some lunch items, snacks, and easy dinners, which included a lot of pasta. Editing would soon start to take up her evenings if she was to hit the deadline.

After she paid, loaded the bags in her trunk, and got in her car, she checked her phone and saw a text from Ashley.

I got your text last night about needing to talk. I just knocked on your suite but no answer. Early morning out? I have a meeting at the resort soon. Do you want to meet for lunch? The diner at noon?

Millie sent a quick reply.

Lunch sounds good. I'll meet you there. I'm out picking up some groceries and then tackling some edits before I go to the Clarkes' estate sale. I want to poke around the old items and get some pictures before the house is cleared.

As soon as she pulled out of the parking space, a call came in. It was Ashley.

"Hey there!" Ashley's voice boomed through the speaker above her head. "I figured it would be easier to call than text."

"Call about what, the estate sale?"

"Yeah. It's been delayed," Ashley said.

"Is everything alright?"

"Yes and no. Dylan is ready to start, but Joyce is having a hard time with it, so they decided to give her another week before they open the sale. It'll begin next Friday. Well, if she's ready. But I like your idea about taking some photos for them before everything is sold. Let me call them and ask if you can still come by today to do that."

"Thanks. I was rummaging through the library in the resort the other day and found some old albums about the Clarkes and the history of how the resort got started, showing how it has evolved since 1940." Millie carefully eased out onto the road. Alpine Ridge was so small, she already knew her way back to the resort and didn't need GPS. "It was so fascinating, and I thought the pictures would be a nice gift to them."

"Agreed. I'll let you know as soon as I talk to them."

Back in her suite, Millie switched the laundry to the dryer and put away her groceries. She scrambled an egg and made some toast, then sat down with her laptop. While the pictures she'd taken over the week downloaded, she ate her eggs and thought about Joyce. She couldn't imagine having to put a house that special up for sale along with all its possessions and move away, so she understood their anguish. Losing their only child in the place they had built their entire lives around must have been truly devastating.

When the photos were loaded, Millie scrolled until she found the few she'd taken at the Clarkes' estate when she'd gone for breakfast. There weren't many, which was why she'd planned to take more today. An idea occurred to her, but she would need to talk to Ashley first. In the meantime, she opened a search page to research print labs nearby and found Green Mountain Photo about fifteen minutes outside of Alpine Ridge. She clicked on their contact page and began typing.

Hello. My name is Millie Rowan, and I am a photographer shooting marketing photos for the ski resort in Alpine Ridge. I'm looking for some print services and would like to know your turnaround time for large print. I can get the files to you digitally or drop them off, whichever you prefer. Looking forward to hearing back.

Sitting back, Millie smiled as her idea grew. The pictures stuffed in the albums in the library could be restored and reprinted at a larger size. A big piece of the Clarkes' family history was being sold, but she could gift them a few prints to allow them to keep part of their past with them.

A quick check of the time told her she had a little over two hours before she had to meet Ashley at the diner, so she got to work editing. As she reviewed each image, she found herself smiling or laughing at the happy faces of the people of Alpine Ridge. She jotted down notes to add to the descriptions she'd be writing for Peak Holdings. They would be able to see how Alpine Mountain could be a jewel in their portfolio, with a community that would offer their employees and guests a good quality of life, positive engagement with the residents, and so many great local resources.

After getting through more than half of the images, Millie stood up feeling accomplished. Most had come out exactly how she'd intended, and she was pleased there would be so many to choose from for the pitch. And she still had more to shoot. The gingerbread house contest at the library the following day would provide more shots with the children, which she'd found to be the most delightful to scroll through while editing. Children had a unique ability for bringing people together with their contagious laughter and joyful outlook.

She saved the photos she wanted to use for the Clarkes' gift in a separate file and headed to the diner to meet Ashley.

———

When the waitress returned with their food, her Christmas bracelet jingled as she placed Millie's giant BLT with sweet potato fries in front of her.

"Thank you, Jill," Ashley said and looked down at her burger.

"This sandwich will fill me up for the rest of the day." Millie took a bite.

"The portions here will never disappoint," Ashley mumbled between bites.

"Nothing about the food here disappoints."

While they had waited on their lunch, Millie caught Ashley up on all the images she'd captured that week. She had saved a few on her phone to give Ashley a sneak peek. She also told her more about the gift idea for the Clarkes, which Ashley fully supported. Since she wasn't going to be using them for commercial purposes, Ashley had given Millie permission to borrow the pictures from the resort's collection.

Ashley picked up her water. "You're doing amazing! I love it all so far. And I know the team will too. You really have such great talent."

"Thank you. I'm glad you're on board with the description write-ups. I think that since I'm new to Alpine Ridge, it would help for the buyers to hear my perspective and see the visuals from my point of view."

"I agree. I keep forgetting this corporation is from out of state. While they're very familiar with other areas of Vermont and other ski towns, they don't know Alpine Ridge." Ashley looked down and poked around at her fries.

"What's wrong?" Millie asked.

"Nothing is wrong. It's just that when I read your descriptions and listened to how the week went for you, getting to know our community and all, this whole thing about the Clarkes selling the resort to strangers is sad. I know this is my job, but it's also my home. I haven't lived here as long as residents, like the Thayers, but it still impacts me to see changes like this."

The mention of Luke's family instantly reminded Millie of the intimate booth at the steak house the night before and the way he had laughed at her corny jokes and how comfortable she was with him.

"Millie?" Ashley snapped her fingers.

"Hmm?" Millie blinked out of her trance to find her friend eyeing her.

"You good?"

"Oh, yes. I'm fine. You mentioned the Thayers and that reminded me of something I wanted to talk to you about." The waitress was approaching with the coffee pot, so Millie waited while she refilled their mugs, trying to find a way to begin. "We need to tell Luke what's going on with the pitch. Just him," she blurted when the waitress was out of earshot. No better way to approach this subject than get straight to the point.

Ashley sat back against the booth. "I see . . ." She picked up her coffee, evidently taking in Millie's words. "Why just him and why now? You know the Clarkes are going to let everyone know soon."

"For one, he's the chair of the select board, so he really should know about possible changes coming to Alpine Ridge, especially one as large as this that will ultimately impact the town in so many ways."

"I already know this, and it's been discussed by the team. Luke will be the first to know, but not yet." Ashley's eyes slanted in a knowing stance. "This is about more than him being the chairman, isn't it?"

Heat flooded her cheeks. There was no hiding this from her friend. "We had dinner last night at the steak house—"

"I knew it!" Ashley exclaimed, then quickly covered her mouth when Millie brought her finger to her lips.

"Would you quiet down?" Millie chuckled at the pure excitement plastered all over Ashley's face. "It was just dinner, but . . ."

"But?" Ashley prompted, motioning with her hands. "Come on, just tell me."

"But it was wonderful. Once we start talking, we don't stop."

"You talked? That's it? What about a kiss at the end of the night?"

Millie shook her head, laughing at her friend. "A kiss? No." She winced thinking about how fast she'd shut down that opportunity.

"This makes me so happy. You know, this is the first time in all the years I've known you that I've heard you talk about a man this way."

Millie twisted the napkin in her lap, realizing her friend was right. "I've just been so absorbed in my photography work."

"Understandable. Look how accomplished you've become."

"Ashley." Millie tossed the napkin on her plate. "I have to be honest with you. I really haven't been all that successful. This is actually my first paying job."

Ashley's expression stayed even while the waitress came over and cleared their empty plates. "So?"

"So . . ." Millie tapped the side of her water glass. "I'm not exactly a sought-after photographer like you probably thought when you hired me for the resort, but I'm giving this job all I can. I promise."

"And you're killing it. I love what you've done so far." Ashley laid her hand on top of hers and stilled her fingers. "Millie, it doesn't matter who has or hasn't hired you before you got here. We hired you for your talent. You're an amazing photographer."

Millie sat in silence, taking in her friend's words. "Wow," she finally said. "That means a lot." It was exactly what she'd hoped to hear from her parents, but never had.

Ashley straightened. "And about Luke. I don't want to say it, but—"

"Yes, I know." Millie nodded, thinking about the way she caught him stealing glances at her while they ate their dinner the night before. "You were right. So was Irene."

"I bet Irene already knows about last night's date. Someone must have seen you two there. Oh, Millie!" Ashley clapped her hands. "Can we start planning the move?"

"Move? Okay, now you're in dreamworld. It was just one dinner that happened to go well. He and I click, but that's all there is right now." Millie looked down to avoid Ashley's hopeful face. "And I'm not sure it'll be more than that."

"Wait. Okay, now I get it," Ashley said. "You're afraid that once Luke finds out about why you were really hired that he'll be upset with you."

"Something like that." Milie's mouth twisted. "But even if he and I didn't have something stirring up between us, I still think he needs to know. Last night he mentioned how sorry he was to see the Clarkes selling their estate, but that he understood why they were."

"See? He's very understanding."

"No, that's not all. He also said he wasn't worried about the resort because you all have a great staff to keep things going while they're gone. He seems so proud of Alpine Ski Resort and what it has meant to the community over the years. He's going to be devastated if it becomes corporately owned."

"I know, but he's the leader of this town and will want what's best." Ashley leaned forward. "He'll be okay, and he'll make sure the residents are too. It'll be an adjustment, but maybe Peak Holdings will grow this town into even more than what it is now."

"Or turn it into something unrecognizable. They'll have so much control with their deep pockets and heavy investments."

"Look, you were hired to do a job. He knows that and he won't be mad."

"I hope you're right." Millie blew out some air and sat back.

"Listen, I'll mention this to the Clarkes and see what they think about telling Luke so he can start to prepare. Sound like a plan?"

"Thank you. I appreciate that."

Ashley's phone started buzzing in her purse and she checked to see who it was.

"It's Joyce. Let me run out and take it, then we'll know whether you're going over to take pictures there today."

While Ashley stepped outside to answer the call, Millie thought about what she'd said. She'd always known Luke was a businessman and that on some level he would understand, but that was before he'd held her hand and taken her to dinner.

"Okay," Ashley said, breathless as she came back to the booth. "Joyce is more than happy to let you come by this afternoon to take some pictures. I didn't tell her about the gift idea, of course, just that you wanted to capture it all before they sold the house. She said Dylan is leaving for the rest of the day, but she'll be there, and you can come over whenever you want."

"Great. I'll head there now."

When they got to the parking lot, Ashley put her hand on Millie's shoulder. "Don't stress about Luke."

Easier said than done. "I'll try." She took a deep breath. "Let me know when you talk to the Clarkes about that."

"I will. In the meantime, just enjoy yourself with him." Ashley grinned.

Millie forced a return smile. She *was* enjoying herself with Luke, but that was the problem. She hated that they were starting things with a lie.

Chapter Fourteen

"Would you like something to eat or drink?" Joyce asked a few minutes after Millie arrived. "I've always got cookies stashed somewhere in the kitchen."

"No, thanks." Millie looked around the front foyer again. It wasn't the first time she'd seen it, but now she was observing it with photographer eyes. "I just left the diner with Ashley."

"Okay." Joyce watched while Millie kept turning around to see all the details. "Beautiful, isn't it?"

"Very."

"Would you like me to give you a tour? I know we didn't really explore when you were here for breakfast. Then you can do your thing."

"I'd love that."

"Now, remember this house is from Dylan's family, so I didn't grow up with it the way he did, but I think I can cover most of it."

"Let's do it." Millie got her camera ready. "I might take some pictures while you talk, if that's okay."

"Fine by me." Joyce waved her hand. "Come on, let's start in the kitchen."

Millie walked through the door and her mouth fell open when she saw how it was classic yet up-to-date with a sleek charm. She immediately snapped a few photos, especially of the cabinets with a faint hint of green.

"Was this the original color?"

"It was a little darker green then, but these are the same cabinets that have since been restored."

"They're really nice with the modern finish but older style."

A small Christmas tree stood in the corner and garland hugged the window frames near the bay window. The countertops also displayed holiday pieces, with three small gold trees next to a hot cocoa station.

"Dylan wouldn't let me take all my décor out since we're getting ready for the estate sale," Joyce explained, and Millie watched her eyes glaze in emotion before she closed them for a moment. "It's been so hard not to; Christmas is my favorite time of year. So we compromised and he let me decorate the kitchen since I'm in here so much and the outside of the house."

"I'm glad he did. It gives this room that magical Christmas feel."

Joyce went over to the tree and touched a few of the decorations. "I only took out a handful of special ornaments. Ones that remind me of Riley."

Millie walked over and stood next to her. "I'm so sorry about your loss."

"Thank you," Joyce said, quickly wiping her eyes. "Sorry, let's continue." She walked to the center of the kitchen and smiled, her eyes now a bit red. "I love how our contractor and designer created a charming blend of nostalgia and contemporary flair in here and throughout the rest of the home. It's been remodeled a few times before we took over, but we put in a lot of work to make it what it is today."

For the next hour, Millie followed Joyce around the home, listening to stories of her husband's family and his childhood growing up there. She caught Joyce fighting more tears a few times, especially when they skipped what was clearly Riley's room. Traces of a deep grief lingered as the woman tried to keep a brave face. This move was so bittersweet for them, but could there be another way? Did they really have to sell this home to strangers?

Once the tour was done, Millie felt she knew the Clarke family so much more, which would help her plan out her pictures better. She wanted this corporation to understand the roots of the resort, the family that loved and grew it for decades, and the town.

"Thank you," Millie said. "I really enjoyed that."

"I'm glad," Joyce said. "I had fun, too, especially since we didn't participate in the holiday home tour this year. Anyway, stay as long as you'd like. I'll be upstairs sorting through some closets. It's incredible how much stuff we've accumulated over the years. Let me know if you need anything."

Millie nodded, and after Joyce went up the stairs, she found herself in the foyer once again. Many pieces of furniture and some décor were marked with blue tape, which Joyce had explained meant they would be included in the sale. After taking pictures and making her way around the old furniture and rooms on the first floor, Millie headed upstairs. An antique tall case clock at the end of the hall had caught her attention during Joyce's tour, and it was the first thing she went up to. Standing next to it, she checked the lighting through her camera lens and crouched into a diagonal position, pointing the camera up. The grandfather clock was so tall that a straight shot wouldn't capture the entirety of its intricate carvings and design. Lowering herself onto the floor, she scooted to the other side and clicked away.

Satisfied with the images, she stood and stared at the old clock for a moment, remembering what Joyce had told her about it: that it had been handmade by one of Dylan's ancestors who was a clockmaker. They'd luckily salvaged it after the flood in 1927, and besides not working anymore, only the front door had needed to be refurbished—the rest had surprisingly received no damage.

She stepped in closer, admiring the painted flowers in the corners outside the clockface. She snapped a quick photo, then studied it. The glass gave off a reflection, as she thought it would, but perhaps a raw fix in edits could clean that up. She didn't want to open the glass, fearing she'd mess up the gears, but she did open the door under it—mainly out of curiosity to see how it was made. The weights that hung in front of the pendulum weren't moving, but it still fascinated Millie to see something that had been made over two hundred years prior even if it wasn't working. She pulled out her phone and turned on the spotlight to see better. Just before she closed the door, something on the bottom of the case caught her attention. She shone the light down, surprised how deep it went, and gasped when she saw an old camera tucked in the corner.

Joyce was humming a tune in one of the rooms nearby, so Millie quickly picked up the camera and blew off a thick layer of dust that had probably been on it for years. In one of the classes she'd taken for her certification, she had studied the history of cameras. To the best of her memory, she was holding a silver and black Kodak 35 mm camera that must have dated to the 1940s. Shining her light once more to see if anything else was hidden inside the clock, she saw a couple old rolls of film.

"I can't believe this," she whispered, then pulled off her own camera and set it aside before picking up the rolls. She walked down the hall and found Joyce deep inside a closet, stuffing clothes into a bag.

"Hi, Joyce, sorry to bother you," Millie said as Joyce stood up.

"Not bothering me. In fact, I need a break. Goodwill is going to have quite a donation from me. How are the pictures coming along?"

"I think I got some really good ones. I can't wait to edit them. But I was taking some shots of the clock down the hall, and I hope you don't mind, but I opened the door just to take a look at how it operates. I've never seen a grandfather clock like that."

"I don't mind at all, and I don't blame you. Isn't it neat how something so old is still in relatively good shape, even after enduring a flood? The craftsmanship back then was incredible."

"That's exactly what I was thinking." Millie held up the vintage camera. "And when I opened the door, I found this."

Joyce looked at what she was holding. "Oh, that's not your camera? Wait." She came closer, squinting at the device. "How old is that thing?"

"It's definitely not mine. It appears to be from the 1940s, although I can check the exact date with a little research. I also found a few rolls of film with it. Did you know that was all in there?"

"No, but hang on." She walked over to the bed where her phone was and picked it up. "Excuse me while I call Dylan to see if he knew about it."

"Okay. I'll be out by the clock once you're done." Millie went back out to the hallway and began to check out the old camera. The central eyepiece with a focus window next to it told her it was the model with a range finder. She didn't want to open the back in case film was still inside. Then she remembered the print shop she'd found. Perhaps they'd be able to do something with the film.

"Okay," Joyce said as she came out of the room. "Dylan said he's never seen it either. May I look at it?"

"Of course." Millie handed it over and Joyce circled it around and around in her grasp.

"I don't even know what I'm looking for. I'm not an expert and neither is my husband." Joyce glanced up at her. "But you are. Do you think there are any pictures that can still be printed?"

"Honestly, I'm not sure. But I was just thinking about a print shop I happened to find in my research of the area. They might have a restoration service. I don't know how far back they can work with film if they do, but I'd be happy to take the camera and rolls of film to them and see. Maybe they could get a few clear prints."

"Yes, please do. We'll pay for the service, of course. Just have them invoice us."

"Sounds like a plan. I think I'm done here, so I'll leave you to your clothes donation."

"Do I have to?" Joyce said, joking. "Moving is no fun."

"I'm sure it's not, especially when you've lived somewhere as long as your family has." Millie held up the old camera. "Thank you for trusting me with this. I'll take good care of it."

Joyce walked her to the front door and gave her a hug. "I'm so glad you're here and that I got to meet you, Millie. I know your talent will help the pitch shine. As you can probably tell, this is very hard on Dylan and me, but with the financial stress from Riley's accident and the grief of losing her, we need to start over."

"I understand, and I'm here to support you however I can. Who knows? Maybe if there are pictures in this old camera they'll be special keepsakes that'll help you transition to a new home."

"That would be great. Can't wait to see what you're able to uncover."

On the drive back to the resort, Millie soaked in everything she'd learned on the tour and thought about the old camera Joyce had put in a paper bag for her to transport. The first thing she'd do would be to follow up with the print shop and see if they could help.

———

IRENE WAS STANDING AT THE FRONT DESK WHEN Millie strolled in holding the paper bag under her arm and her own camera hung around her neck.

"Well, there's Alpine Ridge's hottest new photographer," Irene's voice called to her across the lobby.

"Not sure about the hottest, but the new part is true." Millie smiled as she walked to the desk.

"Food shopping?" Irene eyed the bag as Millie set it on the counter.

"No, it's a vintage camera I happened to find at the Clarkes' house. Joyce let me take it to see if the rolls of film can be saved." Millie pulled it out to show her.

Irene let out a low whistle. "How old is it?"

"I think it's from the 1940s, but I'm going to find out for sure."

"And they didn't know about it?"

Millie shook her head. "I found it hidden inside an old grandfather clock."

"They have the best-made grandfather clock I've ever seen," a low voice said from behind them.

Both women turned to see Luke holding his skis.

"Nice to see you, Luke," Irene said with a grin, waggling her brows at Millie. "Did you just come off the slopes?"

"I snuck a few runs in." Luke glanced at Millie. "Were you over there for the estate sale today?"

"No, the sale has been delayed. Joyce isn't quite ready for it, but she let me come over to take some pictures. I'm going to surprise her and Dylan with some large prints of the house. So you knew about the clock?"

"Oh, yeah, it's a local favorite in past home tours. It's so large and well-crafted." Luke peeked at Irene who was still grinning from ear to ear at them. "What are you so happy about, Irene?"

"Me? Nothing. I was just thinking, though, maybe you should take Millie to the new seafood restaurant in town for your next date. How'd you like our steak house?"

Millie froze, her eyes widening in surprise and making Irene laugh.

"Sorry. Alpine Ridge sees everything."

"Don't scare her, Irene. She's only been here a week," Luke said, winking at Millie. "But seafood does sound good. What do you say?"

"It sounds delicious, but how about tomorrow night, after the gingerbread house contest? Tonight, I need to work on edits, and I wanted to try to get ahold of this print shop nearby for some large prints I was just telling Irene about." Millie showed him the vintage camera after Irene gave it back. "And I'm not sure if you overheard this part, but I found an old camera and some film at the Clarkes', and they want me to see if any of the rolls can be printed."

"Are you referring to Green Mountain Photo?" Irene asked.

"Yes, that's it. Do you know the place?" Millie asked.

"Sure do. My niece, Monica, and her husband, Bruce, own it, and they're the best there is. They do all our banners and signs for events at the resort. He will absolutely be able to help you. I'll go call him now. Stay right here." Irene ducked into the back to make the call.

Millie turned to Luke again. He was looking at her with the same intense gaze that always held her entranced.

"So it's a seafood date tomorrow night then?" His mouth twitched as he leaned his skis against the desk and stepped toward her.

"It's a date," she said, her stomach doing flips as his fingers brushed hers. She glanced at the skis. "We also need to get me on that mountain."

"Done. How about Sunday?"

"I'll be there."

"I'll get Josh to give you a lesson before I take you up. We can start on the kiddie slopes."

Millie laughed. "Start on them? I'll probably stay on them the whole time."

"Good news!" Irene came out of the office and stopped short when she saw how close to each other Millie and Luke were standing. "You two sure look good together."

Millie moved back from Luke and rested her elbows on the counter in an attempt to compose herself. "Did you get ahold of your niece's husband?"

"I did. Bruce said to bring everything down. He'll be in the shop for about another hour. He also told me he's sorry he hasn't contacted you yet after your message, but he just got back in the shop from being sick."

"That's okay. I didn't send the message that long ago. Thank you so much!" Millie said. "I better hurry over."

"Want some company?" Luke asked. "Irene, can I put my skis back there with you until we get back?"

"Of course." Irene's eyes shone with delight. "Have fun, you two!"

Millie picked up the paper bag. "Sure you want to come along?"

"Yes. I love history, and this sounds like a fun project. I know where the shop is, too, so I'd be happy to drive."

"Saves me from trying to figure out roads in another town after sunset."

They started walking to the door and waved at Irene, who was already holding her phone up and tapping away.

"Looks like she's already telling half the town about us," Luke said.

"I bet," Millie chuckled, a thrill shooting through her all over again. *Is there an us?*

After they got in Luke's car, she glanced at him while he reversed and her mind suddenly went back to her conversation with Ashley earlier at lunch. She really hoped they would let her tell him. Keeping the secret just wasn't sitting right with her. But that wasn't all she thought about. In the short time she had been in Alpine Ridge, she'd learned so much about that mountain and its history, including Riley Clarke's possible discovery prior to that awful accident. Millie understood she was there to do her job, and that Alpine Ski Resort was preparing for the pitch to Peak Holdings, but selling it as the Clarkes intended had really begun to feel rather . . . off.

She didn't know why yet, but her intuition was starting to nudge her that the pitch, the sale, and everything with Peak Holdings would not go as planned and they wouldn't be the final sale. That there was more to this story with the Clarkes and this sale that hadn't been said yet.

Chapter Fifteen

Green Mountain Photo had a sign so tiny it took Millie getting out of the car to see it. It was also in a house that looked like every other residential home on the street.

"I never would have found this," she said as Luke came around the car.

"Yeah, Bruce runs the shop out of his home. He and Irene's niece and their brand-new baby live upstairs," Luke explained as he held out his hand to help her over a small snowbank while she balanced the paper bag in her other arm.

The sky was now fully dark after the fifteen minute ride through a lot of twists and turns on back roads.

"What town is this?"

"The tiny and lovely town of Bridgewater."

They stepped up on the deck wrapped in greenery, with red bows along the front rails. A sharp, piney aroma from the Christmas tree in the corner of the deck was lit up with soft lights, and more bows placed throughout created an inviting welcome.

"I love that smell. My parents always get a fake tree, so it's been a real joy to be around all these live ones. Even the tree in my suite is real." Millie walked past him as Luke held the door open.

"I love it too. It always brings back childhood memories during the holidays." They stopped at a front desk where a teenage girl stood up with a smile.

"Hello! May I help you?"

"Hi. My name is Millie and we're here to see Bruce."

"I'll go get him," the girl said and went to a back room.

The same greenery from outside swagged along the desk, and the counter had a sleigh decoration with small, wrapped boxes filling it. A donation box for the homeless sat right in front. Millie pulled out her wallet and put some cash in it, then a tall man with dark hair, wearing jeans and a flannel shirt came through the back door.

"Thank you, Jess," he told the girl and held out his hand. "You must be Millie. I'm Bruce." They shook hands and he looked at Luke. "Mr. Thayer, how are things over in Alpine Ridge?"

"Since when do you call me Mr. Thayer?" Luke made a face. "It makes me sound so much older than I am."

Bruce chuckled. "Well, ever since you got voted in as chairman, you're officially important."

"I have big shoes to fill." Luke glanced at Millie. "My grandfather, Gary Thayer, served as chairman for many years. Every time I run into someone who remembers him, I'm always told how loved he was. He passed away last year."

"Oh, I'm sorry. No pressure, right?" Millie teased. "You'll do just as great."

"Yes, he will," a female voice said, catching their attention. "Anyone want some hot chocolate? I just boiled some water for it." A woman came around the desk holding a newborn.

"Monica, congratulations!" Luke said, smiling down at the baby. "How's motherhood treating you?"

"It's tiring, wonderful, and everything in between. Irene texted me that you were on your way with someone, and I had to come say hello." Monica looked at Millie. "I'm Monica, Irene's niece. She said you were visiting from South Carolina to take some photos at the resort. Isn't it great there?"

"Yes, I love it. I wish I could move in forever." Luke's gaze darted toward her at her words, sending a rush of heat through her face as she looked back at Monica. "And I'd love some hot chocolate, but you have your hands full."

"Not at all. I was just going to put this little one, who is finally asleep, down and make some for myself. Anyone else?" Both men nodded and she looked at Jess. "Your mom should be here any minute to pick you up, but would you like some?"

"Yes, please. And I'll help you so they can talk."

"Sounds like a plan." Monica looked at the group. "Jess is my cousin. She's been such a huge help with the front desk while I'm on maternity leave." The girl followed Monica through a door to get the drinks.

"Family helping family. I love it," Millie said.

"Let's go sit in my office and you can show me this camera Irene said you had, and we can talk about those other prints you need."

After they settled in their chairs, Millie pulled out the camera. "A Kodak 35. With a range-finder view, so I'm guessing it dates back to the forties?"

"Yep, 1940 is the exact year that feature came out." Bruce took the camera and flipped it around, peeking through the lens. "And you just found this?"

"I was doing a photoshoot in the Clarkes' house and found it inside the bottom of their grandfather clock."

"Really? That's incredible." Bruce fiddled with the switches.

"The Clarkes never knew it was there, so who knows how long it's been hiding," Luke said.

Monica returned with a tray of three mugs and a can of whipped cream next to them.

"I wasn't sure who wanted whipped cream." When everyone's hands went up, Monica picked up the can and filled the tops of all three mugs. "And spoons to mix it all together."

"Thank you, honey." Bruce smiled adorningly at his wife.

Millie picked up a mug and spoon and began to stir, taking a sip of the creamy, warm chocolate. "Delicious." She smiled at Monica.

"Very delicious," Luke said with cream on his face after taking a sip.

Millie grinned and handed him a spoon. "That's why she brought these."

"Let me know if you need anything else. I better get back upstairs to the baby."

When she left, Bruce pulled out the rest of the film from the bag. "I haven't done anything to the film," Millie explained. "I'm not an expert in vintage print."

"You brought it to the right place. This is my favorite thing to do, restore and print old film. This will be one of the oldest jobs I've done, but I'd love to give it a try."

"Yes, please do. The Clarkes will pay for all your services."

Bruce studied the camera a bit longer. "I'll tell you what. Let me check out what shape the film stock is in and if there's any damage, and I'll see if I can get the development process going. I'll test one or two prints before I charge them."

"That's very fair of you. Thank you. I'll let them know."

"If things look positive and we can print some of this, would a turnaround time of one to two weeks be okay? How soon do you need these?"

"There's no time limit on these. We don't even know what's in there, so I assume that'll be fine with them."

Bruce put everything back in the bag. "You mentioned in the contact form you sent us the other day that you had another project you were doing that included some large prints."

"Yes. The photos I took today for the Clarkes are what I was referring to. I still need to go through the shots, but I would like to gift them some of the photos in large print to hang in their new house. And possibly resize and enhance a few photos from some of their photo albums I found in the resort, maybe to 8x10?"

Bruce shook his head. "I can't believe they're selling that estate."

"Neither can anyone in Alpine Ridge," Luke said. "But we're all supporting them as best we can. It hasn't been an easy couple of years."

"For you either," Bruce said.

When Millie glanced at Luke, he didn't meet her stare. Instead, he was looking down at his half-empty mug.

"We're all moving forward, one day at a time." Luke looked back up at Bruce with a smile. "Alpine Ridge is a strong community."

Their exchange sounded as if it was about more than just a break-up with an ex, but Millie stayed respectfully quiet. She wanted to press the men and find out what they were talking about, but the look on Luke's face convinced her to leave it for now.

"That you are." Bruce turned back to Millie. "So how many prints in all are you thinking?"

"I'm not sure, but at least three or four large prints and about five of the 8x10."

"That's easy enough. I can get those back to you in a few days."

"Great. I wouldn't need them for two more weeks anyway. I'm planning on gifting the Clarkes these prints at the resort's eighty-fifth anniversary party, right before I go back to South Carolina."

"Then you'll definitely have them in time, as long as you don't take too long to get them to me. Just email me which ones you need." Bruce handed her his business card with all his information. "And I'll let you know once they're done and keep you informed on the vintage photos."

"Here's my cell number." Millie pulled a sticky note off the stack on his desk and jotted it down. "I think that's everything." They all stood up and reentered the shop to find Monica closing up the front desk. It seemed that Jess had left.

"Keep an eye on my aunt," Monica said. "Nice meeting you!"

Millie and Luke said their goodbyes and headed back to the car. The first few minutes of the drive back was quiet. Millie was lost in thought about the camera and the possible photos that might be on it.

"I wonder what those pictures will be, if Bruce can develop any." She turned to Luke, who looked as if he was deep in his head too.

"Yeah . . ." he said, slowing at a traffic light. "It'll be interesting to see." He pointed to the right. "There's some takeout we could grab just up the road. I don't want you having to work on those edits hungry."

"We couldn't have that," she teased.

His expression lifted. He made the turn and leaned toward her a bit. They caught eyes just before he looked ahead again.

"I haven't been there in a while, but if my memory serves me correctly it should be right up here." He scanned the businesses as they passed. They came upon a large wooden sign with a weak spotlight shining up on it from the ground. It read "The Country Cabin," and Luke slowed before pulling into the full parking lot.

"Looks like a popular place."

"It is. They have some of the best stews around here, and everything on the menu can be ordered to go."

Inside, Luke told the woman up front they were ordering takeout. Millie scanned the small menu, reading through the stews since he'd mentioned them.

"Chicken cider stew? I need to try that," she told the woman.

"And I'll have fish-and-chips," Luke said.

The host wrote it down and told them to wait in the bar area. They sat down and Luke waved at the bartender.

"Want a drink while we wait?"

"Just some water for me."

"Two waters, please," Luke said when the bartender came over.

"Thanks for driving me out here," Millie said after their drinks were placed in front of them.

"Well, that camera intrigued me. Like I said before, I love history stuff."

Millie grinned. "After watching your performance during the home tour, I can see that." She took a sip of her water and the cold liquid settled her nerves—a feeling she was all too familiar with by now whenever she was with Luke.

"Did you enjoy the tour?" he asked.

"I did, especially your outfit."

"Hey now, I work hard on perfecting that every year."

They both laughed, and she caught the blues of his eyes against the low lighting above their heads. His charisma was nearly impossible to ignore, and she could understand why he turned so many heads as Ashley had told her when she first arrived.

"It's a shame the Clarkes didn't participate one last time," Luke said.

"I agree. Their house is gorgeous. I love that brick style."

"They may be moving, but they'll still be around for the

resort, and I'm sure they'll come visit during the holidays. Maybe next year I can convince them to join my family for the tour as our guests."

The way Luke casually spoke tore up Millie, and she nearly blurted the truth right there. Taking another long drink of her water, she quickly regrouped, but she found she just couldn't stay quiet.

"I wonder how long they'll still run the resort once they move out of town," she said, then held her breath.

Luke stared at her with confusion. "What do you mean?" he asked. "They're leaving their management team here—why would anything have to change?"

She regretted saying anything; now he was on to her and avoided his question altogether. "I just meant that, judging by what I've observed with Joyce, especially how she seemed today while packing up and marking all the furniture . . . They need to start over."

"Yeah, well, that's the whole reason for selling the house and moving. To get a fresh start living somewhere else. But the resort is their business. That's different."

"It is different. You're right."

He studied her face. "Do you know something I don't?"

Great, now what should I say? "No, I . . ." She didn't want to lie, not when he'd asked her so directly, but she didn't feel she had a choice. It wasn't news she had a right to share. What was she thinking? "I don't know. It's just an assumption."

Luke stirred his water with his straw, doubt filling his expression. "They wouldn't sell anyway."

"How do you know?"

"Because after the accident . . ." He hesitated before he shifted toward her. "My parents offered to invest in the resort or even buy them out to help with the financial setbacks from the hospital costs and other struggles they'd been dealing with."

"They did?"

"Yes, and the Clarkes said no. That they didn't need financial help. We didn't believe them, but we didn't want to meddle with their private business. It was just . . ." He trailed off again.

"What is it, Luke?" She remembered his strange exchange with Bruce earlier. Was this what they had been referring to?

"I don't want to bring the evening down, but maybe it'll be good to talk about it."

"I'm listening."

"Remember how I told you Riley wanted to talk to me about our property lines and the stuff she found in her research?"

"Yes, I remember. But then you never got a chance to talk."

"I know that's what I told you, but it isn't the whole story." He sighed and leaned on the bar, and she remembered her hunch from when they first left the resort for the photo shop that there was more that she hadn't heard yet. Maybe her intuition was spot on after all. "She came over the morning of her accident and sat down with me. Her parents were already struggling financially, even before her accident. Mr. Clarke made some mistakes over the years with his money management, including some very poor investments. She shared that they were in big-time debt. She then proceeded to tell me that everything would be alright because she'd found out the resort does, in fact, sit partially on our property. Meaning—"

"Meaning if that were true, your family co-owns Alpine Ski Resort . . ." It slowly started to make more sense. "Which would mean that your family could perhaps dig the resort out of debt?"

"Well, yes. That's exactly what she wanted to talk about. But she didn't handle the conversation well." Luke stared down at his water glass for a moment.

"I could imagine the stress of debt had been building up for her."

"Yes, I think it had been because she started to demand that my family help fix things right in the beginning of the conversation. Which was irrational because clearing up something such as the property shares for Alpine Ski Resort would require lawyers and a lot of time to sort through all that. Anyway, she took out her family's struggles on me that morning. She then wanted to have a sit down with our parents and lawyers, and she said we needed to pay them for decades' worth of our share of the taxes."

"That's a lot to take in all at once." Riley must have overlooked a lot of important facts. "What about all the years of profit your family missed out on, if you really do own some of that mountain?"

"It was a lot to take in and, yes, that occurred to me too, but I wasn't ready to bounce that back in her face at the time. I tried to be calm and rational and told her we shouldn't get ahead of ourselves. But she exploded, telling me it was my family's fault because we knew the property lines were always blurred and didn't push hard enough to clear that up."

"I don't think that's true. From the little I've learned, it seems as though your family argued for a very, *very* long time."

"We have." Luke rolled his shoulders.

She could tell this was still a hard topic to discuss. "We don't have to talk about this anymore."

"It's okay. I started it." He gave her a weak smile, but the weight of what had happened was still so evident in his eyes. "Anyway, Riley then started pointing fingers at my father and his wealth, saying he had plenty of money to fix things. That was when I got angry and lost my temper, accusing her family of whatever I could think of, including an old rumor that her ancestors hid the original deed map."

"What? They *did*?"

Luke shook his head. "It was just a silly rumor that had been passed down through the years. It was so long ago; at this point it's been dropped."

"What if it's true?"

"Then we would own part of that mountain. But it's probably not true and it's best to keep that feud dormant." He picked up his glass and took a long sip of his water. "After that accusation, she stormed out, and I guess decided to get her stress out on the slopes."

"Luke, her accident wasn't your fault. Wasn't she still recovering from being sick?"

"Yes, which is another reason I shouldn't have been so harsh. Anyway, you know the rest. Her accident happened, throwing the Clarkes under even more financial stress. The guilt of that fight ate at me, and I begged my father to help by investing in the resort after I told him about Riley confronting me."

"So you did tell him about the argument with her." She remembered how hesitant he looked in the café that first day he brought her on a tour of the town.

"Yeah, I know I told you otherwise, but I finally did. It was very brief though. He waved me off, not wanting to hear more gossip over some old diary entries. But I did convince him that helping with the resort's financial issues would be a good investment, so he made an offer to Dylan."

"And the Clarkes refused the offer."

"Yes, and it sparked another huge argument. Mr. Clarke said they weren't one of Dad's charities that my parents donate to every year."

"Ouch, that must have hit your dad hard. He was only trying to help," Millie said.

"The whole thing was just awful."

"So nobody else knows about that fight you had with Riley?" she asked.

"No one. I should have told the Clarkes about it, but they were deep in the throes of grief. I didn't want to make things harder than they already were. But, anyway, they didn't accept our offer, which tells me they aren't looking to sell it. And that's perfectly fine by me. If my family can't invest in it or buy them out, I wouldn't want anyone outside the town to."

The bartender came over with their bagged food and, after they paid, they both sat in silence for a few minutes. Selling to Peak Holdings would be the answer to the Clarkes' debt, but Luke had made it clearer than ever before that the sale would not be well received. As Millie connected more pieces of the story together, she looked at Luke staring into his now-empty glass and fought the urge yet again to tell him about the sale.

"I hope you heard me before," she said as he closed his eyes and slowly inhaled. "Riley's accident wasn't because of the fight."

"I know." He opened his eyes but kept his gaze on the glass. "It's just that I can't help but think if I hadn't yelled like that, she wouldn't have felt the need to de-stress on the mountain."

"From what I've been told, she loved to ski. She may have made the choice to do so that day whether she saw you or not."

Luke didn't argue. Instead, he nodded and looked over at her with tears in his eyes. She wanted to reach for him and encourage him to share more, but she didn't want to push.

"All I know is now that I'm chairman, I have goals to help grow Alpine Ski Resort so the Clarkes can get themselves in a good place financially again. With you helping Ashley and the rest of the marketing team, it'll help push them forward and perhaps sell out their reservations."

"I hope so," she said in barely above a whisper.

"Thank you for listening to me."

"Anytime." Millie finally extended her hand and gave his arm a squeeze.

He put his hand over hers as his gaze fell to her lips. She flushed, knowing what he was thinking, and she wanted that too, but she pulled back—not knowing how much longer things could hold out between them.

"We better get going before our food gets cold."

Luke snapped out of his daze and glanced at the bags. "Yeah, and you wanted to get some work done."

They stood up and went back outside. The nighttime temperature seemed to keep dropping, and she shivered once she was inside the car.

"Cold one tonight."

"It's supposed to snow all day tomorrow, but the ginger-bread house contest will still be on at one," Luke told her.

"Can't wait. I haven't made one of those in years."

After they arrived at the resort, she picked up her takeout bag and opened the door to get out. But Luke stopped her before she could.

"Running away from me again?" he asked, shifting closer.

"Running away?" She forced a chuckle in an attempt to show him she wasn't. Even though that was exactly what she intended to do until everything was laid out on the table and he knew the real reason she'd come. Hearing him share that story about Riley and how the Clarkes had turned down the Thayers' offer to buy them out had just added to the pressure of the looming sale.

"I need to get going with edits. I only have two weeks left."

"Unless I kidnap you," he teased.

"Then I better run away," she poked back, stepping out of the car. "Goodnight, Luke."

"Goodnight. And, Millie?" She ducked back in. "I'm looking forward to our seafood date tomorrow night."

Millie smiled and shut the door. Another date. Another

night of this buildup of tension between them. She walked inside the resort with part of her wanting to remove herself from this town's drama before it got worse and hearts were broken, and the other part of her wanting to drop the whole job for Luke. But the only thing she could do at the moment was get lost in her edits.

CHAPTER SIXTEEN

October 29, 1940
Evelyn

"Darling, sit down," Lawrence said after Evelyn paced by him for a third time. "You're going to tire yourself out. Let's just take a moment and breathe."

"I can't breathe, that's the problem." Evelyn ignored his request and walked over to the window. The last of the leaves that still clung to the bare branches were finally falling, and she watched them circle through the air with light flurries that had just started. Winter would arrive in full force soon. It was usually her favorite season, but not this year.

Lawrence came up behind her and placed his hands on her shoulders. "Yes, you can. Let's do it together." He leaned over, wrapping his arms around her.

Her parents weren't due back for hours, but it was still risky to have him here with her like this. For the moment, however, his strong arms were just what she needed, and after a few minutes of watching the scenery unfold, Evelyn's racing heart began to calm.

She finally turned to face him and reached for his cheek. "Lawrence, your number was called. I can't even think about what will happen now."

All of America had listened in as President Roosevelt came over the radio just before noon and the first drawing under the Selective Service Act took place. Evelyn's parents left straight after to meet with some friends in town, and she rang Lawrence as soon as they'd left. Fifteen minutes later, he stood on her front porch to tell her the worst possible news: His number had been chosen.

"Remember, we're not actively at war yet. Did you hear what the bishop said in the address earlier? It's better to be prepared than not. If I am called to serve, I'll go train and come home. I'm sure that's all that will happen."

"How can you be so sure? What's going on overseas is intense and terrible. How can America stay out of it much longer?"

"To be honest, I don't know, but I'm hopeful. As a healthy young man of this fine country, I'm proud to go if needed, except for the fact that I know it's hurting you." Lawrence extended his hand. "Come on, perhaps some fresh air will help."

Before they began their walk, Lawrence opened his car door to retrieve his camera. They crossed the fields and walked along the edges of the mountain. Evelyn held up her face toward the gray skies, clinging to what he'd just said: their country hadn't joined the war yet. She wanted to believe that everything would be alright, but something inside kept weighing down those thoughts. Hitler was not being stopped and the Nazis were only gaining more power. America would surely need to step in.

Once they crested a hill, another small open area was before them.

"This view will never grow old. Just look at it, my love," Lawrence said, holding up the camera.

Evelyn looked at the mountains that rose in the distance, their rugged peaks seeming to reach for the sky.

"It's beautiful!" She spun in a circle, her dark green plaid skirt moving with her, mirroring the swirling snowflakes. Raising her arms, she let her worry move through her as she twirled out the shakiness of her anxiety and Lawrence snapped pictures, capturing her at every angle.

"Keep going!" he called out, taking a few more before motioning for her to stop. "Okay, now pause and look at me with that gorgeous smile."

As she posed for him, a playfulness took over and she gave him a flirty smile before facing the view once more. Serenity washed over her as she stared at the hills that stretched for miles. The beauty grounded her restless nerves, and something suddenly occurred to her.

"Wait!" She whipped back around. "I heard somewhere that if you're married, you may be exempt from serving."

Lowering his camera, Lawrence stood still in thought. "I heard that myself, too, but I believe it's more for if there are dependents in the home. Even if we were married now, we don't have children."

"But *I'd* be your dependent as your wife. I don't want to be hasty with something like marriage, but it might save you from the military." She began to head back toward the house. "Come on, let's go to town and find my father."

"Evelyn." He gently reached for her arm to stop her. "I told you. I'm proud to serve and defend this country. I don't want us getting married to be for any other reason than because we love each other."

"We *do* love each other," she said, her eyes moving back and forth on his as she tried to find the right words. "I don't mean to sound ungrateful for our military, but I don't want that love to be taken from us." Tears brimmed as she drew in a long breath, trying to stay composed.

"My sweet Evelyn." Lawrence stood closer, drew up her hand, and softly kissed it. "I know you're worried. But I need to get your father's blessing about us being together first. There's no way I'd accomplish that for trying to keep me from serving. How do you suppose that would look in your father's eyes? He would think I'm a coward."

Evelyn wanted to get upset and argue, but Lawrence was right. Her parents didn't even know they were together, and with the ridiculous feud between their families, getting them to accept their love was going to be the first step.

"You're right." She sighed as he held her hand close to his chest. "The last thing my father would want is a son-in-law hiding from serving our country."

"But it doesn't mean we can't talk to them. And we need to do that soon. Let me think through this a little more and how best to approach him." He smiled down at her. "If there's anything I'm a coward about, it's facing your father."

Evelyn laughed. "My father? He's not so tough, you'll see. Having three daughters has softened him over the years."

"Except you're his firstborn. This will be challenging, but I know our love is stronger than silly arguments over land."

She slipped her arm through his as they walked back down the fields. When her driveway came into view, her worry faded, replaced by a fierce determination. Despite what was happening, she would follow Lawrence's lead and stay positive. They'd get through this together and alongside their country.

———

Present Day

Even after two cups of coffee, Millie's eyes drooped in fatigue as she glanced out the window at the gray clouds that seemed to have grown darker since she'd woken right after dawn. It would be a snowy Saturday, just as Luke had warned, but she didn't feel uneasy about driving in it. Maybe she was morphing into a Vermonter.

Looking back at her laptop screen, she forced herself to keep going. There were only a few more edits to go and she'd be done. The late night and early wake up were already hitting her, but she had a full day ahead and couldn't stop. After she returned with her takeout the night before, it was hours before she went to bed. She ate the delicious stew and edited photos until well after midnight, and even put together a mini slideshow presentation to give Ashley and the team as a preview. If they liked what they saw, she could continue in the direction she was going.

She had an abundance of pictures from the past week and grouped together a few from various settings, like the kids from the mountain taking ski lessons and the locals sledding. She started a document titled "Alpine Ridge: Christmas in Focus" and began writing about the pictures. Before she knew it, she had nearly three full pages written from her perspective. Her aim was to bring the community alive to those listening to and seeing the pitch, to tug at the heartstrings of the representatives from Peak Holdings and show them what visiting the resort and town would be like for their guests. She wasn't a writer, but the words flowed, and when she finally paused she realized Alpine Ridge was in fact pulling at her own heartstrings.

Luke's face flooded her thoughts when she reread what she'd written. She didn't mention his name, but it was as if her time with him was transferred into her experience of the town so far. Meeting him, sharing memorable places together as he taught her about this wonderful community, and the comfort she'd felt being in it since arriving, all spilled into the way she described the people, the events, and the town.

After finishing the last edit, she put some of the photos together with the preview in an email to Ashley and hit "send." Then she rooted around the couch for her phone to text Ashley about the email. She finally spotted it between the cushions and sent the text, then noticed it was nearly eleven. She had two hours left to shower and eat before the gingerbread house contest started.

When she stood, her muscles were stiff from sitting in one place for so long. As she stretched, an incoming call from Lila popped up on her phone.

"Hey there!" she answered with more enthusiasm than she had. Hopefully a shower would wake her up.

"How's everything up there?" her sister asked. "Getting some good pictures?"

"More than I can keep up with in edits. It's so beautiful here that I can't stop." Millie turned on the water to warm up and walked back to her dresser to find some clothes for the day. With the snow, she chose jeans and a khaki round-neck sweater. Her snow boots would be a must.

"Awesome! Think you're getting what the resort needs?"

"I think so. Well, at least, I hope so. I just sent a preview for the marketing team right before you called." Just saying that out loud suddenly made her nervous. "So I'll let you know what they say."

"I'm sure they'll love it. And just wait until the hotel here sees this job added to your résumé. They can't say no then. And speaking of the hotel . . ." Lila was banging pots in the background, making Millie a little homesick for her sister. There were so many times Millie had reorganized that cabinet, but with how busy Lila was at the hospital, she always messed it up again in her constant rush.

"I can hear that you haven't kept my cabinet organized," Millie teased.

"No, which makes me miss you."

"I miss you too. I wish you could experience this place with me."

"Me too. Hang on, just need to reach for my frying pan." Another loud bang and she could hear the phone shuffle. "Okay, got it. I have you on speaker while I scramble some eggs."

"So, what were you saying before about the hotel?"

"Oh, I spoke to my friend, Hannah, who interviewed you."

"You did?" Millie's voice fell flat.

"Well, geez, you sound rather annoyed. Do you not want me to talk to her about the job?" Her sister's voice grew defensive.

"No, it's fine."

"You sure? I won't mention it to her again if you aren't interested in that position."

Thinking back to the description essay she'd written for Ashley and how much she had fallen in love with Alpine Ridge, it felt almost as if she already lived there. She realized that since the minute she'd landed in Vermont, the hotel in South Carolina and the possibility of reapplying for a position there had been out of her mind. Her life there seemed to go off her radar completely.

"Well, truthfully, I haven't thought about that since I've been here. I've been absorbed with this town, meeting people, taking pictures everywhere . . ." *And there's Luke*. But she kept him out of the conversation. Her sister would dwell on him way more than she was ready to talk about.

"Oh," Lila said. "Well, it wasn't a long conversation. I was just updating her about your job in Vermont and that her team would probably like what they see once you're done."

Dishes clanked in the background. "But, anyway, that's all up to you if you want to contact them again. Or not. She did sound interested in what you're doing, so I figured I'd let you know that."

"Thanks, sis. I appreciate the good word and support." The steam from the shower began to drift out of the bathroom. "I have to get going—another busy day ahead."

"Have fun!"

When she hung up, Millie instantly felt bad. Her sister had taken the time to talk to Hannah and was trying to keep that job as an option for Millie, but she was really starting to see herself in Alpine Ridge long term . . . that is, if the town didn't cast her out once they learned about the sale. Not once had she sat in frustration over her career since she had begun this job or felt frozen in her abilities while thinking about her parents. A drive she'd thought was lost years ago was building in her again.

———

The parking lot was full when Millie arrived at the library. The snow was falling fast and luckily she spotted the snowplow in town and followed it most of the way there. The dark clouds made the town sparkle with Christmas lights that shone brightly in all the storefront windows as she made her way down main street.

After she parked, she grabbed her camera bag and hurried through the snowy lot. Inside, the library was warm and loud with kids all around, excited to make gingerbread houses. Parents were carrying boxes and following the kids into a large room where tables were set up with the gingerbread pieces. Just to her right was another table of Christmas treats, compliments of the library. Hoisting her bag under her arm, she reached for a piece of peppermint fudge and popped it in her mouth. The minty chocolate immediately melted on her tongue.

"Millie!"

She turned and spotted Ashley at the check-in desk, waving at her and holding up two coffees.

"What a fun event!" Millie said as she approached the desk.

"So much fun. Even tourists sign their kids up for it." Ashley handed her one of the cups. "I got you a caramel latte. It was today's special at the café." They walked toward the other room.

"Thanks. I'll need all the caffeine I can get today. I had a late night putting that preview together for you. Did you get it?"

"Yes, I did. And let me just say . . . wow. I'm blown away. I'm going to meet with Cassidy and Danny on Monday morning to show them. You've more than nailed this job."

"You mean it?" Millie followed Ashley to stand along the wall so others could get by, and then she took a peek at the room as everyone set up their stations. Each participant was bringing their own decorative pieces for the houses, which explained the boxes the adults were carrying.

"More than mean it." Ashley turned to her, confused. "You really don't see the talent you have, do you?"

"I guess I'm just too critical of my work." Millie took a sip of the much-needed latte. The sweet and nutty vanilla flavors instantly gave her an extra boost.

"Well, cut that out. I'd tell you if you weren't getting the right pictures. But let's focus on today," Ashley said, changing the subject. They both looked around as the room continued to fill up. "I just love this event. Wait until you see what some of these families create with their themes. My favorite last year was the Grinch gingerbread house."

"This will be so fun to shoot." Millie shrugged out of her

coat and laid it on a back table. "Did we get permission for me to take pictures?"

"Yes." Ashley pointed back toward the front desk. "The librarian is having the parents sign the form. I printed it out this time. She said she'd let us know right away if anyone says no so you can avoid that table, but so far it's all a yes, so go for it."

"Great." She pulled her camera out of the bag.

"And speaking of Danny and Cassidy, I know you'll be working, but I signed you up to join our team whenever you want to take a break and help."

"I'll definitely come help after I make a few rounds."

"Good because they are terrible at this." Ashley rolled her eyes at her coworkers who were seated at their station. "They are wonderful at marketing, but not this. Alpine Ski Resort needs a better outcome than the caved-in mess we put together last year."

Millie chuckled. "Not sure I'll be any more helpful, but I'll catch up with you in a bit."

Ashley walked off to join her team, and Millie turned on her camera and held it up. The large overhead lights made for perfect lighting and she took a couple test shots. As she did so she felt someone move in and stand close to her.

"Good afternoon." The familiar voice startled her, but his formalness made her grin as she looked through the eyepiece.

"Good afternoon to you as well, Mr. Thayer." Millie lowered her camera and burst out laughing when she saw Luke's outfit. He was wearing a gingerbread man jumpsuit, complete with peppermint buttons and a white icing face around the hood. "Run, run as fast as you can!" she teased, pretending to back away.

Luke raised his brow, hands on his hips. "You're just jealous that you don't get to wear it." He waved both arms at a toddler who came over with his mother, then gave the boy a high five, making him giggle as he walked away.

"You might be right because I love it." She held up her camera and Luke struck a pose.

"It's also an Alpine Ridge tradition that the chairman wears it," he said, and a few teenagers gave him more high fives, laughing as they walked by.

"Looking good, Thayer," one said.

"Thanks! Good luck today!" Luke turned back to Millie. "And the kids love it—or rather, love making fun of it. Are you going to join Ashley's team today?"

"I think I may have to. She said last year was a flop . . . literally. But I'm not sure how much help I'll be. I haven't made a gingerbread house in years."

"Just have fun with it. There are a few teams that are impossible to beat anyway."

"I will. And you have fun being the gingerbread man," she said and laughed again, holding up her camera as he made a funny face for the picture.

He kept his gaze on her as he slowly backed away. "Still on for tonight?"

"Maybe . . ." She pretended to think about it. "Will you be wearing that?"

"You'll have to find out later!"

Shaking her head, she was still smiling as she turned back to the crowd. A few parents had been curiously observing their exchange. She could tell they were wondering about them, and as she snapped pictures of the contestants and their fans, she found herself pondering the same question herself. It had only been a week of getting to know Luke, but each time he snuck a glance at her from across the room while she worked the crowd, it seemed as if it had been much longer.

Chapter Seventeen

After opening the door of The Ridge Reef, Millie could hardly get inside with all the people waiting. Luke had told her the seafood restaurant had only opened a couple weeks prior and, with it being a Saturday night, the place was slammed.

"Good thing I made reservations," he said close to her ear against the noise from the bar.

A large black chalkboard lined with holly berries and ocean animals drawn all over it hung near the hostess station. In green and red chalk it read "Christmas Specials All Month Long" with various dishes listed. Luke approached the hostess and she motioned for them to follow. They walked through the crowded restaurant, the dark blue low lights creating an intimate setting, and she seated them in a small booth. The center of the table had a small glass bowl filled with turquoise holiday baubles and silver starfish.

"What a lovely restaurant." Millie was glad to be away from the noise near the front.

"It's my first time here, but I'm impressed too. I hear the food is really good."

"I have no doubt. Everything I've eaten this past week in Alpine Ridge has been delicious." She picked up the menu.

"It's only been a week?" Luke asked. He was holding his menu, but when she looked up, his eyes weren't scanning the options, they were focused on her. "Feels like you've been here a lot longer."

A server filled glasses of water for them as Millie kept her focus steady on him.

"It must be because of all these fun Christmas activities that have kept us busy."

"Maybe . . . or spending time with you," he said.

Her heart thudded and she tried to find the right words to respond—while also ignoring the lurking secret that still hung over their budding relationship. Ashley better let her tell him soon or she might lose her job spilling the truth.

"Welcome to The Ridge Reef!" Saved by the waitress. "Oh, hello, Mr. Thayer. So glad you're here!" Her T-shirt showed a lobster wearing a Santa hat, and she also wore a holiday-light necklace.

Luke finally broke his gaze from Millie and smiled up at the waitress. "Me too. I'm pleased to see how busy this place already is."

"You'll see why when you taste the food."

As the waitress rambled off the daily specials—oysters in a spinach, bacon, and cream sauce and a surf-and-turf platter—Millie tried to focus, but her thoughts were spiraling. *I'm overthinking*, she told herself in order to relax. *Just focus on him. Enjoy the evening.*

"And for you, miss?" the waitress glanced at her. "Something to drink? We have a holiday cranberry martini special tonight."

"Sounds perfect." That would surely settle her down.

When the waitress left to get their drinks, Millie kept her attention on the menu. "The haddock sounds good."

"I'm going for that platter." Luke put down his menu.

"Sounds like a lot of food."

He patted his belly. "I worked up quite an appetite as the gingerbread man."

Millie smiled. "The kids loved you today." She'd taken a lot of pictures of him interacting with them at the tables and with this year's winning team. "I'm glad the Candy Land house won. Theirs was remarkable with all the ribboned pink hearts the mother did herself."

"Every year the participants create something new and brilliant."

For the next few minutes they discussed the other gingerbread houses and how great the turnout had been, making for some good pictures. The waitress came back with their drinks and took their food order before dashing off again.

"And then there was our station." Millie made a face, making him laugh before he picked up his beer for a sip.

"Their house wasn't as bad as last year and, I must say, you saved the day with those icing skis. Let's toast to that."

"The rest of the lodge did not work out, so I had to do something." She clinked her martini against his bottle with a shrug. "At least it didn't cave in."

Luke laughed and then leaned on the table. "Okay, Miss Millie Rowan. Tell me about you."

Keeping her fingers on the base of the martini glass, she stared at the red drink. "What would you like to know?"

"Tell me more about Charleston. Did you always live there?"

"I grew up about an hour outside of it next to a lake."

"Sounds nice. Not to mention the warmer weather. I'd love to get down South after Christmas for a break from this cold."

"See, this is a break for me. All this snow. I love it."

"That's good to hear."

"Is it?" She raised her glass to her lips, trying not to let his gaze shake her this time.

"Yeah, it is. It means I don't have to beg you to come back for a visit."

"I don't want to leave at all." The words came out before she realized she'd said them.

"Is that so?" He straightened, the corners of his mouth turning up.

"Tell me about you," she said, dodging the question. "How are you liking being the chairman?"

He studied her for a second, but didn't press her. "It's quite a job, as you saw today," he answered.

"I wish I could dress up for my job. Anything to entertain the kids, right?"

"Yeah, that's what it's all about this time of year. The children." He took a swig of his beer. "But I'm enjoying it. Like I mentioned back at the print shop, I have big shoes to fill after the job my grandfather did as chairman."

"Based on what I've witnessed so far, you'll do just as well." Millie's gaze moved past Luke when she saw Mr. Clarke walking right toward them. "Oh, it's Dylan." She waved, but he didn't return the gesture, his expressionless face surprising her.

"Hello, Millie," he said when he got to their table and looked at Luke. "Mr. Thayer, how are you?"

Millie watched the two men staring at each other. There was nothing friendly about their exchange. She found it odd that Dylan didn't call Luke by his first name. After all, they were neighbors, despite whatever old tensions lay in the family history.

"I'm doing well. And yourself?"

"Fine, thank you." Dylan glanced at her again. "Enjoy your evening, Millie."

Watching him walk off, she felt a little confused. "That was a strange conversation." She turned back to Luke.

He hesitated. "Nothing new with him."

"I don't understand." She suddenly worried that perhaps Dylan was upset about them being together. She was technically only here because she was working for the Clarkes, but she was off the clock for the evening. And even if he wasn't fond of Luke, did that mean she couldn't be? "Every time you've talked about them moving, you seemed supportive and caring. Is it not mutual? I mean, I get that your dad's offer to invest in the resort after Riley's accident didn't go well, but why did Dylan look so distant just then?"

"He and I are just not close is all," Luke said with a sigh. "And despite how estranged things are with my family and his, they are part of Alpine Ridge, and the resort is very important to this town, so I try to be supportive, especially as chairman. I want nothing but peace for them as they continue to heal."

"But *why* are things still so estranged?" Millie asked. But then it dawned on her. She remembered what he'd said about the argument with Riley before her accident. "Besides your parents, no one else knew about your argument with Riley that day . . . so what else could it be?"

"Actually, that *is* partly why." Luke looked at his beer, tapping its side. "Dylan also knew . . . I lied before. I didn't want to get into that part of the story the other night, since we're still getting to know each other. But talking to you feels more natural every time we're together." He stopped his fingers and met her eyes.

Millie felt the same way, but stayed quiet, taking in the newest pieces of this ever-unfolding story. Before she could ask anything else, the waitress returned with their food.

The baked haddock was made with a crumbled almond and herb topping and served alongside buttered asparagus and a rice medley. Luke's platter was filled with a plate full of steak bites, grilled shrimp, and scallops. They both dug in. The haddock's topping was the perfect blend of crunchy alongside the soft fish.

"I give yet another restaurant a one hundred out of ten," she mumbled between bites.

"Agreed." Luke pushed around his potatoes, looking deep in thought.

Did she push him too far with her questioning?

"I didn't mean to pry before," Millie said. "You don't have to explain any further if you don't want to. I was just a little thrown off with how Dylan acted. He was so warm and friendly when I met him at his house for breakfast."

Luke continued to stare at his food, and she felt worse by the second.

"It's okay," he finally said and met her eyes. "I was just thinking about everything that happened, and I want to explain it. Remember how I told you that after the accident I asked my father to help out by either investing in the resort or buying it to help with their debt?"

Mille nodded.

"Well," he continued, "that resulted in a big fight between Dylan and my father, more so than I originally let on." Luke paused, picking up his beer for a drink. "I don't want to drag you into the middle of this mess. I hope you're alright hearing it."

"Yes, it's more than alright. I'm not taking anyone's side, but I want you to be able to share whatever you want to share, especially if it helps to get it off your chest." Millie truly meant it, even more than wanting to know what happened in order to be prepared for sharing the news of the pitch. There was more to this story than even Ashley seemed to know.

"The fight was awful. I think it may have been the worst one despite centuries of tension between our families. Dylan was enraged that night because he had just found out about mine and Riley's discussion that led to our argument. He accused my father of wanting to buy the resort to 'make up' for me causing Riley's accident. The Clarkes were so distraught over her death, which I don't blame them for one bit, that they needed to point fingers at someone to offset how much grief they were in. I understood that. My father never had." Luke leaned his arms on the table, clutching the now-empty beer with both hands. "So it's been a hard couple years. My parents are glad they're moving, just so they don't have to live so close to them."

"I'm sorry that happened," she said, taking one of his hands off the bottle.

When they joined them, Luke's face relaxed and he glanced up at her.

"Well, you're here now. You'll put together some great material. Ashley and her team are wonderful, and I feel very hopeful that the Clarkes will be happier in their new home—and that their marketing plans will bring even more success to the resort and get them out of their financial struggle. I was worried for a while that they *would* sell out to a large corporation or something. That would be a total disaster for Alpine Ridge."

"Did they mention something to make you think that?" Her pulse sped up fast, but she kept holding his hand.

"No, it was just something I drummed up in my own head."

Millie's stomach churned while a rush of guilt ran down her back. Suddenly, keeping the pitch quiet didn't matter anymore. Hearing this story about Riley, their families fighting, and seeing the look of hope on Luke's face about her being there was more important.

"Luke—"

"Millie! Luke!" A female voice erupted near them.

Millie turned and let go of Luke's hand when she saw Ashley, Cassidy, and Danny walking toward them.

"Ashley, I didn't know you'd be here," Millie said, glancing at Luke.

"Oh, are we interrupting?" Ashley asked with a smirk.

"It's okay. We were just in a heavy conversation. Have you all eaten yet? The food is amazing."

Ashley looked between them as if she could guess what they had been talking about. "Yes . . . we just did and we're heading to the bar for some drinks. We'll leave you two to get back to your intimate discussion," she said, looking right at Millie with trusting eyes. "Millie, we were just talking about the preview you sent over. We can't wait to talk to you on Monday about it. Enjoy your night!"

The group headed to the bar and Millie was completely torn. Watching her friend walk away made her feel even guiltier. She'd almost broken her promise to Ashley, but as she turned to Luke, frozen in his gaze, she was locked in a standstill with no clue what move to make next.

To her relief, they fell into an easy discussion for the rest of their date. He had her laughing about stories of his first few months as chairman and the silly mistakes he'd made trying to figure out the job. She shared her passion for photography and her choice to pursue this career over college, opting for a certification instead to help her get started. As she found herself letting it all out, including how her parents didn't exactly approve of her career goals and not going to college, his stance didn't falter once.

"We're all on different paths. For some of us a degree is useful and needed, like in the case of your sister. You chose something entirely different, but that doesn't make one way better than the other. And, by the way, I looked you up on social media," he said, giving her a sly look.

"Oh, yeah? What did you find?" Her face flushed in warmth.

"I found a woman who has exceptional talent. Millie, the pictures I've seen on there are incredible. So raw and candid. Your parents should be proud."

"Thank you," she said as the waitress put the check on the table. Compliments still made her feel awkward.

"I mean it. You don't need anyone's approval to do what you are meant to do."

Luke put his card in the bill holder and flagged the waitress. "Ready to go? I wanted to take you to the town center to see our big tree. Would you like that?"

"It's a good thing I drove to meet you here and still have my camera."

———

The Christmas tree in Alpine Ridge's quaint town center shone brightly next to a large white gazebo along with snow still lightly bouncing through the air like winter confetti. It was a wondrous sight. A peaceful hush fell over them as Millie and Luke stared at it. The tree with its branches packed with lights and heavy with freshly fallen snow stood tall and proud, a beacon of joy and magic.

The large star at the top pulled Millie out of her trance, beckoning her to take pictures from every angle. She continued to move around the tree, snapping photos. Her gaze drifted to Luke, his eyes crinkling at the corners as he smiled at the sight before them. She raised her camera once more, this time framing Luke's rugged features against the winter wonderland backdrop. As the shutter clicked, Millie's heart skipped a beat, for in that instant she felt the weight of their previous conversation settle over her.

"Was I making a goofy face watching the tree?" Luke came closer.

"Not at all. You looked mesmerized. With the stores all lit up behind you, I think I got just enough light to make out your face."

"Did you get enough? You'll see more of this tree at next weekend's Christmas parade when you can take daytime pictures."

"I got plenty for now." Millie turned off her camera and put it back in her bag. "Thank you for showing me this. This entire town feels so cozy with the Christmas décor, especially with the snow."

"I knew you'd like it," he said and held out his arm. "I'll walk you to your car."

"Why, thank you," she said, slipping her arm through his.

They walked in silence, the puffs of their breaths visible in the cold air. Her car was parked one block away, next to his, and this time she didn't jump inside so fast.

"You're not running from me. Does that mean I won some points?" he joked.

"I didn't know we were keeping track," she said as he took her hands. She looked down at them, joined together once again. Ever since Ashley had interrupted them at the restaurant, she'd put the sale out of her mind, but now in the stillness of the winter night with no one else near them, it all came back. When his hand lifted her chin up toward him and his gaze fell on her face, she knew that if she let him kiss her, he'd feel even more betrayed when he found out the truth.

"I better get back so I can rest up for our day of skiing tomorrow." She loosened her grip on his hands, halting his next move.

"I forgot about that." He grinned. "More Millie fun."

She opened her car door, relieved he didn't seem upset by

her sudden interruption. "What time should I meet you out there?"

"How about eleven? Gives you some time to sleep in, eat, and be ready for Josh."

"Can't wait," she said and slipped into the car.

Her mind was stuck the entire drive back to the resort, replaying the way his gaze had lowered to her lips, the same desire gripping her. What had started out as a job to further her photography résumé was turning into a lot more.

Once she got to her suite, the exhaustion that had started her day fell over her once again, and before her mind could contemplate the mess she was in the middle of between her heart and her job, she fell into a deep, much-needed sleep.

Chapter Eighteen

Millie wrapped her scarf tighter around her neck the next morning, feeling a thrill of excitement as she gazed up at the towering slopes. The sun was out, inviting skiers for a new day on Alpine Mountain, and she was ready for her first ski lesson.

Josh scanned the crowd next to her. "Oh, there he is," he said, pointing to Luke walking through the skiers toward them.

As Luke approached, Millie drew in the crisp mountain air filling her lungs, and the sounds of laughter and chatter from the other skiers were drowned out by the smile on his face.

"Hey, Josh," Luke said, shaking the instructor's hand. "Perfect day for this first-timer."

"Let's not keep reminding him. The kids he just taught will probably do this better than me." Millie glanced at the children making their way down the small practice hill. "I'll be staying over there with them." The rope pulling kids up the beginner slope nearby looked easy enough compared to the chair lift that kept moving above their heads. Watching it carry people up the big mountain suddenly looked terrifying.

"No way, we're going to at least bump you over to the green slope," Josh said. "You might be surprised how well you do."

"*Might* is the key word there." Millie winced, realizing she may be in over her head with this activity. She could barely stand straight as she clicked her boots into the skis before Luke got there.

"Don't chicken out on me now," Luke said, giving her a slight nudge that nearly toppled her to the ground. He quickly took her arm to save her from the fall.

"See?" she said. "The practice hill will be enough for me."

"No better way to find out than to try," Josh said. "Luke, can you hold her hand? I'd like her to unclip from her skis for this first part of the lesson."

Luke held her tight as she got off the skis.

"Now I want you to bend your knees and feel the weight of your shins against the boots," Josh said. "Then walk in a straight line a few steps and come back."

Millie did as instructed, and when she circled back she looked at Josh. "And here I thought I'd have to glide down that mountain. I can do this all day!"

Josh laughed. "Oh, we're going down the mountain alright. I just want you to get used to the feel of your boots. It's important to know their weight so they don't throw you off balance. Often, first-time skiers feel intimated with how heavy they are."

After she took a few more laps, Josh had her clip back into one of the skis. "Toe first, then heel." Millie put her boot on top of the ski and felt it snap into place. "That's it. Now, let's get this show on the road and get in line for the lift!" Josh exclaimed. "Follow me."

"You'll do great!" Luke followed Josh's lead.

When the men turned around, Millie rolled her eyes.

"Ha-ha," she said, shaking her head with a grin. "That would be the last time you would see me. I would one leg it right off this mountain with this single ski."

"Okay, so let's begin the lesson. First was getting used to the boots, and I also need to get you comfortable on those skis. But we *are* going to do this one at a time. Stay clipped in to just one ski. Now, just as you did before, start walking. Glide the one ski forward and use your other foot as an anchor with the poles."

Millie hesitated, her eyes darting between Josh and the snow-covered slope. "Uh, I'm feeling a little . . . wobbly?" She tried to move forward, but everything was shaking now with the ski on her foot.

Josh chuckled. "Wobbly? That's a great start! Wobbly is just a fancy word for 'I'm about to feel the snow on my face.'" He winked. "Don't worry, we all fall in the beginning. Bend a little more, and feel the shin against the boot and use that as your balancing point."

Millie did as she was told and, before she knew it, she was moving forward with ease. "I got it!"

"Great job! Now let's clip in the other ski," Josh instructed.

As Luke once again offered his hand, she clipped into the other ski.

"Okay, now we're going to do the same thing with both skis, but before you move forward, I'm going to have you simply move side to side. Like this." Josh lifted his leg, gripping his poles for support, and moved one ski to the side, then the other. "This is called side slipping and helps you understand where your balance is with both skis."

After Millie went back and forth once, Luke joined her in the motion, and she began to feel more stable.

"I think I'm getting this balance thing!"

"You definitely are," Josh said. "I told you, you can do this. Okay, now it's time to move forward so we can tackle that practice hill."

Over the next half an hour, Josh taught her how to keep her legs apart and steer with her toes in, without crossing the skis. She practiced in a straight line until she was ready to go down the tiny practice hill with Josh alongside her. Millie focused on Luke who was waiting at the bottom and went for it, feeling like a drunken flamingo as she steadied herself, but within a few seconds she was gliding with ease toward Luke.

Josh cheered her on. "Look at you go, Millie!" he called out as they reached the bottom.

Millie stumbled to a stop, her face flushed with joy.

"You did it! Now, let's do this little hill a few more times before we go up the beginner slope and work on that whole not-falling-over thing while stopping," Josh said.

Millie giggled, feeling a sense of camaraderie with Josh, which gave her the confidence to keep going. "I'm getting the hang of it, but it's because you're so good at teaching."

Luke came toward her. "I'll be on the other side of you going down the beginner slope, so if you fall, we'll go down together."

"I'll make sure to lean your way then," Millie joked.

Luke shrugged. "I can take it."

"He definitely can. I've seen him tumble many times," Josh joked. "Okay, before we fall down the slopes, let's practice stopping."

The instructor demonstrated on the practice hill, widening his stance, drawing his skis a little closer, and increasing the pressure to slow himself. After a few more runs, Millie finally felt comfortable stopping without falling. Facing the ropes up to the beginner slope, she was ready.

"Let's do this!"

Together, the three got on the rope pull and went up the slope alongside all the children. Josh grinned as he watched Millie's eyes widen the higher they got. When they reached the top, she stumbled off the rope just as Luke caught her.

"This is higher than I thought. I don't know, Luke." Her heart hammered against her chest as she looked down the hill. "This is a beginner slope?"

Josh slid up next to them. "You got this. We're both right here with you."

Millie followed them, struggling at first to stay upright.

"Whoa, easy does it, Millie," Josh said as she regained her balance. "That's it, nice and slow. Ignore the other skiers."

With sudden determination, she focused straight ahead, feeling the sturdy boots hugging her legs as she pushed down the hill. At first, she felt as if she was going to fall over again, but as she picked up speed, she started to get the hang of it. Josh cheered her on from one side and Luke the other, both offering words of encouragement as they made their way down. When she reached the bottom, she remembered to widen the gap with her skis, but the speed this time was more than before and reaching for Luke, she found herself in the snow and on top of him.

"Just as we discussed!" Luke said, laughing as they lay in a tangled clump.

"Sorry," she said sheepishly. "I tried not to grab you like that."

"I'm not complaining," he said with a playful smile.

"Now there's a way to stop!" Josh said, circling around them. "Ready for more?"

"Sure am!" Millie took Luke's hand after he got on top of his skis first and then helped her up.

Hours slipped by, and after Josh assisted them down the

beginner slope a handful of times, he jetted off to another lesson, leaving Millie in Luke's hands. The wind rushing by her face each time she went down the hill put her in a world of her own. She could easily see why people loved skiing so much. Before long, she had mastered the beginner's section, and just as Josh had insisted at the start of the lesson, she was ready for the green slope with Luke by her side once again.

As she carved her way through the powdery trail, the thrill became her escape for the day—momentarily releasing her from the pressure of the sales pitch and all the intensity around what was to come with it.

———

"I'm still impressed with how fast you picked that up, especially learning to twist stop like that."

Luke's cheeks were still reddened from the cold air. They had warmed up inside the resort's café with the day's special of creamy pumpkin soup and cheddar biscuits. Both were now sipping coffee, watching the skiers outside still making their runs before the afternoon ended.

"I think once I got the hang of balancing, it all clicked." Millie was proud of herself and already hooked on skiing. "I can't wait to do that again. That was so much fun."

"It's why you always see me here with my skis." Luke's attention moved past her. "There's Irene." He waved and the woman came over to them.

"Hello, you two," Irene said. Her delight at seeing them together hadn't waned at all. "I came to grab a bowl of this soup everyone keeps talking about."

"I don't blame you," Luke said. "Josie added a creamier base this time."

Irene looked at Millie. "Josie has been cooking for the café since she was in her twenties. She's now pushing retirement age."

"Well, she's got cooking talent, along with every other chef in this town," Millie said, taking the last sip of her coffee.

"Looks like you two were skiing," Irene said, eyeing their snow pants.

"Millie here had her first lesson and is a pro already," Luke said.

"That mountain drew me in, but I'm far from a pro. I need to get past the green slope first."

"Alpine Mountain certainly has that effect on people." Irene glanced out the window. "I may do a few runs since we got all that fresh snow yesterday."

Millie stood and looked at Irene. "It's been a day, but I need to get some pictures emailed to Bruce. Thank you again for connecting me with him. He and his wife are very nice."

"He'll do a great job on those prints," Luke said, standing up next to her. "I have some work to do myself with this week's upcoming events."

"I haven't looked at my calendar yet. What's on the schedule this week?" Millie asked.

"Aren't you enjoying all of this nonstop holiday fun?" Irene said.

"Yes, it's wonderful. The kids in town must really enjoy it too."

"Irene!" a woman behind the counter called out, holding up a paper bag.

Irene went to the counter to pick up her food, and when she came back, she smiled at Millie. "I'll walk with you to the elevators." She looked at Luke. "That is, if you don't mind, Luke?"

"Not at all. And, Millie?" he asked, with a glimmer of anticipation. "Christmas movie night at the parks and recreation building this Wednesday night is next on that holiday event list of yours. Save me a seat?"

"Depends," she said as Irene happily eyed them both. "I saw on the event listing there would be chocolate- *or* caramel-drizzled popcorn. I like chocolate."

"Done. Bucket of chocolate popcorn and a seat next to Mille. I'll see you there."

When Luke was far enough away, Irene turned to Millie. "I can't even begin to tell you how thrilled I am to have Luke back," she said in a low voice, glancing over her shoulder. "I know others would agree with me, but I don't want to be heard spreading gossip about our chairman."

Irene's words from the other night came back to Millie. *He's not the Luke we all remember.*

"I don't have anything to compare him to, but I'm glad he's coming back to his old self."

"He is. Because of you."

"Maybe he's just starting to let go of the past." Millie didn't feel right taking the credit, or maybe it was the nagging guilt of the sale still hanging over her head. The excitement from the day on the slopes faded a bit as she remembered what he'd said at dinner. How he was worried the Clarkes would sell out to a corporation. His worst nightmare was coming true.

"No." Irene was beaming. "It's all you. Millie, he's smiling again. A *real* smile. Not the forced one he's been doing the past year since he was elected as chairman. He's jovial, flirty, and relaxed. That's the Luke I know."

"We do seem to click, don't we?" Millie grinned. She and Luke had had an instant attraction, but with everything that was still unspoken, their relationship already felt doomed to be short-lived. Not to mention her home was so far away. "It's too bad I live in South Carolina."

"So what? You can always visit each other, and then if things work out, one of you can move." They reached the elevators and Irene leaned in, talking behind her hand. "And I selfishly hope you move here because then I could see you more."

"Thanks, Irene," Millie said as Irene gave her shoulder a squeeze. "I really appreciate how kind and inviting everyone has been." The elevator doors opened, and they moved to the side, letting people off.

"That's Alpine Ridge for you." Irene studied her face. "And that's why I wanted to walk you to the elevator. To check on you and make sure our community has been treating you okay."

"More than okay. I feel like I'm part of this town." Millie cast down her eyes, collecting her thoughts before she looked back at Irene. "Can I ask you something?"

"Sure."

"From your opinion, and assuming you're aware, how bad is the tension between the Thayers and Clarkes?"

Irene's face fell. "Ah. So you found out about that." She motioned toward the two chairs near the elevators. "Let's sit so I don't have to hold this bag of food." Once they settled in the chairs, Irene turned to Millie with concern. "Everyone in town knows about that fight between Dylan and Brandon, but I don't want you to stress over it."

"I'm not stressed, just curious," Millie fibbed. She needed to understand the situation, so she gave Irene an encouraging nod.

"I won't lie. It was really bad for a few months after that fight." Irene shook her head. "It was an overheated, unnecessary argument too."

"It may seem that way, but from the little I've learned, I can understand both sides. Brandon wanted to help with the Clarkes' struggling finances with his offer, but the Clarkes were deep in grief over Riley's accident and losing her."

"And they still are. I really hope moving out of this town

will help them." Irene paused and looked right at Millie, as if she was debating whether to say anything else. "Did Luke tell you about his argument with Riley before she went skiing?"

Millie nodded, not surprised at all that Irene knew, even though Luke had told her otherwise. "Yes. I guess that has sat with Luke for a long time. I think he's blamed himself for her accident because of that."

"I know he has. He's really been hard on himself." Irene cast her gaze at a woman who pressed the button for the elevator and waited until she stepped inside before continuing. "Which is another reason it's so great he seems happy."

"I bet." Millie decided to press Irene a bit more about the argument. "It sounds like Brandon and Dylan's fight was a big misunderstanding. Like fingers pointed in anger and hurt."

"That's exactly what it was. Look." Irene clasped her hands. "I don't know how much Luke has shared with you about his family and the Clarkes' history, but those two families need to quit their nonsense."

"I agree," Millie said, even though she wouldn't have phrased it quite that directly.

"I know the Clarkes were hurting and that's why they wanted to point fingers at Luke being the cause of Riley's accident, but she was still getting over a bad bout of the flu. She shouldn't have gone out there as weak as she was. That accident could have happened regardless of whether she had that conversation with Luke or not."

"I know a little, but what do you know about their conversation that day?" Millie wasn't sure if she should be pushing this much in case Irene didn't know this part, but the way the woman immediately nodded told her she already knew everything.

"I know all about it. And I'm one of the few who does because Luke came to me shortly after to unload. He was hurting and frustrated and needed to talk to someone outside the family." Irene sat back in her chair. "Riley was convinced she found something that pointed to the fact that the original deed map—the one from well before the great flood of 1927 that wiped away many tree markers, all the way back to when the farmhouses were first built and the properties were established—indicated that the Thayers' property line extended into where the resort is."

"That's what Luke told me, too, but they never were able to go anywhere with it because she got hurt. He told me he tried to tell his dad about the argument with Riley, but I guess Mr. Thayer didn't want to hear it."

"Yes, Brandon can be stubborn at times. But a centuries' old fight between families can do that to someone." Irene took a deep breath. "Anyway," she exhaled.

The intensity of this story was a lot, and Millie could feel the weight of it just by talking to Irene. She couldn't imagine being Luke or the Clarkes.

"They understandably let it go once the accident happened." Millie continued, looking at the elevator that dinged open again, as a group of people laughing walked out. After they passed, she turned back to Irene. "Which means the argument over the property line, once again, was never settled."

Irene waved her hand. "It's neither here nor there. Things have finally calmed down since that fight. No need to dwell on all that any longer. Here's how I see it. The families will never be close, even though everyone in Alpine Ridge wishes they were. The last time there was any hope of them coming together was when Luke's great-uncle Lawrence and Riley's great-grandmother Evelyn were secretly dating and set to marry."

"Really?" Millie's brow shot up. "How tragic. How do you know about that?"

Irene laughed. "Repeated gossip through the years, so I

really don't know what was true and what wasn't and neither does Luke or his parents. The full details never came out about it either, outside of a heartbroken Evelyn sharing about the relationship after World War II took Lawrence's life. Lots of rumors have spread over the years about them since. It's like the whole town is invested in what has happened and what will happen next between the Thayers and the Clarkes."

"I mean, I don't blame y'all. Over two hundred years of fighting is bound to stir up some drama." They both laughed, and Millie pointed to Irene's bag. "Your soup is probably cold. I'm sorry to keep you so long."

"Don't be. I can reheat it. But the front desk is probably wondering why it's taking me so long." Irene stood and hugged Millie again. "If I don't see you in passing, just know that I won't be at the movie night. I have to cover for the woman who usually works Wednesday evenings—she has three young children she wants to take to it. But I'm here anytime you want to chat again. Just come find me." She hurried off with her food.

When Millie got to her room, she opened her laptop and drummed her fingers in thought over what Irene had shared. She glanced out the window. Alpine Mountain was radiant under the setting sun, its orange glow spreading downward. There was so much history with that mountain and so many unanswered questions.

But she needed to focus on work. She created a zip file of the photos she wanted Bruce to print of the Clarkes' house, along with the ones she'd scanned from the albums, and wrote her instructions in the email with the sizes requested. After she pressed send, she went out to her balcony and watched the rest of the sunset.

What if Riley had been right and the Thayers' property did run into the resort? It was interesting to think about, but if they did own some of that land, maybe selling it to Peak

Holdings wouldn't be a possibility anymore. Despite how much she wanted to please the Clarkes with her pictures, she was also invested in Alpine Ridge and understood why Luke had been worried about a sale like that. It was quite a toss-up to be an outsider who was stuck right in the middle and clearly seeing both sides.

Chapter Nineteen

Wearing the most adorable Christmas pajamas under their big coats, children were walking inside the parks and rec building on Wednesday evening. Millie held the door for a mother carrying an infant in a car seat in one hand and holding her toddler's hand in the other.

"Thank you," the mother said, out of breath. "This thing weighs a ton."

"I bet," Millie said to the mother. Peeking into the carrier, Millie saw the baby girl wore the same large red bow and red pajamas as her older sister. "How sweet, they match. They're adorable." Millie glanced at the toddler who was pointing to her camera.

"Cheese!" the little girl said with a wide grin.

"Aww! Perfect smile!" Millie said.

The toddler clapped with excitement, quickly getting distracted by the big blue screen on the wall inside the event room.

They moved inside and Millie said to the mother, "My name's Millie. I'm Alpine Ski Resort's photographer for this

Christmas season. If you'd like to participate, I'll be capturing this event, and hopefully your daughter can give me another smile like that."

"I've heard about you. The town is thrilled you're helping the Clarkes with their marketing. It'll make for a wonderful start to the new year for them. Of course we'll participate."

"Gr-Great," Millie's voice shook as she spoke. "See you in there." She stepped aside to allow the crowd through the door, while her thoughts were in disarray from what the mother had said. The residents truly had no idea about the sale, the corporation interested, and what was about to change for their tight-knit community. She'd be known as the monster who took all the photos and unwittingly used the townspeople to convince the corporation to buy the resort.

A knot began to form in her stomach just as Ashley walked through the door. Millie immediately pulled her to the farthest corner. "I need to talk to you."

"Millie? What's wrong?" Ashley glanced around, making sure no one was close enough to hear them.

"I can't keep up this charade anymore." Millie's frustration was apparent, but she couldn't help it. The whole job suddenly felt like manipulation, which in a way it was.

"What do you mean?"

"I mean I can't keep lying to these nice people—and to Luke. I just can't."

"Hold on. You're not lying to anyone."

"Ashley . . . yes, I am. I understood clearly when I arrived that the Clarkes weren't going to tell the town anything until the pitch was over and the sale was final. I get that. But no one has a clue what's happening. They think they're consenting to be in regular marketing materials. They have no idea they're helping us sell the resort, which will cause a lot of changes in town. Big changes. Ones they may not agree with or like, especially if Peak Holdings impacts other small, beloved local businesses. The longer I do this, the worse I feel."

"I've told you. It'll be alright. I know the residents don't know." Ashley shrugged. "But they'll move forward. Yes, we're a close community, but that means we will adjust to the changes together. Did something happen before I got here?"

"I was chatting with a mother when I walked in, and she said my marketing photos will help the Clarkes start the new year right. Once they find out what my photos are really for, I'll never be able to come back here. I'll be a villain." Millie held up her hands. "I can see it now on my résumé: Villain Photographer who stirred up a tiny town in Vermont with her pictures taken behind their backs."

Ashley chuckled. "Take a breath."

"It's not funny. I feel like a fraud getting everyone to smile for the camera. Just so I can sell out their beloved ski resort to a large corporation." Millie's hushed whisper was on the verge of yelling and Ashley took her arm.

"I'm not laughing at you. I'm just as nervous about this as you are, but it's my job. I can't change the Clarkes' mind, so I've had to adjust to the idea, and so will the rest of the town. Is this still about Luke? I can understand how worried you are about him considering how close you two are getting."

Millie drew in her breath and held it for a second before slowly letting it go. Her heart was beating fast after her sudden outburst. "I've already told you I wanted to tell him sooner, so yes, *I am* still worried about that, but—honestly—I feel bad for everyone. I know people can acclimate, but change isn't easy, especially for a whole town. I just . . . feel bad is all."

Ashley put her arm around Millie as they slowly walked to the event room. "Okay, how about this. Let's get through the Christmas parade on Saturday. That parade is a huge selling point for this town. Then we will tell Luke."

Millie looked straight ahead, still feeling annoyed, but also resigned. After all, she was getting paid for this. She'd agreed to the job of her own free will, even knowing what it involved.

The buttery smell of popcorn wafted through the air and when she looked inside the room, she saw Luke standing up front wearing a dark blue-and-white Christmas reindeer jumpsuit, making a group of kids laugh. When he spotted her, his goofy grin instantly lifted her distress, and she burst out laughing. He motioned his hand up and down to show off his outfit, making her laugh even more. She gave him a thumbs-up, matching his cheesy smile. The experience, the job . . . was the money even worth it anymore?

"Fine." She locked eyes with Ashley. "But no more delaying it after that."

"Despite all the drama with this resort sale, my team and the Clarkes were blown away with your preview. Remember how happy we were at the meeting Monday morning?"

"Yes." Millie thought back to the pure delight on everyone's faces after they viewed her preview. Even Dylan was pleased. Which was a relief after how irritated he'd seemed when she saw him at the seafood restaurant. "It would be a huge waste if I quit now," she reasoned. Though a part of her didn't really care anymore, Ashley was depending on her, and her friend had been working so hard for the Clarkes. "Especially since I spent most of yesterday finishing edits and piecing more photos together for the presentation."

"See? It'll all be worth it." Ashley pointed to the room full of happy kids waiting for the movie to begin as Luke made a group of them roar with laughter in his silly jumpsuit. "I'm going to collect the photo release forms and head out."

"You're not staying for the movie?"

"*The Polar Express* isn't my favorite holiday film. Besides, I have so much work to do for the anniversary party."

Millie had forgotten that was coming up. She'd been so preoccupied with the other events, edits, Luke . . .

"You know"—she stepped closer to Ashley and whispered —"that party feels like a giant goodbye party rather than a celebration."

"Because it is." Ashley's eyes drooped with sadness. "The Clarkes are planning to announce everything publicly then."

———

Millie managed to get a lot of pictures in the fifteen minutes before the lights dimmed for the movie to start. She had made her way around the room, getting as many shots as possible of all the fun pajama sets the kids were wearing, especially when the parents were matching them. When she found her way to be next to Luke, he didn't notice her right away as he made the children in front of him dance to a Christmas tune playing in the background. He was a natural around them. Without realizing it, she'd lowered her camera and was caught in a trance watching him interact with them.

"He's fantastic, isn't he?" an older woman next to her said, startling her out of her stupor.

"Oh, yes, he is. I was just . . ." Millie's embarrassment that she'd been caught gazing at Luke fumbled her words.

"Luke will do that to you," the woman said, studying her face, but Millie kept it as neutral as she could despite how heated it became. "I don't blame you one bit for staring."

Millie wanted to shrink out of the room. "It's just fun to watch how good he is at his job."

The woman patted her shoulder and took a seat with some children who jumped up, and yelled "Grandma!"

"I hope you got my good side in this thing." Luke's voice was suddenly right next to her.

Millie narrowed her eyes at his outfit. "Hmm . . . not sure there is a 'good side' in that getup."

"You're just jealous again. Where are your pajamas anyway?"

"I didn't know the adults wore them too." She held up her camera. "Besides, I'm just the photographer."

Luke eyed her for a moment. "Not to me." Before she could think of a response, he took a step backward. "I have a bucket of chocolate-drizzled popcorn to get. Pick a seat and I'll find you."

She watched him walk to the back where the ladies handling the popcorn machine were set up, then she got a little closer to snap some photos, catching him handing a bucket to a child just in time. *"The Clarkes are planning to announce everything then."* Ashley's worried expression after she'd said that clouded Millie's vision, and she put down the camera, shaking off the words. She couldn't imagine how the townspeople would respond.

Looking around the room, she found two seats next to each other all the way in the back. She sat down and put her camera on the other seat.

Luke came up behind the chairs. "Popcorn and some water, because we'll need it after all this salt."

She moved her stuff off chair and took the bucket from him.

"And napkins." Luke handed her a bunch.

The gooey chocolate was drizzled all over the popcorn, and she picked up a few kernels, then popped them in her mouth. The salty popcorn balanced the sweet chocolate perfectly.

"So good," she said, glancing at her chocolatey fingers.

He reached in the bucket and threw a handful in his mouth, and she giggled at the chocolate on his chin.

"And messy," he said, wiping it off with a napkin.

"It's Christmas. Messy desserts are acceptable."

The room darkened and as the movie started, Luke swung

his arm around the back of Millie's chair, making her earlier conversation with Ashley lose its grip as she found herself leaning into him. The fuzzy pajamas felt cozy, and soon Luke's fingers began stroking her hair.

As the movie played, Millie wasn't paying attention. All she could think about was the town and Luke, who put everything he had into keeping it the way the residents loved. Something occurred to her while she snuggled into him. Glancing up while he continued to run his fingers through her hair, she recognized the same suspicions from the day Luke had driven her to Green Mountain Photo grabbing hold of her again: how everything about the sale felt slightly off.

Her thoughts moved to Riley Clarke. Millie never knew her or what her intentions had been with wanting to get to the bottom of the situation with the property lines, but she imagined the woman had loved her town, just as Millie had grown to. Maybe Luke shouldn't keep brushing off what the woman had started.

The idea of somehow proving Riley to be right circled Millie's mind, even though she had no clue how to accomplish it. The Clarkes may have been planning on announcing the sale and saying goodbye at that party, but what if it could all be stopped? They may not want to sell the resort to Mr. Thayer because of whatever old hurts lingered—but what if they had no choice? What if Riley was right all along and the Thayers did in fact already own part of the land? Maybe she could help Luke figure out . . .

It was a far-fetched idea, one that needed to be done within the next week and a half, but now that she had been proven correct and there *was* more to this story, her earlier hunch was only growing stronger—the sale to the corporation wouldn't be final.

CHAPTER TWENTY

Morning of November 15, 1940
Lawrence

"Bobby, our son is reporting to service tomorrow. Let's not begin another war with Leroy right before Lawrence leaves," June said.

Lawrence overheard his parents from the other side of their bedroom door.

"Tommy has passed, and there's no way now to know what he found on that mountain."

Old Tommy Davis had died in his sleep just the other day, but what business did he have with them? Lawrence stood perfectly still.

"I'm going up there. That mountain is not all Leroy's, and I'll find proof."

"This needs to stop," his mother insisted.

Lawrence had been in a daze for the past two weeks since his number was called in the first draft. He'd been trying to sort himself out, totally oblivious to this land mess his parents were still focused on. The shock had eventually worn off as reality became clearer—that he was reporting to service. The odds of the military disqualifying him were low, and he knew it, even though Evelyn had spent many days trying to convince herself that he would be. Despite what was ahead, he'd come upstairs to inform his parents before he left that he intended to marry Evelyn Foster when he returned.

But as he listened to his mother begging his father not to start an argument with Evelyn's father, irritation started to boil. He'd had enough with this property war over a silly mountain.

"I understand that, June. Let me handle this," his father said.

Footsteps came toward the door. When it swung open, Lawrence took a step back.

"Father, I was just coming to find you. I didn't mean to overhear your conversation."

Lawrence moved aside as his father continued past him, not saying a word. His mother was wiping her eyes and sitting on the side of the bed.

"Mother." He went to sit next to her. "Is everything alright?"

"Lawrence, I'm fine. Go help your father outside in the barn with Kenneth."

"I will, but you're upset. I want to make sure everything is alright. What argument were you referring to with Leroy?"

His mother glanced up, her eyes swimming in tears. "Don't worry about that nonsense. It's just the same old fight coming out once again with the opening of the ski resort next month."

"You mean about the property lines?"

"Yes." June sighed and reached up to touch his cheek. "Let your father sort it out. I just want you to focus on what you need to do for tomorrow, so you can go to training and get yourself home again."

"I'll be fine. I'm strong and will serve however our country needs. But the stress over this mountain is not something I want you and Father to be dealing with while I'm away."

June lowered her hand, looking down at her lap. "Your brother is still here, and he can assist with the matter."

"Until his number gets called," Lawrence said before he could stop himself.

His mother stifled a cry. "Don't say that. America is not entering another war."

"I know this is hard for you to imagine, but the possibility is great. The tension in Europe is escalating. But both Kenneth and I will get through it no matter what."

When her eyes met his, she stared at him as though he were still a little boy. "My sweet Lawrence." She smiled at him and grasped his hand then kissed the top of it. "I know you will."

"I'll go talk to Father about this issue with the Fosters. I think it's in the best interest of our family that he keeps that argument at bay for now. With the possibility of war at our doorstep, it'll be a stressful time for both families."

"Go easy on him. I think he's just feeling like everything is slipping away from him. First you're leaving, and Kenneth may be right behind you, so I think this feud is his way of gaining something back."

"I see what you mean. I won't start a fight, if that's what you're worried about." Lawrence stood, but his mother gripped his hand.

"I love you and your brother so much. Always remember that," she said as if he were already gone.

He nodded, neither of them wanting to discuss what most of the country was afraid to say: that the war was indeed coming for America.

Outside, he found his father stacking hay bales with

Kenneth inside the barn. Lawrence pulled on some gloves, picked up a fork, and got to work alongside them.

"It's okay, son. Go inside and rest. You have a big day ahead of you tomorrow."

"I don't mind. It helps distract me."

His father nodded and the men got to work. An hour of moving bales and shoveling stalls calmed down Lawrence. He finally paused, knowing it had to be now, or he wouldn't have a chance to address it until he returned from service.

"What's wrong, Lawrence?" Kenneth stopped shoveling. "You look deep in thought over there."

"I am." Lawrence walked over to the stall Bobby was in. "Father, I overheard what you said to Mother."

"Mind your business about that," Bobby said, straightening up to face him.

"What happens in this family is my business. I'm the oldest son."

Bobby exhaled, shaking his head. "So what do you need to know?"

"What's going on with Leroy? The land again?"

"Look." His father tossed down his shovel and faced him. "This ski resort that's opening in a few weeks—"

"Will be a strong addition to Alpine Ridge," Lawrence cut in, defending Evelyn's family and catching his father by surprise.

"I didn't say it wouldn't be." Bobby stepped closer. "What has you so uptight about the resort?"

"I'm not uptight. I'm simply pointing out that it will increase this town's economic growth."

Kenneth appeared by the stall door. "Lawrence, you didn't even let Father explain. Jumping in to defend the Fosters. I know—"

"Stay out of this, Kenneth!" Lawrence cut him off.

His brother knew about his relationship with Evelyn and

didn't approve, telling Lawrence it would severely upset their parents. Bobby Thayer and Leroy Foster were always at each other's throats over this land dispute, and while Kenneth had grown tired of it as well, he'd still inserted himself into the arguments a little too much over the years. All Lawrence wanted was for it to end, even before he fell in love with Evelyn.

"Don't talk to your brother like that, young man!"

Lawrence closed the gap between them. "I'm not a young man. I'm a *grown* man about to report to military service."

Bobby's eyes widened and he cast them to the ground. "I know." His voice softened. "I'm just frustrated, son, and I have to figure this out. They're about to open that ski resort when part of it is on *our* land."

"How do you know that to be true?"

"We're missing a surveyor report."

"Not that again!" Lawrence threw up his hands. "None of this was even an issue until the Fosters begun to clear trees for the slopes."

"It has always been an issue!" Bobby retorted. "But now it's become an even bigger concern because they just spent the summer clearing more slopes than we previously thought. Cutting into our land."

"The town clerk already clarified for you last year when the clearing started that the rock wall marking our property line is the one near the stream—"

"The town clerk was wrong." His father reached in his back pocket and pulled out a sheet of paper. "Read it again."

"I've read this report dozens of times." But Lawrence opened the paper anyway to appease his father. "And yes, I know, page two of this surveyor report is missing." It was a repeated conversation he'd had with his parents over the years, but the town clerk had made it clear that the boundaries were reestablished after that page went missing, and the clearing for the resort continued.

"I said, read it again." Bobby took the paper and held it up, pointing to the last sentence on the page that was cut off.

Lawrence held it closer, squinting and walking to the barn door to see it better in the sunlight. And read nothing different. *Martin Farm, 1804.* The Martin name was from before his ancestor Samuel Thayer married into the family.

One mile down Alpine Mountain to the east a half mile until you reach the rock wall near the white birch trees, turn—

"Yup, nothing has changed."

His father snatched the paper, nearly ripping it.

"Father, we've gone over this, and I know it doesn't mention the stream on that old report, but the town is not going by that anymore since page two is missing. And, besides, the rock wall we own *was* found after the 1927 flood. There are no birch trees there anymore, but it's the only rock wall up there. And it's not where the slopes are." Lawrence was so tired of talking circles around this. "Maybe the stream wasn't as apparent back in the 1800s, and I know the '27 flood made things even harder to track but—"

"There is another wall!" his father exploded. "Listen to me, Lawrence. Old Tommy helped the Fosters clear for the slopes. He came by three days ago with urgent news. He found the missing rock wall that this surveyor report is referring too with those white birch trees and no stream anywhere near it. The rock wall that is the *real* boundary for our property but is currently on the ski resort's side."

"What?" Lawrence asked, surprised over this new information.

"You heard me, son. There's another wall up there on the resort's land and it's ours."

"I can't believe he found it." Kenneth came closer.

"Me either. He said it's mostly in shambles, but it's there."

Bobby glanced at the document again. "I don't know if we'll ever find page two of this report, but the first page was found, which is proof enough that the wall that's by the stream isn't the right marking."

"Did Tommy tell Leroy he'd found that wall?" Kenneth asked.

"That's a good question," Lawerence said. Perhaps Evelyn's father was hiding the truth.

"I don't believe he did. He came straight to me to tell me first. We need to demand that the town reevaluates this and finds what Tommy discovered," his father said, then folded the report and put it in his back pocket.

"But Tommy is dead." Lawrence watched his father run his hands through his hair and stare out into the distance. "You'll never find what he found on that mountain."

"It doesn't matter. The land marking is still there, just as I've always suspected, and it's probably why Leroy never allowed me back there to search." His father turned to him wearing a serious expression. "Because maybe he already knew it was there."

"That's just an assumption. Another possibility is that he didn't let you back there because you two don't get along," Lawerence pointed out, holding out hope that Evelyn's father wouldn't do such a thing as cover up land markings.

His father glared at him. "I'm heading into town tomorrow after you leave. A share of that resort should be in our family's name. Or Leroy will have to buy out our portion because, you are correct, the resort will be good for this town. I don't want it stopped. I just want what's fair."

Lawrence could see in his father's eyes that he wasn't going to be dissuaded, and a part of him didn't blame Bobby. "I wish I could help you," he said, thinking about Evelyn again and wanting this to be straightened out between their families so they could move forward together.

He understood his father's frustration, but he also knew this argument could continue on and on, especially if they couldn't find the place where Tommy supposedly discovered another rock wall. Vermont was filled with white birch trees and old walls, but his father did have a point that there weren't any white birch trees by the wall near the stream that had always been claimed as the boundary. It was the section of the landscape that had never changed, as the flood waters back in '27 never rushed down that side of the mountain. Either way, without more specific direction, they could walk that mountain for weeks, passing dozens of those trees and not find the wall. Besides, Old Tommy had a reputation for not being right in the head, so who knew what he'd seen. Maybe he'd even made it up.

Lawrence felt useless since he was leaving the next day, but all that mattered was getting Evelyn's parents' permission for her hand. Once they were married, none of this would be important anymore. The whole mountain would be in both their names, ending this ridiculous feud.

Present Day

LUKE HAD BEEN PULLED INTO A DISCUSSION SHORTLY after the movie ended, enabling Millie to slip away. She had wanted to hang around, but once her mind got going with the idea about figuring out what Riley had started, she couldn't stop.

Back in her suite, she began to piece together everything she'd learned about the fight for Alpine Mountain. She thought about the old pictures she had looked through in the library and tried her hardest to remember if there were any clues in them that would lead her in the right direction. But she came up empty.

Sitting next to the Christmas tree in her suite, the rest of the room in darkness, she watched the twinkling lights and already felt defeated. Who was she kidding? She was completely new to Alpine Ridge, an outsider looking in on a battle about land that extended well over two hundred years. She must be falling for Luke Thayer. Why else would she try to do something so outrageous?

She'd only been in Alpine Ridge for twelve days and had become too wrapped up in the residents of this town, Luke and his family. And now she was magically trying to save Alpine Ski Resort. Sitting back against the couch, she couldn't help but chuckle at her wild notion to solve something so complicated in such a short time. Her life in South Carolina had felt so distant since she'd been here, but now reality came crashing back. Was she about to risk ruining the opportunity she'd been given here? A chance she'd hoped would launch her career so she would potentially get hired at the hotel in Charleston. All to follow up on an old rumor that might not even be true?

Her phone lit up on the coffee table in front of her. A message from Luke.

> Ran from me once again I see! Sorry. I got caught in conversations with one person after the next. I hope you enjoyed the movie. Do you happen to be free tomorrow morning? Want to squeeze in a few runs down the slopes?

Millie closed her eyes, trying not to immediately reply yes. Luke Thayer was a wonderful man, and she had no doubt he was interested in her. Their instant connection was something she'd never had with any other man. But it was based on false pretenses. He didn't even know the real reason she'd come to Alpine Ridge. She needed to pump the brakes. Once he found out the truth, whatever was building between them would come to a hard stop.

After rolling the tension from her shoulders, she started typing.

> I did enjoy the movie. I'm really busy tomorrow. Sorry. But I'll see you at the parade Saturday.

She hit "send" with immediate remorse. The last thing she wanted was to be rude, but she didn't know how else to behave. She wasn't all that busy tomorrow, especially with no events scheduled to shoot. Another message came through.

> Okay . . . Let me know if you're free at any point from now until then.

Millie clicked off her phone and laid on the couch, then pulled a blanket up over her and closed her eyes, shutting out everything until she fell fast asleep.

Chapter Twenty-One

Millie's eyes fluttered open the following morning, a sense of heaviness weighing on her despite hours of sleep. The light that streamed through the sliding doors of the porch reminded her she'd fallen asleep on the couch and not in her bed. She lay there and stared at the ceiling, her body feeling like lead, her thoughts muddled and unclear. The vivid dreams she'd had all night lingered, making her feel even more tired.

Finally sitting up, she knew a shower might shake off the fogginess and the dream she'd had of skiing down a mountain with no ending, trying to find something out there, though she had no clue what it was. It was the type of dream that left her feeling disoriented and confused.

With a heavy sigh, she threw off the blanket and made her way to the bathroom. The water came out ice-cold at first, and while she waited for it to heat up, she realized for the first time since being there that she wasn't feeling excited for the day ahead. She remembered her message to Luke the night before and suddenly wished she could go back to ignoring everything and spending time with him—but it was her job that sat foremost on her mind. In a week and a half, she'd be on her way back to South Carolina, where she'd need to get steady work to move forward in her career. Her crazy idea to save Alpine Ski Resort from Peak Holdings now seemed absurd. The job was what she'd originally come to do, and that was where her focus needed to be.

Once showered and dressed, she decided to grab some breakfast at the café and plan out her day. The pitch was scheduled for Tuesday, and Ashley and her team were working overtime with the Clarkes to get it ready. Peak Holdings would be there bright and early that morning to be convinced to invest in Alpine Ridge, and Millie wanted to make sure her end with the visuals went as smoothly as possible. That would guarantee a reference for her résumé, and a chance to further her photography career and move on from the trip.

The café was swarming with guests in their snow gear about to hit the slopes, making Millie remember Luke's offer to ski with her again. Ignoring the urge to call him, she stepped in line and scanned the menu hanging behind the cashiers.

"Good morning!" the cashier's friendly voice boomed when it was her turn to order. Millie was so tired the loud voice nearly made her trip as she stepped forward. "Will this be for here or to go?"

"For here," Millie said, checking the menu one more time, realizing she didn't have much of an appetite, but forcing herself to order something anyway. "I'll just have a simple cheddar omelet. No side of hash browns. And a cinnamon dolce latte with oat milk, please."

After she paid, she chose a seat in the corner in case anyone came in who recognized her. She wanted to avoid small talk. She pulled out her phone and checked her email, not expecting anyone to be contacting her since it was only half past nine, but as she scrolled through her emails, she received an incoming call. The area code told her it was a Vermont number.

"Hello?" she answered.

"Millie? This is Bruce over at the print shop."

"Hi, Bruce." She'd forgotten all about the prints.

"I'm calling to let you know that all the prints are all set and ready to be picked up. I also have two photos from one of the old rolls printed, and I'd love to show them to you."

"Really? Wow, okay. Would it be alright to come in this morning?"

"Absolutely. I'm here all day. See you soon!"

The GPS guided her to Green Mountain Photo an hour later. Since it was dark the last time she drove there with Luke, she needed the help. Thinking about him made her long to call him again, but she kept her eyes on the road until the impulse passed. They'd known each other for such a short time that they couldn't have possibly had any real impact on each other's lives. Once the resort was sold and she was long gone from Alpine Ridge, he'd forget all about her soon enough.

As that thought crossed her mind, she nearly slammed the brakes when a sudden realization overtook her.

"I've felt like this before," she said out loud. A time when she was fifteen years old, just after her first high school photography class came flooding back to her. She had been absolutely elated over everything she'd already learned, and she remembered how she'd raced home to tell her parents about it and her new dream to pursue photography as a career someday.

Millie turned right when the GPS prompted her to. It then told her to continue straight for seven miles—long enough to zone out as the memory continued to haunt her.

———

"Millie." Her mom had snorted, evidently trying to conceal the laughter that was surfacing. "Photography is a hobby. It's like picking up a book to read and then wanting to write one. Both *can* be careers, but most of the time they are just hobbies."

How negative. Millie stayed quiet, her initial smile fading after her mother's reaction to her excitement. She watched her mother move around the kitchen as she cooked dinner, completely unaware how her response impacted Millie. She thought about her teacher and how the woman had inspired her with stories about other photographers and how they got started before they became well-known in the field. Even just picking up the camera and looking at all the functions had excited her.

"I know a career like that takes work, but I think I can do it. I really like it so far," Millie said, trying to reason with her mother.

"Do what?" her dad asked as he strolled into the kitchen.

"Millie took a photography class in school today." Her mother paused what she'd been doing and faced her dad.

"Really? Sounds interesting," he said, leaning against the counter.

Maybe he'll understand.

"Yeah, and I loved it, Dad! Can I get my own camera?"

He shrugged, glancing at her mom. "I don't see why not. A good hobby is always nice to have."

"But that's the thing. Millie wants to make it a career goal and become a well-known photographer," her mom explained.

Her dad burst out laughing, not even trying to conceal it, then turned to Millie.

"Sweetheart," he said, "you'll never be successful enough to make a career with that or even be memorable within a field that hard to compete in. Besides, you have a lot of catching up to do behind Lila to make anything of yourself. She's going to become a doctor. Now that's both a sure career path and memorable!"

————

"THE DESTINATION IS ON YOUR RIGHT," THE GPS said, breaking her out of the flashback.

That one day in the kitchen with her parents was the start of years of tearing her down about her passion for photography and pushing her to be "more like Lila" as they'd done since Millie was a child. And here she was, still absorbing it all, assuming she really was as forgettable as her parents claimed—and that it wouldn't be long at all before Luke forgot her too.

She turned into the driveway and parked. Monica came out the front door with the baby carrier, moving Millie's attention away from the painful recollection.

"Hey, Monica!" Millie called out.

The woman turned, holding up her hand to shield the sun. "Oh, hi, Millie!" She came down the steps, gripping the carrier. "We're stepping out to do some grocery shopping. So far all she does is sleep, so it makes errands easy . . . for now." Monica opened her car door and clicked the baby's seat in its place then turned to Millie after shutting the door again. "Here to see those vintage shots?"

"Did you see them?" Millie asked, feeling hopeful when Monica instantly nodded.

"Yes. I'm always so impressed with how Bruce does that."

"I can't wait to see." Millie waved and headed for the door. "Enjoy your shopping!"

The bell rang when she opened the door, but this time there wasn't a young girl at the front desk.

"Be right there!" Bruce called just before he came out from the back room. "My help is in school right now, so it's just me.

Glad you could make it over. Come on back. I have everything ready to show you."

Millie went with him to a different room from the other night. This one had a large rectangular table where her prints were laid out. The first one was a shot of the front door that she'd angled just right to highlight the old features.

"I really love that house." She leaned closer to the image. "And look how nice this came out. I think it'll make a great present once framed."

"Would you like us to do that for you? I'm sorry I didn't ask before. With the new baby my head's been a little scattered." Bruce walked over to the cabinet and pulled out some frame samples.

"That's understandable." Millie walked to the next picture. It was taken in the all-season room and she'd blurred the snowy backyard, though a large evergreen was visible through one of the windows just right. "I think I will have you do that. Complete the gift."

"That one's my favorite," Bruce said when she reached the third picture. "The way you got the winding of that staircase is incredible. I bet the lighting in that house wasn't easy."

Millie shook her head. "It wasn't. But the windows are large for an older home, which added some natural light, and the wide-angle lens also helped, especially getting a good shot of that grandfather clock." She got a clear image of the clock straight on for the fourth picture.

"We can frame both the large prints and the smaller ones from the photo albums I restored if you'd like." Bruce handed her the frame samples. "I know choosing a frame can be tricky based on preferred taste, but we can give it our best guess. What do you think?"

"I did notice the pictures already hanging on the walls looked traditional, and none were tagged for the estate sale. So it looked like they want to keep them."

"I'm happy you noticed because that was my next question. What did they already have hung? Here's what I'm thinking." He went back to the cabinet and got some more samples. "These are more sophisticated, more classic than the modern sleek ones."

Millie took the samples from him and looked at the carved details. "These are all pretty."

"Now remember, these are just recreated vintage-style wooden frames, but they do give that old feel, don't they?"

"I like this one." She held up a dark brown sample with deep ridges and grooves. "Can't go wrong with this shade."

"That one it is. I'm assuming you'll be framing all of them, correct?" Millie nodded, and he pulled out a piece of paper from the pad behind him and jotted some notes. "Normally this can take up to two weeks to get back to you, but I'm expediting it at no extra charge since I know your time here is limited. And because I forgot to ask you at our first meeting." Bruce gave her a sheepish grin.

"Thank you so much, and it's all good. You have a lot going on with the new baby and Monica not being able to help as much. I want to gift them at the resort's anniversary party." She looked up in thought. "Today is Thursday, which means the party is in nine days. Is that too quick of a turnaround?"

"I can get it done by then," Bruce said, jotting down more notes. "Okay, now for my favorite part, the vintage photos. Let me grab those."

When he walked out, Millie glanced at her messages. A text from Ashley was the only one she'd seen, asking Millie to change something in one of her descriptions. There was nothing from Luke. Even though she hadn't expected him to contact her after the way she'd shut down his offer to see her before Saturday, it was still hard to grasp. The majority of her trip had been spent with him.

"Okay, here we are."

Millie popped her head up as Bruce strolled back through the door holding acid-free envelopes and gloves to prevent any oils from his fingers damaging the photos. After pulling them on, he gently took out the two pictures.

"Look at their outfits. I love this," Millie said, clicking on her phone's flashlight to see better.

The first photo was of a woman with her arms up, twirling in a dark green plaid skirt. Behind her were peaks from a mountain.

"I'm pleased the Kodachrome film was used to bring out these colors," Bruce said.

"Me too." Millie studied the scenery. "Is that—"

"Alpine Mountain? I think so, and look at the next one. The mountain is closer up." Bruce pointed to it.

Millie moved her camera's light over it. "It looks cleared. But there's no ski lift."

"Not yet anyway. If I could guess, this was taken around 1940. From what I know of that mountain, the tow rope was installed shortly after they opened that winter, and the chair lifts didn't come until a few years later."

"I wonder who she is." Millie looked at the woman again.

"Well, she must be related to the Clarkes since that's where these rolls came from."

"Must be. But I'll wait until you work on the rest to show them all at once."

"Good idea. Unfortunately, one of the rolls was damaged throughout. These two were printed from the roll that was still in the camera, and I think there are some I'll be able to work on from the second loose roll. It's my main focus all next week, along with those frames."

"Thank you for the speedy turnaround times. I wish I was here longer so you wouldn't have to rush." Millie turned off the light on her phone.

"I don't mind at all. I love vintage photo restoration and seeing history frozen in time with these pictures." Bruce escorted her out. "Would you like me to just finish up the rest and tell you when they're ready so you can come see them all at once? Or would you rather get them one by one?"

"I'll probably come look at them all once you're done, unless you discover something major. Like a ghost in one of them," she said jokingly, making him laugh.

"Then we will hire ghost hunters to scope out the Clarke estate," he said, holding the front door open for her. "I'll talk to you soon."

Back out in the icy air, Millie was pleased with the work Bruce had done so far. The large prints would be a little pricey, but it was her way of thanking the Clarkes. Hiring a photographer they'd never met and giving her the experience she'd lacked had truly unlocked her from the rut she'd been in. The moment she'd arrived in Alpine Ridge and begun shooting, her previous hesitancies had vanished. She would always be grateful for them and couldn't wait to gift them the prints, no matter the cost.

Zoning out on the short drive back to town, she noticed the gray clouds covering the sun were letting out light flurries. A faint glimmer of sunlight broke through, accenting the delicate flakes twirling around.

"What a picture." Millie quickly pulled over to park on the main street, realizing she was near the town's Christmas tree that Luke first showed her. Reaching for her camera in the bag next to her, she hopped out, relieved she'd brought it.

She pointed the camera toward the clouds and adjusted the lens. The tree fit it into the frame, its glittering lights making for a perfect fuzzy holiday background. She turned around and saw a few people strolling and decided to do what she'd always done best—candid photos. She made her way up and down the main section of town, making sure to keep faces out of the pictures. She got a few shots of hands pointing to the storefront windows dressed in Christmas lights, frosted snow, and small trees.

Inside a couple of the boutiques, with the owners' permission, she took some pictures of festive displays, even filming some video. The café came into view and the reindeer lit up in golden lights was something she didn't remember seeing before. She asked the baristas for a latte with a heart in the center and a Christmas paper menu, then set them up on the table. Standing on a chair, she hovered her lens over it for the perfect flat lay shot.

"Thank you!" she called over to the baristas, waving when she was finished with the pictures and drinking the latte.

Before she knew it, the whole afternoon had gone by and Millie had dozens of new photos of the town, showing its holiday spirit. The resort would be open well after the Christmas season each winter, but since Peak Holdings was coming for the pitch right in the middle of it, why not hook them with the magic the holidays were known for?

She remembered Ashley's text, and when she got back to her car, she sent a reply.

No problem. I'll take a look when I get back to my suite. Sorry for the late response, I was at the print shop, and then I did a whole afternoon of brand new photos in town. You'll love what I captured. Off to edit!

Her plan for the evening would be to edit the day's work and then send photos and videos to Ashley. The marketing team needed the presentation finalized by Monday, and after Saturday's parade, she'd have to edit those images too. It would be a long night with this extra photoshoot. Room service dinner, more coffee, and her laptop would consume her whole night—a perfect way to distract herself from thoughts of Luke.

CHAPTER TWENTY-TWO

Friday morning seemed to come in a blink, but when Millie checked the time on her phone, she shot up. It was almost noon! And she had three missed calls from Ashley. She hit "call" and her friend answered on the second ring.

"There you are! I was getting worried and about to come barging into your suite," Ashley said, sounding breathless.

"Sorry! I didn't get to bed until about three this morning. Did you get the photos I sent?" Millie rubbed the sleep from her eyes. "And where are you? Sounds like you're running."

"Coming back to the resort from a coffee and lunch run for the team."

"The restaurant in the resort wasn't open?"

"They were." She could hear Ashley's breath quicken as she walked. "But the café in town had their famous holiday special: white chocolate croissant bread pudding. You have to try it. I just dropped the drinks and food off to my team."

A ding in the corridor outside made Millie smile. "You're bringing me coffee and pudding aren't you?"

"Correct. I'll be there in a few seconds."

Millie grabbed a sweatshirt and pulled it over her head, then went to answer the knock on her door. "Room service coffees are my favorite. Thank you."

"It looks like room service was already here." Ashley scanned the living room where Millie's half-eaten dinner still sat on the coffee table next to her laptop and camera, along with her notes scattered everywhere. "And it appears you really did have a long night."

"Did you look at the photos from yesterday?" Millie asked, taking a long sip. The hot brew was just what she needed. "This is delicious. What flavor is this latte?"

"Gingerbread. They insisted. And, yes, we got them. It's why I was calling you. Millie, those pictures need to be entered into some sort of contest."

"Really? You think so?"

"Yes, we really do. We love them! Danny has been hard at work incorporating some of them into the presentation. The B-roll you taped was the perfect touch. You've worked so hard, and it'll pay off big time next week." Ashley's head tilted. "Are you okay?"

Millie hadn't realized she was staring outside at the skiers. She'd heard Ashley, but her voice seemed miles away. "I think so."

Ashley came over and put her arm around her. "Are you sick? You look pale."

"Not sick, just a lot on my mind." *Luke.* Yesterday it was easier to ignore him, but the first person she'd wanted to share her photos with last night was him. He was the chairman of the town after all, and he'd enjoy seeing them. But that wasn't what had suddenly taken over her train of thought. It was what she'd been dwelling on during the drive to the photo shop the day before when she nearly halted the car in the middle of the road. Her parents.

The memory of that day after her first photography class

had started to weigh on her since. She wasn't sure if it was because her time in Alpine Ridge was almost over and she'd have to go back to her life in South Carolina, which included her parents, or if it was because she was worried this job would be her only one. The truth of the matter was, there was no other job to return to. What if years went by before she landed another photography job? Her parents would surely have a lot to say then.

"Let's sit for a minute." Ashley walked with her to the couch.

"Do you remember my parents?" Millie asked, holding her latte with both hands and drawing her knees up on the cushion.

"How could I forget them, especially your mom." Ashley made a face. "No offense, but she intimidated me that first time I went with you for that summer barbeque at their house."

"Oh, yeah. Fourth of July, right?"

Ashley nodded. "Why are you asking about them?"

"I don't know. It's just that since I've been here, I haven't spoken to them once."

"Well, if it makes you feel any better, my parents are about thirty minutes up the road a few towns over, and I don't talk to them a whole lot."

"Yeah . . ." Millie suddenly felt embarrassed. Talking about her parents this way to Ashley made her feel like a child. Maybe she should have talked to Lila about this.

"But one thing about mine," Ashley said, "is that they are my biggest fans."

Millie looked at Ashley with wide eyes. "You understand what I'm getting at then?"

"Of course I do. Millie, the little I know about your parents is how much they used to criticize every little thing you did. It was always an argument with them, a one-sided one. They constantly critiqued you and it used to make me uncomfortable. Are they still doing that?"

"That's them alright. And yes, they are." Millie raised the cup to her lips. The spiced liquid helping her relax. "Ashley, this job has turned out to be much more than taking pictures. Charleston is my home. It always will be. But I needed this job *and* to get away from all that."

"I know." Ashley patted her knee. "I don't know the ins and outs of your daily life there anymore, but I had a hunch you could use some time away. I'm sorry we haven't stayed in contact like we should have, but from what I observed while living down there, you needed to be pulled out. So when you contacted me, I felt like it was fate's way of telling me to do exactly that."

"Thank you. For the first time, I feel like a photographer. Yes, I'm always taking pictures, but the time here, just me on my own . . . well, and you"—she smiled at her friend—"have given me the confidence to keep going. This is what I love."

"And it's what you are incredibly talented at. Anyone would be lucky to hire you." Ashley's eyes narrowed. "And I'm not all you have here."

"Don't say it." Millie shot up a hand.

"Luke is smitten over you."

"I told you not to say it."

Ashley chuckled. "Can't help it. Because he is."

"I'm focused on this pitch for next Tuesday." Millie changed the subject, not wanting to weigh down Ashley with a conversation about Luke. Her parents were enough.

"Me too." Ashley stood up. "I better get back to my team. Get some rest today and then later, how about a girls' night?"

"That sounds perfect."

"We can eat junk food and watch Christmas movies. I'll even bring some takeout Chinese. Does seven work?"

"Can't wait." She followed Ashley to the door.

"And charge up that camera. The parade is going to be a blast tomorrow!"

Millie closed the door behind her friend and went back to the couch and stared at her phone on the coffee table. She wasn't sure what prompted her to talk to Ashley about her parents, and she still felt silly she'd bogged down her friend with it, but clearly her relationship with them was heavy on her mind.

She picked up her phone and found her mom's number, then hit "call." When the voicemail came on, something in her revved up.

"Hi, Mom, it's Millie. I wanted to check in with you and Dad and let you know how amazing this job in Vermont has been. The resort is more than happy with the marketing photos I've taken for them, and this opportunity will be huge for my career. I know that's not what you or Dad care to hear, but it's who I am and photography is what I'm meant to do . . . I'm tired of waiting for you two to accept that."

When she hung up, her pulse was racing. She'd never spoken to them that way. Usually she cowered when they belittled her about her photography. Should she call back and apologize? She looked down at her phone and shook her head, then placed it on the table. Her nerves dissipated, replaced by a rush of pride. An inner fire had been unleashed, and nothing was going to extinguish her drive, passion, and determination to succeed in the field she loved. She should have made that call years ago.

———

MILLIE STEPPED OUT OF HER CAR THE NEXT morning, feeling rejuvenated after her girl's night with Ashley. They'd spent the evening gorging on takeout and laughing until late into the night. The crisp winter air carried the scent of woodsmoke and the sound of jingling bells from the street lined with people just ahead. Alpine Ridge's annual Christmas parade was about to begin, and the small Vermont town was alive with festive cheer.

As she walked the couple blocks from the parking lot to the main road, she took in the vibrant scene before her, her camera ready to capture every moment. To her left, the horse-drawn wagon she'd seen her first day was approaching, signaling the start of the parade. As it drew closer, she saw it was covered with twinkling lights around garlands of ever-green on both sides. The horse guided it smoothly along the parade route, its occupants—a jolly Luke and a bevy of merry elves—waving at the crowd. She lifted her camera and clicked away to the sound of the horse's hooves on pavement and the soft dinging of the bells. Just before it passed, Luke caught sight of her and gave her a slight head nod and a smile, then continued down the road.

Trying to shake off the sight of him, Millie scanned the street. Colorful floats, each one more elaborate than the last came toward her. A giant inflatable snowman, its carrot nose glowing bright orange, bobbed and weaved through the crowd on the other side, trailed by a troupe of giggling children waving pom-poms. Zooming in, she worked the angle and snapped a picture. Nearby, a group of carolers bundled up in scarves and hats harmonized in perfect pitch, their voices carrying the joyous tune of "Jingle Bells" and growing louder the closer she got.

A vendor with freshly baked cookies was ahead, the delicious scent wafting from its tent and enticing Millie's senses, making her stomach growl. She paused to get one and lowered her camera before choosing a peanut butter flavor, decorated as reindeer. Then she took more pictures, getting all the details of the vendor's cookie designs and the beaming faces of the people as they sampled the treats after they'd agreed to be in the photos.

She continued walking alongside the floats, her attention drawn to the town's iconic gazebo next to the Christmas tree she was getting closer to. The gazebo's white wooden slats were lined with a dazzling display of large Christmas bulbs and held a band. The musicians played lively renditions of holiday classics, and she circled the spot, taking shots with different lenses.

Millie stayed near the gazebo while the last of the parade marched toward her, and she soon found herself swept away by the energy surrounding her. This was what Christmas was all about: community, love, and coming together to celebrate the season. Her mind was racing with the possibilities for the images she had captured. Maybe the opening part of the presentation could include pictures of this day. A horn blared in the distance, and a vintage fire truck, its sirens echoing on and off, moved slowly down the street, followed by a group of giggling kids in matching elf costumes, tossing candy canes to the crowd and blowing bubbles.

"Millie!" Ashley was jogging toward her, wearing a bright green jacket.

"Love that coat!" Millie said, holding up her camera.

Ashley stopped and posed with her hands on her hips and a wide grin. "Thanks. It's the closest thing I have to a Christmas costume. Have you seen Luke? His elf costume is the best." She laughed.

Millie looked around for him. "I only saw him on the float, but you know, now that I think about it, I did see pointy ears."

They both laughed.

"He's doing a speech soon, so you'll be able to get some good shots."

"To add to the hundred I just took over the past hour."

"Awesome! Come on, let's get closer to the gazebo." Ashley tugged her sleeve toward the crowd that was already starting to gather around it.

A few minutes later, Luke walked on stage. Clapping and cheering erupted at the sight of him as Millie squeezed her way to the front. When she got closer, she smiled at his outfit. Ashley was right, his bright green-and-red elf costume with matching hat was quite the crowd-pleaser. The kids especially loved it and called out to him. He tossed candy their way, and she was very aware of the moment he glimpsed her from the corner of his eye, but his usual reaction to her was muted.

Millie hid behind her camera, trying not to let her disappointment show as she took a handful of pictures. Luke approached the microphone.

"Welcome, everybody, to the forty-second annual Alpine Ridge Christmas parade!" The crowd erupted in applause again. "It's been a wonderful year for us, hasn't it?" Cheers rang out.

"He's so loved," Ashley whispered, crouching next to her.

Millie nodded, peeking at him from behind her camera. She didn't blame the residents.

"We've had a few new businesses open, including the popular Ridge Reef seafood restaurant," Luke continued, clapping for the owners. "And it's officially the end of my first year as your chairman. How'd I do?"

Applause exploded with a lot of whistling.

"I take that as you're all happy with me," he joked, glancing at Millie. "It's also a big year for Alpine Ski Resort. Their eighty-fifth anniversary party will be next Saturday, December twentieth. All are invited!"

Dylan and Joyce appeared on the side of the stage, and Millie held her breath. She wasn't expecting them to make a speech. Luke stepped back, allowing Dylan to take his place.

"Joyce and I are excited to celebrate such a big milestone

with the town we love," Dylan said. "As many of you know, the past two years have been tough for us since we lost our daughter, but the people of this town have kept the spirit of our beloved resort going. And we couldn't thank you all enough. We hope you come out to celebrate with us and have a good time."

Everyone clapped, and Luke came back to the mic.

"Hear that?" Luke said. "We want all of you to come so we can help the Clarkes prepare for another successful winter season, and I think it'll be the best one yet thanks in part to their amazing photographer, whom many of you have seen roaming around town, taking all kinds of pictures. Millie? Wave!" He looked down at her and she held up her hand, heat tingling down her back. She hadn't been expecting that either.

"Her talent will help the Clarkes market the resort and give them the resources to keep our mountain running the way we here in Alpine Ridge intend. We're so proud to call that resort ours."

Millie's eyes darted to Ashley whose mouth popped open. *Not good*, Millie mouthed to her.

Ashley nodded and leaned close to her ear. "Not at all."

When Luke finished telling everyone to check out the shops along main street that were offering all kinds of treats and specials, he disappeared so fast Millie didn't see which direction he went.

Ashley pulled at her arm, bringing her behind the gazebo. "I didn't expect him to say all that. Did you see the Clarkes' faces?" She looked over her shoulder to make sure no one was approaching them. "They seemed very uncomfortable."

"Well, the speech Dylan gave didn't exactly help. Ashley, this is what I've been talking about since I got here."

Ashley squeezed her eyes shut, clearly trying to take it all in.

Without meaning to, Millie's voice rose. "It's wrong that the town doesn't know why I'm here."

"Why *are* you here, Millie?" a male voice behind her said.

Ashley's eyes popped back open, looking over Millie's shoulder. "Luke, hi. We didn't see you there," Ashley said.

"Obviously you don't want anyone near this discussion since you two are hiding behind the gazebo," he said.

Millie turned to face him. "Luke, I was going to come find you after the parade to talk," she said.

The hard look on his face didn't soften at all. "Do you have something to tell me?" he asked.

Ashley stepped forward. "This is not how we planned to share this news with you, out here at the parade. Let's go to the café. We can talk there where it's warmer."

"I'm plenty warm." He crossed his arms in defense. "Millie?"

"Okay, I'm just going to say it." She stepped toward him as he stared her down. "Ashley and the Clarkes hired me to take marketing pictures, but not to increase their visitors. Luke, they're selling the resort."

"What? Selling?" His arms loosened as he turned to scan the crowd before his eyes darted toward Ashley. "Where are the Clarkes?"

"I don't know. I don't see them anymore." Ashley looked around. "I didn't even know they were planning on making that speech."

"I feel like a fool." Luke glanced at the gazebo. "Saying all that up there." He faced both women again. "Who's buying the resort?"

"We're making a pitch to Peak Holdings on Tuesday," Ashley said.

Luke's mouth fell agape, and he shook his head in confusion. "*What?* You're selling us out to a corporation!" He threw up his hands.

"*We* aren't. The Clarkes are." Ashley walked toward him. "Luke, calm down for a second and understand that Millie was just doing her job. She was hired to take photos for the presentation and told not to discuss this with you or the town until we gave her the green light."

"So let me get this straight." He whipped around to face Millie. "You just played everyone here, getting them to smile while you took their pictures, so you could use them to sell the resort to Peak Holdings? After everything I shared with you . . . You knew how I worried about a corporation taking over. You knew what happened between me and the Clarkes!"

"Luke, I—"

"Were you just using me to make that presentation shine? I can't believe you, Millie." Luke backed away. "This conversation's over."

When he abruptly turned and left, Millie waved her hand toward him. "See!" she said to Ashley. "He's mad. Just like I said he would be."

Ashley held up her hands. "I know. That was a crappy way to learn about the sale."

"There was no good way to tell him. I feel terrible."

"Luke will be okay. I'll reach out to him. It wasn't your choice to stay quiet."

"I don't think that'll make anything better." Millie's eyes burned as Luke got farther away. She wanted to run after him, to tell him she hadn't been using him at all.

As he stormed into the distance, she knew she'd been wrong to assume he'd just forget about her. No, he'd remember—and the memory would keep hurting him for a long time.

Everything was ruined.

CHAPTER TWENTY-THREE

Sunday was a haze. Millie didn't leave her suite once. After trying to call Luke a few times, she lost hope that he would give her a chance to explain. She worked through photos of the parade for half the day, and it took everything in her to control her tears while she attempted to edit. Her heart wasn't in it, but she needed to get them to Ashley.

Slamming her laptop shut after she finished, she noticed the room darkening. The sun was setting and she stood up to get some air out on her porch. Was the day already over? All she could think about was Luke's face, the exact expression she'd feared—betrayal. Alpine Ski Resort had hired her, but what had developed between her and Luke was something that meant far more to her than a job. She should have followed through on her intuition and told him the truth right from the start. How could she have hurt him like that?

The tears that had threatened all day finally streamed down her face as she went back inside. She really hadn't meant to hurt anyone, but her inability to decide to do what was right and speak up had hung over her. Just as she wasn't able to challenge her parents for over a decade—who hadn't even bothered to return her call from the day before. Her mom was probably fuming in surprise at how direct she had been.

She headed to the kitchen to find something to eat, even though she wasn't hungry. But she hadn't eaten all day, and figured food might help her mood. The cabinet still had some pasta and sauce, so that would have to do. She got out a pot and filled it with water, and while she waited for it to boil, she heard her phone buzz from the living room. It was Lila calling, and Millie cleared her throat and tried her best to sound cheery when she answered.

"Hey!" she said, a little too loud.

"Millie, I'm so glad I caught you," Lila said, her tone jittery.

"Everything okay?"

"I'm so proud of you!" her sister blurted. "Mom just called me."

"Oh." Millie winced. "I was just thinking about that. I shouldn't have done it. I was so rude."

"Excuse me, but you should have done that years ago."

That had been her first thought too, but after what happened with Luke, she felt like a monster all around.

"Is Mom okay?"

"She's . . ." Lila's voice trailed. "A little taken aback is all."

"What did she say?"

"At first, she was upset. She went on and on about how random the message was. And you know me, I listened. And listened." Lila chuckled through the phone. "She finally slowed down and asked me why I was so quiet. You would have been proud of me because I was perfectly calm, which is not the norm when it comes to my baby sister."

Millie smiled. "I know. You've always had my back."

"I simply told her that it was about time."

"You what?"

"Yup, you heard me. I told her how proud I was about the job you have up there, how excited you've sounded in the conversations we've had the last couple weeks. And she grew even quieter before she asked what I thought about your career prospects after failing to land any solid long-term jobs after all those interviews."

"Clearly she didn't pick up on the 'proud' part of your statement."

"I told her that careers like yours take time, dedication, and talent. And that you've got the talent alright. I said you were born to be a photographer, and I was looking forward to seeing what you do next after this job."

"Knowing Mom, it went in one ear and right out the other."

"I don't think so, Millie. In fact, she didn't say anything for a minute. That's not like her. And I know I've said things to her many times in the past, but this time I was adamant when I told her that you aren't me, and she really needed to ease up on you."

"Thanks for saying all that." Millie poured the pasta into the boiling water. "Honestly, I don't know why I still feel the need to prove anything to them."

"In my opinion, it's not about trying to prove anything, but more about letting how they've been in the past go. It's had this grip on you, and I've hated how it has weighed on you. When she told me you called and left that message, I practically jumped with excitement. I love them, but they really need to relax."

"Mom? Relax?" Millie rolled her eyes and stirred the pasta.

"I know. It's a rarity. Anyway, how are you doing?"

Millie considered giving a real answer to the question, but she didn't want to kill the happy vibe by explaining Luke and everything that had happened. "The pitch is Tuesday. I've given my all with the photos, and they are pleased, so I'm looking forward to the presentation."

"Will you be there?"

"In the meeting? No, but I'm going to a practice run tomorrow, and so I'll see my work put into action."

"That's exciting. Could you possibly get a copy of it? I think any place that sees something like that would hire you before they even met you."

"I don't know if I'll get a copy, but that's a good idea. I'll ask if I can use it going forward for my own marketing and portfolio."

"Absolutely," Lila said. "What's the next fun event you have coming up?"

"The resort's eighty-fifth anniversary event this Saturday night. It's supposed to be a big party and open to the whole town."

"How exciting! Listen, Jake just got home, and I'm off to work. I'll cross my fingers for you all for Tuesday! Love you, Millie."

When she finished her pasta, Millie cleaned up the kitchen and zoned out to a movie, before falling into a much-needed sleep. She dreamed of skiing again, but this time with Luke by her side.

———

"So, what do you think?" Ashley asked the next morning as the Clarkes, Danny, and Cassidy turned to face her. They'd just finished the practice pitch in their meeting room and the way it had all been put together was impressive.

"I just might invest in Alpine Ski Resort after watching that!" Millie said, making them all laugh.

"Your visuals are what will sell this resort. You are a genius behind that camera," Joyce said.

"Thank you, that means a lot." Millie smiled at Mrs. Clarke and tried to appear more enthusiastic than she felt. There had still been no word from Luke, and she was beginning to think she would be leaving Alpine Ridge on Sunday without saying goodbye. At least the presentation was a success. Now the team just needed to show it to Peak Holdings the next day with the same spark she'd just witnessed.

The ten minute slide show, complete with a lot of her own words and descriptions, had drawn in Millie immediately. Even though she'd personally experienced the events, the people, and the places around town while capturing the photos, watching them appear on the screen gave her a different perspective. Peak Holdings would surely be delighted and amazed with the visuals—just as she had been witnessing them behind her camera.

Dylan glanced at Danny and Cassidy. "Mind if we have a few minutes with Millie? Ashley you can stay." Both nodded and left the room, and Dylan turned to her. "Millie, we understand there was a heated discussion with Luke after the parade." He put his arms on the table. "Ashley filled us in. We didn't mean to put you in the middle of that, but I know you two had spent some time together."

"Yes, we had. He was really helpful showing me around town and keeping me company," Millie said, trying not to let her emotions get the best of her. The fact was, Luke had been much more than a tour guide.

"I don't know if you've heard the rumors whispered around town about our relationship with the Thayers, but it's not exactly the friendliest." Dylan glanced at his wife.

Joyce's apologetic gaze met Millie's. "And we didn't want you to have to get in the middle of that either, but after hearing how upset Luke was about us selling the resort, it sounds like you were tossed in between this pitch and him, and Dylan and I wanted to apologize for that. I guess we didn't think you'd take to the town so fast . . . and the people in it." A tiny grin crept onto the woman's face as she watched Millie with knowing eyes.

But Millie wanted to keep the conversation focused on the job. "Please don't feel bad. I understand why you made the decisions you made," Millie said. "On the other hand, I also understand why he's not happy about it."

"We do too," Dylan said. "Peak Holdings is not his ideal choice. Luke and his parents stand firmly behind the traditions of Alpine Ridge. Seeing change like that will be hard, but they will accept it in time."

"That's what I told her too," Ashley said, giving her a sympathetic smile.

"We just need you to know you have done an incredible job for us. One that I'm so thrilled to share tomorrow. Whatever you need from us, especially a reference, let us know and you'll receive a glowing one." Joyce stood up and came around the table to hug her. "I hope we can keep in touch after you leave here."

"We will, of course," Millie said, trying to ignore the memory of Luke's hurt expression behind the gazebo at the parade. "Good luck tomorrow. I'll be waiting to hear all about it."

"I'm going to walk her out," Ashley told the Clarkes.

They reached the lobby and Millie turned to her. "I still can't get ahold of him."

"Neither can I. I was talking to Danny and Cassidy about it before the meeting, and we agree this may not go as smoothly as the Clarkes hope if we don't talk to him before the anniversary party. He's important as the chairman of the town. People will look to him for guidance on how to react when they hear the news." Ashley blew out some air. "I think

I'm going to head to his office after I finish up with Dylan and Joyce."

"He's mostly mad at me. Let me be the one to face him," Millie said.

"Want me to come with you?"

"No, I think I need to do this one on my own."

Ashley gave her an encouraging smile. "If anyone can calm him down, it'd be you."

"Let's hope that's true."

When Millie got to the valet, the thought of showing up at Luke's office unannounced suddenly made her nervous, but she needed to talk to him. Convincing him to get on board with this sale would be impossible, but she wanted to at least apologize in person, which would hopefully calm him down enough to talk to Ashley.

The valet brought her car around and the short drive to the town hall barely gave her enough time to think about how she'd approach him. Luke's office was on the third floor, and she decided to take the stairs to give herself more time. When she reached the right floor, she walked to where a sign pointed to his office and stopped outside the door.

"No better way than to just go in and try," she mumbled to herself.

His secretary looked up with a friendly grin. "Good morning! May I help you?"

"My name is Millie. Is Luke in his office?"

"Do you have an appointment?" she asked, clicking her mouse as she looked at her screen. "I didn't think he was meeting with anyone today."

"No, I didn't schedule a meeting." Millie already wanted to turn and run.

"That's okay." She stood up. "I'll go let him know you're here." The secretary disappeared through a door behind her desk, and a moment later, Luke came out with her.

"Thank you, Charlotte," he said to the secretary and glanced at Millie. "Come on back."

Now her heart was racing. The scowl on his face couldn't have been more apparent as she walked by him into his office. When he shut the door, he didn't say a word as she stood there.

"Have a seat," he said after a minute, gesturing toward the chair in front of his desk as he sat in his. "What can I do for you, Millie?"

"I've been trying to call you," she said, sitting down.

"I'm aware. Was me not calling you back not clear enough? I have nothing to say to you."

Now her anxiety was full blown, but she had come for a reason and she was determined she wouldn't leave until he heard her.

"I know 'sorry' doesn't cut it. I was wrong to keep that information from you. I won't even blame the resort because I still could have told you anyway, and I almost did. A few times."

"Then why didn't you?"

His simple question left her speechless. "I don't have an excuse besides the fact that it just wasn't my place to share it."

"Job or no job . . . What the Clarkes are doing is wrong! And you know that after everything I've shared with you!" He closed his eyes, lowering his voice. "How could they sell to Peak Holdings and not my father? You're fully aware that we offered to buy them out two years ago."

"I know, and I wish I could tell you the answer to that."

"It's because Dylan is a stubborn fool. Do you have any idea what this corporation has done to other resorts? It's like they took over the entire town, closing small businesses, changing the entire atmosphere." He ran his hands through his dark hair, his blue eyes piercing through her like knives. "And you helped make this happen."

"Luke, I came here for a job. It doesn't excuse me from keeping important information like this from you, but I was hired by the Clarkes and asked to keep this quiet. At first, I was just doing as I was asked. I didn't see anything wrong with it because I didn't understand what things were like here, but then I got to know you. And this town."

"Really, Millie? You're here to try to convince me that what was building with us was real?"

His words shot through her heart and her eyes swam with tears.

When he saw her reaction, his face finally softened. "That was a little harsh. I'm sorry."

"A little?" She stood up, anger bubbling to the surface. "I understand you're upset about the sale. I've struggled nearly every day since I arrived about what it would do to Alpine Ridge, the people, and all you represent. You don't think I've fallen in love with this community?" *Not to mention been falling for you.* She pushed the statement out of her mind before she said it out loud. "How could I not? I'm not that much of an evil villain!"

"Millie—"

"I came here to apologize. To let you know that despite what you think, these last couple weeks of capturing the essence of one of the most magical places I've ever been and getting to know you have been real for me. As real as it could get. None of our time together was staged just to get a smile. The Clarkes asked me not to share this information in fear of the town not cooperating with me, but honestly, Luke? I forgot all about it whenever I was around everyone . . . and you."

She turned toward the door and left before he could say another word. Leaving things this unresolved wasn't exactly what Ashley had hoped would happen, but seeing him again had triggered a flood of emotions Millie had been trying to push away, and she didn't know how much longer she could last without sobbing.

Outside, she stopped at her car, trying to regulate her breathing. She wiped away the tears that had fallen all the way down the stairs, and wrestled with whether to go back to try the conversation again or return to her suite and hide. What would she tell Ashley? Here she was once again caught between the job and Luke.

Her phone buzzed in her purse and, half expecting it to be him, she reached for it without checking to see who it was. "Hello?" Her voice was stern.

"Hi, Millie? It's Bruce. Am I interrupting you?"

"Oh, Bruce. Hi. No, I was just leaving a meeting."

"Do you have time to come by today? I just printed a few more of the older pictures, and . . . I think you need to see them."

"Okay. I'm on my way."

"Millie!" A voice called to her from across the parking lot.

She turned, and Luke hurried over.

"That was terrible. I'm really sorry. Can we—" He stopped short when he saw her expression. "Everything okay?"

"Yeah, everything's fine." *Besides what just happened in your office.* "I got a call from Bruce. He printed some of the photos from that old camera and asked me to come right away."

"Oh, then he must have found something important." His face was much more relaxed than it was in his office, and he seemed to want to say more.

"Would you like to come?" she asked tentatively.

His smile wasn't as bright as she was used to, but it *was* a smile. That was a start. And maybe they could try that conversation over in the car.

"I'd love to."

"Hop in. I'll drive this time." They got in her car and she

started to plug the address into the GPS when she noticed he was now grinning. "Oh, right, you can be my directions." She turned on the ignition.

"Millie." He put his hand on hers, preventing her from putting the car in reverse. "I'm really sorry for how angry I was up there. All the past tension with the Clarkes since Riley's accident just came exploding out on you. I know you were put in a tough spot and that it wasn't something you had permission to share."

"I don't blame you for being upset about the sale and about me keeping it secret. This conversation should have happened much sooner." She remembered the message to her mom the other day. "Putting off hard conversations is one of my weaknesses, but I'm getting better at it. Come on, let's go see what Bruce has to show us."

CHAPTER TWENTY-FOUR

Evening, November 15, 1940
Evelyn

"Lawrence, wait. I can't do this." Evelyn touched Lawrence's shoulder, stopping him from going inside her house. She'd told her parents she was heading to town to run an errand and would be back just before dinner. Lawrence had met her in the coffee shop, where they discussed telling her father about their relationship and their intention of getting married.

"I'm not afraid of Leroy. I can talk to him," he said, pulling her closer. "I love you. Everything will be alright."

"But what you told me about Old Tommy and the rock wall." Evelyn shook her head. "It's going to ruin everything."

"Which is why I need to do this before my father upsets him, so I can try to reason with him and get everything out in the open before I leave tomorrow." Lawrence walked them to the door. "We need to face this."

Evelyn turned the knob and stepped inside. "Mother? Father? I'm back!" she called out, taking off her long coat.

"In the kitchen!" her mother's voice echoed from the other room.

"Ready?" Evelyn glanced at Lawrence, who suddenly appeared somber.

"Yes," he said and followed her to the kitchen.

"Evelyn, could you help me with the vegetables— Oh! Lawrence, what are you doing here?" Clara nearly dropped the spoon she was holding.

"Good evening, Mrs. Foster," Lawrence said. "I'm here to speak to your husband, if that's alright."

"It's fine, I suppose," she said, eyeing him. "Is everything alright with your family?"

"Yes, we are all keeping well."

"Leroy is in his study. Let me walk you back there." She turned to Evelyn. "As I was saying, can you help me with the vegetables? Rinse them, and peel those potatoes, please."

"Certainly," Evelyn said and walked to the counter, trying to keep her composure.

A few minutes later, her mother returned, coming immediately to her side. "Why is he here and, more importantly, *why* were you with him?" Clara whispered.

"Mother." Evelyn put down the potato peeler. "Lawrence and I are together."

"Together? How?"

"He's asking Father for my hand."

"What!" her mother nearly shouted, her face flushed red with shock.

Voices from Leroy's study grew louder, and the women looked at the kitchen door.

"I must go back there," Clara said.

Evelyn followed her mother to the study to find her father and Lawrence shouting.

"You heard me, Lawrence Thayer. You do *not* have my

blessing or my permission to marry my daughter!" her father roared.

"Sir, I understand your position. All I'm asking for is a chance to prove to you how much I love her. I promise to take care of her. And I want this argument between my father and yourself to end so our families can learn how to live side by side in peace. I do not agree with how determined he is to prove something that may not exist."

"It *doesn't* exist!" Leroy seethed. "And I appreciate your position with the land dispute, but it doesn't change my mind!"

Evelyn pushed past her mother, bursting into the room. "Father, would you please lower your voice? Listen to me. I love Lawrence. And I will marry him whether you approve or not. I don't actually need your permission. I'm of age." She held her head high as Leroy came toward her.

Clara lurched forward to stand between her daughter and husband, who'd become enraged.

"Darling, take a breath." Her mother let out a nervous laugh. "She's in love. People in love are known for making poor decisions. He's leaving tomorrow for service, and that will be the end of it, along with any marriage discussion."

"It won't end. I'm marrying him when he comes back!" Evelyn knew her yelling would only make the situation worse, but she couldn't help it. She loved Lawrence Thayer more than she could describe. Nothing would stop her.

"I need a moment with my wife. Please leave this room. The both of you!" Leroy shook his fist. "And, Lawrence, see yourself out immediately!"

Evelyn led Lawrence to the parlor, and her father slammed the door behind them. Her parents' muffled voices went back and forth as she and Lawrence stood in silence.

"They're just surprised with this news," she told him as she paced the room.

"Yes, but did you see the look on your father's face? Pure hatred. He will never approve of us being together."

Tear suddenly blurred her vision. "What are you saying?"

"I'm not saying anything," Lawrence said, coming closer when he saw she was upset. "I just don't know what to do. And when my father confronts him tomorrow, things will get even worse between our families."

"Listen, you better go before he comes out of his study and sees you still here. I'll talk to him. Don't give up hope." She fell into his open arms and let him hold her tight. For a moment, all was well.

"I won't give up, my love," he said and then slipped out the door.

She crept closer to the study, her parents' voices barely comprehensible.

"Tommy found something up on the mountain," her father said as she leaned her ear next to the door. "Which could ruin everything."

Ruin everything? Evelyn continued listening.

"You know that old man was confused a lot," Clara said. "Besides, he's gone now."

"Bobby won't let it go, and now our daughter wants to marry into that family. Has she gone mad?"

"It'll pass. Thankfully he's getting called to service. And don't worry about Bobby Thayer. Nothing will stop this resort from opening. The town clerk has clearly specified the boundary lines and is on our side."

A bang on the desk made Evelyn jerk back. She moved away from the door and returned to the parlor before one of them came out. Fierce determination rose up in her. She was marrying Lawrence whether they liked it or not.

———

Present Day

FOR THE FIRST HALF OF THE DRIVE, NEITHER MILLIE nor Luke said another word. Millie kept one hand on the steering wheel and nervously flicked through the radio to fill the silence, settling on a familiar Christmas tune. Luke stared straight ahead, appearing lost in his thoughts.

"Well, this is awkward," she finally said, casting him a side smile.

A grin broke out on his face. "I'm sorry. My mind is going one hundred miles per hour thinking about so many things."

"Mine is racing right alongside yours."

Luke pointed ahead. "Actually, take this next road on the left. I want you to see the view of Alpine Mountain from up there. It'll only add ten minutes to the drive."

The landscape on the sides of the road quickly thickened with tall evergreens winding upward in every direction while Millie gripped the wheel. "Is the road getting smaller?"

"It seems that way, but in a few minutes you'll see a clearing and a lookout spot to park. Do you have your camera?"

"Always." She nodded toward the bag near his feet.

When she made one more wide turn, the trees thinned out just as Luke had told her.

"Easy now, the road does get a little narrow here. You'll park right up there where that wooden sign is."

"There's a parking lot on the side of the mountain?" Her stomach flip-flopped as she looked at how high they were.

Luke put his arm around the back of her seat. "I better hang on. New Vermont driver here," he teased. She rolled her eyes. "Okay, here we are. See? A parking space."

Millie slowed and noticed about five spots. Only one other car was parked in front of it, the passengers standing outside enjoying the view. Once she'd parked, she was able to take a good look and gasped as she got out.

"Here you go," Luke said, holding out her camera after he closed his door.

Without looking at him, she reached for it, completely mesmerized by the breathtaking vista before her—Alpine Mountain's terrain and all its slopes in perfect view. She turned on her camera, adjusted the settings, and fired away. Lowering the camera a few minutes later, she couldn't stop staring. In the distance, more rugged peaks capped with a thick layer of winter's white blanket rolled on behind Alpine Mountain, stretching out as far as the eye could see.

"Look at the size of those mountains." Millie held up her camera again and zoomed in. She wasn't sure she could get a photo that would compare to the majesty of what she was witnessing in person.

The sun moved out from behind a cloud, lighting up the landscape.

Luke came closer to her. "I stand out here sometimes to think."

"I feel so tiny and insignificant in the face of such natural beauty," she said.

"You're not insignificant to me," he said.

She turned to face him. The other people got back in their car and left, leaving the two of them alone with the mountains.

"I still feel really bad for how fast I blew up at you," Luke said quietly.

"It's okay," she said and broke their gaze, looking at the view again. "I mean, look at that mountain. Alpine Ridge centers around such beauty, so I can truly understand why you love it so much and why you're so determined to protect it. I wish I'd known all I do now before I took this job." She caught his gaze again and shifted backward. She could feel him closing in, and she wanted to let go and embrace him, but everything still seemed so jumbled together and messy. The pitch and what would happen with Alpine Mountain stood between them, but what was really holding her back was the knowledge that she was going back to South Carolina soon and didn't know what was next for her.

"How could you have known the deep, dark secrets of this town? And you were right before. You were just doing your job. I respect that, and I can see why they hired a photographer as skilled as you. You've maintained your professionalism as best you could through all the drama."

A breeze caught some of her curls and he brushed them away from her face.

She couldn't do this and took another step back.

"Luke, they hired me thinking I had experience. If it weren't for Ashley, I wouldn't have been considered. The truth is, I've spent the last four years wasting time, too afraid to move forward. The camera was like a hiding spot for me and as we stand here next to this stunning view, I can't even give you a solid reason as to why I've been so stagnant." *Besides trying to push away years of judgment by my parents.* "This is my very first paid job as a photographer."

"So?"

His immediate response surprised her.

"It's not like being a professional photographer is easy. I imagine there's massive competition, and it takes time to build a reputation. Experience or not, you were hired and you did the job with everything you've got. I've watched you this whole time working extremely hard and never once would I have guessed this was your first job."

"Really?"

"Absolutely. You're made for this career." Luke gestured to the car. "I could stand out here with you for hours, but we better get to Bruce."

Millie walked to the driver's side, still in awe. For the past few days, she'd felt bad about leaving her mom that message. After hearing Luke, the guilt finally released.

———

Bruce was waiting for them by the front desk when they arrived. "Hey, Luke. Glad you could join Millie. The three pictures I got are pretty interesting."

They followed him to the room Millie had been in the other day.

"Wow. Is that your work?" Luke asked her, standing close to one of the large prints already framed and leaning against the cabinet.

"She's amazing, isn't she?" Bruce stood next to him. "How do you like the frame? The company express-mailed it to me in forty-eight hours." He glanced back at Millie.

"It's perfect. The Clarkes will love it." She smiled at Luke when he turned around. "Thanks for the compliment."

"Are you kidding me with those shots?" Luke came closer and whispered in her ear. "And you think you're an amateur? Please." He rolled his eyes. "Okay, Bruce. What have you got?"

The envelopes were already on the table, and Bruce quickly put on his gloves and retrieved two more pairs from a drawer behind him. "You'll need these to bring the photos closer." He pulled out the first one. "This one here is of some birch trees, which at first I thought nothing of. We have thousands of those. Then I was able to get this other one mostly printed." He pulled out the next photo. "As you can see, there are a few blotches. I'm guessing the birch trees must have been in the same area as that first picture, but now I'm looking at cleared slopes."

"Which means that's Alpine Mountain for sure," Luke

said, picking up one of the pictures. "To see it back then is fun."

"Yeah, well, here's where it gets interesting." Bruce slowly pulled out the last picture and handed it to Millie.

At first glance, the image was unclear to her. She got out her phone and shone the spotlight on it, drawing it closer. "It looks like . . ." She squinted. "A picture of a document."

"Look closer." Bruce handed her a magnifying glass. "Read the top of the document. You can just make it out."

"Martin Farm, 1804. P. 2," she said.

Luke nearly knocked over a chair coming closer. "Let me see that." Luke carefully took the photo and the magnifying glass. "Could you shine your light again?" He studied the image for a minute while Millie shrugged at Bruce, holding her phone over it.

"Recognize the Martin name?" Bruce asked.

Luke placed the photo back on top of the acid-free envelope. "Of course I do. They're my family."

Millie's mouth dropped open. "I don't understand."

"When my family settled in Alpine Ridge, the town had just been chartered. Back in 1794," Luke explained. "My ancestors, John and Abigail Martin, came first. John passed unexpectedly, and Abigail then married Samuel Thayer." Luke looked at the picture again. "I can't believe what I'm looking at." Millie and Bruce stayed silent as he studied the picture. "I need to get the first surveyor's report we have to compare it, even though it's not the deed map we go by today."

"Explain some more," Bruce prompted him. "Because when I saw it, my first hunch was that it looks like an old surveyor's report. Which was why I called Millie right away."

"Wait. If that's what it is, why would a report with your family's name be on a camera in the Clarkes' house?" Millie asked.

"The land fight. Now I understand," Luke mumbled.

"Is that argument still going on?" Bruce asked.

"No," Luke said. "But it started with John Martin and Earl Foster back in 1794, and—"

"Continued for a long time," Millie cut in. "This history is slowly coming together."

"Foster?" Bruce asked.

"Foster is the name of the family that started the resort. Riley's great-grandmother, Evelyn, was a Foster before she married into the Clarke family. As the oldest daughter, she inherited all the property," Luke explained.

"Does Evelyn happen to be her?" Bruce pulled out the photo he'd shown to Millie of the woman twirling in the green-plaid skirt.

Luke took the picture and stared at it for a moment. "You know, I really don't know. But there's a strong chance it is, which explains how that document is on this camera."

"Oh, wait. Isn't there that rumor that Evelyn dated your great-uncle? But he died in World War II, so they never got married?" Bruce asked.

"Exactly. And I remember my grandparents saying he loved photography. This must be his camera."

"So why would it be in the Clarkes' grandfather clock?" Millie asked.

"I don't know, but we need to find that document. If he took a picture of it, then there's a chance it's still around here somewhere." Luke took off his gloves.

"Wait, what would this old surveyor report tell us if we find it?" Millie asked.

"That Riley's hunch was right. That my family owns part of Alpine Ski Resort. We can't let Peak Holdings buy it."

"The Clarkes are selling to a *corporation*?" Bruce asked. "That won't fare well for the Alpine Ridge community."

"No, it's won't," Luke said. "Bruce, I'd like to take this photo."

"It's all yours," Bruce said and placed it back in the protective envelope before handing it to Luke along with more gloves. "Wear those when you handle it. And I'll call you immediately once I get this last photo printed. The rest are damaged. I'm going to finish it now. It'll probably take me about an hour or two."

Millie left right behind Luke who was practically running to the car. "Luke, wait. How will we find this document?"

"If the camera was at the Clarkes' house, then the document must be too."

"Okay, but why would it be there?" Millie turned on the car and cranked up the heat.

"According to Riley, one of the entries in Evelyn's diary that she was trying to show me was all about how her father had been hiding that second page of the original surveyor report that clearly defines the property lines."

"I don't think I asked before, but where did Riley find this diary? How did her parents not see it before?"

"I guess it was in her room, which she thought must have been Evelyn's old room. She found it in her closet when she was cleaning it out one day. She told me there was so much stuff stashed in there for so long that her parents simply didn't know it was in there. They really had no reason to go in the closet to begin with, so it was just sitting there . . . for over sixty years."

Millie nodded, remembering when Joyce had been cleaning out another closet the day she found the camera and couldn't believe the amount of stuff they'd collected over the years. "Well, I suppose homes as old as theirs in the same family can have a lot of things go missing or stay hidden." She put the car in reverse, but stopped in confusion. "What copy does your family have of the surveyor report?"

"We have a copy of the supposed first page that my family has held on to for centuries. I don't even know why we still have it because, like I said inside, it's not the deed map we go by today. What if the deed map we have today was forged somehow?"

"What do you mean?"

"What if the Foster family somehow created a fake one and the town never knew?" Luke said, glancing at her. "Just like Riley was trying to tell me."

"So before that flood, your family was aware of what part of that mountain they owned?" She started to back up again.

"That's been the rumor, but it's also confusing. I think since it's been so long, my grandparents and parents eventually gave up on ever solving the mystery, especially since we never found page two of that first surveyor's report. But Riley was trying to reopen the case. She told me right before our conversation got heated that, according to Evelyn's diary entry, her great-great-grandfather, Leroy Foster, committed fraud, stealing the land after the flood by changing the deed map. And she wanted to dig further into it with me and go on what I thought was a wild goose chase to find the report. I should have listened to her."

"We need to talk to the Clarkes." Millie felt her pulse speed up with all this new information as she drove back to Alpine Ridge.

"That's exactly what we're going to do, and we'll start by showing them this photo."

Chapter Twenty-Five

Late Evening, November 15, 1940
Evelyn

After hours of tossing and turning, Evelyn still couldn't sleep. She'd spent the better half of the evening trying to reason with her father while her mother finished preparing dinner. Nothing made him budge. As she was above the age of twenty-one, she could marry Lawrence without his blessing, but the idea of that broke her heart. She'd dreamed since she was a little girl about her father walking her down the aisle.

She tossed off the covers and quietly made her way downstairs to get something to drink. The house was dead silent and after she heated up some milk, she took her glass and wandered around the dark house until she found herself outside the study. A room neither she nor her mother ever went in, other than to find her father or clean it. When he was in there, her father expected not to be bothered.

Without thinking, she crept inside. A chill ran through her and she looked back, half expecting to see him behind her.

This was *his* study and he'd made that clear. Hesitating, she debated turning around, but her frustration led the way and she clicked on a tall lamp next to the large wooden secretary desk where he kept all his filings and books.

She opened the top glass doors and aimlessly pulled out books, finding nothing interesting. She closed the doors, then tugged at the heavy slanted lids under the shelves and was surprised when they opened. All the times she'd dusted this piece, it had been locked. She remembered the loud bang she'd heard earlier and realized he must have been closing the lids a little too fast and forgot to lock them in his fury.

While she knew she had no business snooping, she couldn't stop herself. At first, she found nothing in the shelves except cigars, bills, and pens. She shook her head, feeling silly. She was about to shut the lids again and click off the lamp when her hand brushed against something unusual. The brass pieces placed on either side of the drawers jiggled. Weren't they just decoration?

"That's strange." Moving her hands over one side with the brass again, she grasped it and pulled out a long rectangular secret compartment that contained two small box drawers inside. She pulled out the first box and found various items, such as jewelry and some cash, and the second one held a wooden box. Her curiosity overtook her and she picked it up, only to be disappointed to discover it was locked.

Glancing up, she saw her father's overcoat hanging on the coat rack in the corner. "I don't know if I'm that lucky, but let's see," she whispered and got up. When she reached inside the first pocket, it was empty, but when she stuck her hand in the other one, she pulled out a set of keys. "It can't be."

Listening at the door for movement, she heard nothing but silence, which gave her the courage to hurry back over to the box.. The third key was the one. The box popped open and a handful of papers were folded inside. She brought them under the light on her father's desk and flipped through them. Halfway through, she was about to give up and put the papers back in the box when the last one halted her. *Martin Farm, 1804 P. 2.*

"Oh, my." Evelyn covered her mouth.

It was the second part of that surveyor report that Mr. Thayer had been on about for years. The document then gave clear instructions about the second rock wall on Alpine Mountain with the birch trees. It even described the wall that had the stream alongside it and how that was the second marker for the Thayer property, but that their land did indeed stretch in between both rock walls. If that was the case, the wall with the birch trees crossed right into their new ski resort.

Evelyn glanced at the door, trying to understand. "Father had it this whole time?"

She returned the stack of papers and closed the box, locked it, and put it back in the secret compartment, but she kept the report in her hand. When morning came, she would march up to her father and demand answers. There was no way she would sleep now. Instead, she went to make herself some tea and wait until morning.

Hours later, while she rested her eyes in the parlor, the first rays of dawn appeared over the horizon, awakening her. It was morning and time to face her parents. She stood and halted when she saw Lawrence outside the window. He was sitting on her porch with his back toward her.

She opened the door and ran across the porch. "Lawrence, how long have you been here?"

"Since well before sunrise." He stood up. "I was waiting to see you."

"But Father—"

"I don't care. I'm leaving today, and I had to come say goodbye."

Suddenly she remembered the document. "I'm glad you did. Come inside, I need to show you something."

When she handed the report to him, Lawrence didn't say anything for a long while. "Where did you find this?"

"In Father's secretary desk, in a hidden compartment. Lawrence, do you know what this means?"

"That my father was right all this time."

"Then it's settled. There's no reason to continue this war between our families. Let's go wake my father—" A tug at her arm startled her.

"Evelyn, wait." Lawrence glanced behind her. "Let's think this through before your parents wake up. I'm leaving in two hours."

"So? What does that matter?"

"Let's keep this to ourselves until I get back."

"Why would we do that? Father committed fraud by keeping this document hidden, and I intend to get to the bottom of it."

"And put him in jail?" Lawrence sighed. "That won't solve anything. When I return, I am going to marry you. We will reveal this document then, but only in the privacy of our families, and then when we're married, I'll take over Alpine Ski Resort with you. It'll be fair to both families then, since the resort was built on part of our land."

"That's silly. The resort shouldn't open at all. Our parents need to sort this out properly, with lawyers."

"Evelyn, we're both going to inherit our parents' land anyway. If I take over the resort alongside you, our families can finally come together, especially if we don't report what your father did. Stopping Alpine Ski Resort from opening would only make things uglier."

Evelyn understood then. "I see. Okay then, I'll hide it. You won't be gone long anyway."

"If I'm called in, I'll be away a year at most. We'll sort this out when I return."

"Father won't be expecting anyone to have discovered the document. He thinks it's hidden still. But I'll hide it somewhere new in case he moves it or destroys it." Evelyn looked around the room. "I know. Upstairs inside our grandfather clock, behind the face. No one would ever find it there."

"Good idea. And I wanted to give you my camera to hang on to while I'm gone." He held it out to her along with two rolls of film, just as footsteps sounded above. "Take good care of them. There are special pictures on those rolls." He leaned in and kissed her hard. "I love you. See you soon."

When he walked away, she watched him for a minute before more footsteps caught her attention. She closed the door and went up the back stairs and through her father's study to the clock, while the footsteps went down the main stairs. She flicked on the hall lights.

Without any idea of how to properly work it, she held up Lawrence's camera and took a photo of the page for extra proof that she had found it. Then she carefully, and as quickly as she could, reached up for the hood and lifted it off the clock, exposing the face and the gears behind it. Since it wasn't working, the gears were still and she refolded the paper, and quickly tucked the document inside them, then snapped one more photo of it hidden there. One of her sisters stirred in the bedroom behind her. Out of time, she placed the camera and film rolls inside the bottom of the case. Lawrence would be back before she knew it, and everything would work out.

———

Present Day

Joyce turned from the counter holding two mugs and placed them in front of Luke and Millie. "Dylan won't be back home for a while. I tried to call him and it went to voicemail. Let me see the picture again." She sat down at the table with them.

"Thank you," Luke picked up his mug and slid the picture to her.

Joyce put the gloves back on and studied it in silence. "I just can't believe this," she said and glanced up at Millie. "When you found that camera and the rolls of film in the clock, I didn't think anything of it. I thought it would turn out to be some old pictures of the town or house, but this?"

"It's pretty incredible," Millie said.

"I knew the clock hadn't been worked on or working at all since before the 1927 flood. I'll need to check with Dylan, but I don't think it was working properly when he was a kid either. We've just kept the glass cleaned and the outside dusted. If we'd had it serviced to make it run again, we would have found all of this and fixed this centuries-old land fight years ago." Joyce shook her head, lowering the picture. "We need lawyers."

"Hold on. I haven't even shown my parents yet. We came straight to you," Luke said. "Let's not jump into things. Dylan needs to see it too."

"And you all need the original document," Millie pointed out.

They both looked at her.

"She's right," Joyce said. "If it's still around. It could be anywhere in this house."

"Riley had mentioned a diary entry to Luke. Did you ever find the diary?" Millie asked.

Joyce shook her head. "We searched for weeks. I have no idea where Riley stored it."

"I'm not sure that would point us to where the surveyor's

report is anyway. Who knows if Evelyn spelled it out in her diary—or said that this camera was in the clock. All she said was that her great-grandmother mentioned land fraud had taken place. Riley would have already had the report and showed me that day we spoke if the entry had more information than that." Luke sat back, holding his mug.

"That's true," Joyce said. "Which brings us back to square one."

Millie's phone buzzed in her purse. "It's Bruce." She accepted the call and put him on speaker. "Hi, Bruce, I have you on speaker. Joyce Clarke is with us too."

"Are you at the Clarkes' house?" Bruce's voice echoed loudly through the speakers.

"Yes, they're here," Joyce said.

"It's in the clock."

"What do you mean?" Luke asked.

"The second page of the surveyor report. I went to work on developing that last photo immediately after you left. I just finished, and that's what I saw in the image. Take the hood off the face of the clock and look in the gears behind it."

"Thank you, Bruce!" Millie ended the call and the three of them ran up the stairs.

Joyce lifted the hood off and looked behind the face of the clock in the gears. "I don't see . . . wait." She reached for something, and her eyes opened wide as she pulled out an old, folded-up document. Opening it, she read it through and then turned it around to face Luke with pure shock on her face. "It's the second page of the original report."

CHAPTER TWENTY-SIX

A knock on the door of her suite made Millie stop applying her makeup. The eighty-fifth anniversary party was starting in thirty minutes and she had to hurry.

"Coming!"

Millie opened the door and saw Ashley wearing a long black dress, with a red necklace and matching shade on her lips. Her hair was pulled back and pinned to the side, falling in front of her shoulder.

"Wow! You look gorgeous."

"I could say the same but even more about you! Dark green suits you!"

Millie did a little twirl in her short, dark green cocktail dress, her silver jewelry sparkling.

She and Ashley had gone shopping after the pitch was canceled. They'd worked off the stress of it all with some retail therapy and searched for new dresses.

It had been a very busy four days since the discovery of the original surveyor's report. Joyce and Luke had showed the document to Dylan and Luke's parents, who then contacted their lawyers. Ashley came to Millie's suite on Wednesday while the families were meeting with their attorneys. To distract themselves, the friends headed to a nearby mall. The meeting went on for hours, and Ashley kept nervously checking her phone. They weren't sure what would come of it or the party, but they decided to shop for outfits anyway.

"I'm so glad we got these dresses. I didn't pack anything appropriate for this event," Millie said and went back to finish her makeup.

Ashley sat on the foot of her bed. "I know you're giving them the smaller ones from the photo albums tomorrow, but where are the large prints for Dylan and Joyce that you're presenting tonight?"

"I have them stored behind the ballroom, ready to come out when the Clarkes make their speech. That is, if there will still be one. I haven't exactly thought this through."

"Neither have I." Ashley watched Millie apply the finishing touches to her blush. "I don't know what kind of speech they'll give now, but the party is still on, and the right opportunity to give them the pictures will happen at some point."

Millie gave her friend an apologetic look through the mirror. "I'm sorry you never got to show off that amazing presentation after all your hard work."

"Who said I still can't?"

Ashley's sly smile made Millie turn around.

"What do you mean?"

"My lips are sealed. You'll have to wait and see."

Millie studied her for a moment and turned back to the mirror. "Okay . . ."

"How was dinner with Luke last night?" Ashley asked, changing subject.

Millie looked in her small mirror and laughed at her friend's huge grin. "It was amazing as always."

"Did he mention anything new about the resort?"

"He said it'll be a long road sorting it out with the lawyers, but that there had been no fights between his family and the Clarkes so far. The good news is that the sale remains off the table."

"I talked to Joyce yesterday, privately," Ashley said.

"Oh, yeah? What did she say?"

"That she's relieved. On so many levels. She's happy they aren't selling the resort, and she's happy this crazy land fight is finally coming to a close and that the future of Alpine Ski Resort will hopefully be handed over to the Thayers."

"Do you think they'll sell their share to Luke's family?" That had been what the lawyers were trying to figure out because it was the option Brandon Thayer had immediately requested. "I know they were counting on using the money from the sale for their fresh start. If they sell to the Thayers, hopefully that can still happen."

"I hope so." Ashley smiled when Millie turned. "Beautiful!"

"I hope so too. Luke told me they're still moving. It's like they'll just disappear from the town."

"Yeah. I wish they didn't feel the need to do that," Ashley said as another knock came at the door. "Who could that be?"

"No idea," Millie said. Both women got up, and she opened the door. "Mom? Dad?"

"We heard there was a big party tonight," her dad said, leaning in to kiss her cheek before he walked past her and into the suite.

"Yes . . ." Millie eyed him, ignoring the joke. "Why are you two here?"

"Four!" Lila came through the door with Jake behind her rolling in a suitcase. "What time does this party start? I need to change into my dress!"

"Lila?" Millie laughed at her sister's excited expression as she silently stood, taking in the suite.

"*This* is where you've been staying? *Wow!*" Lila pointed to the deck off the living room. "Jake, let's go look at the view before the sun sets."

"I'll meet you in the lobby," Ashley said, then looked at Millie's parents after Lila and Jake went outside. "Nice to see you again, Mr. and Mrs. Rowan."

"You, too, Ashley. See you in a bit," Mrs. Rowan said, looking at Millie. "Can we talk to you?"

"I guess so, but I only have a few minutes." Millie led them to the couch and they all sat down. "How did you know about the party tonight?"

"Lila," her dad said, nodding toward the deck. "But we didn't come for that."

"I would hope not, since that'd be a little odd." Millie crossed her arms, already feeling her defenses rise.

"I'm officially frozen," Jake said when he and Lila came back inside. "But this resort is stunning."

"Jake and I are going to go get changed in the bedroom. We both came right from the hospital." Lila paused and smiled at them. "This is good to see—us all together on a little vacation. Have a nice talk."

When her sister and Jake disappeared into the bedroom, Millie turned to her parents.

"What made you come then?" Millie looked at her mom first, especially since she was the one Millie had left the voicemail with.

"Millie, when I got your voicemail the other day . . . I'll be honest. I was mad at first," her mom said

Her dad snorted. "Mad? She was livid," he said.

"Okay, yes, but I didn't understand. I spent days going over it in my mind and out loud with your father. I couldn't figure out how you could say that to me. I reasoned with myself that we had given you everything, raised you well. But then—"

"Then she finally listened to Lila. We both did." Her dad reached over and placed his hand on Millie's knee. "When you got this job, I was proud of you, even though I didn't say it, which I should have done before you landed this opportunity. I was also relieved that you were finally stepping into this career that you'd insisted on for so long. Then when I heard that voicemail you left your mother and realized how happy you were doing what you love, I was first to accept how wrong we've been in the way we've treated you."

"You two have been nonstop judgmental, criticizing me every chance you had since I was fifteen years old. Never supporting me." She looked at her parents and felt stronger by the second as she let out years of pent-up emotion. "But I've done a lot of soul-searching while I've been here, and I've come alive in my work. I know now that I don't need you to agree with what I do. I just wish I had realized that sooner."

"No, you don't need our approval to do what you love," her mom admitted. "Hearing you stand firm made me proud too, after I let my hurt out. I finally understood, Millie, and it hit me all at once how critical I've been." Tears brimmed in her eyes. "Lila laid it out for me and explained how much we've always compared you to her, always made you feel like you didn't measure up. There's no excuse for that. We were worried you wouldn't be able to sustain yourself as a photographer. We thought we were doing the right thing, pushing you toward a career that had more security. But we closed our eyes to what made you happy, and that was wrong."

"Your mom's right. After listening to how confident you sounded in that voicemail, and now, my worry has faded. I know you'll be okay." Her dad moved closer and opened his arms. "Do you forgive us?"

Millie didn't move for a second as she looked into his eyes.

When he smiled at her the endearing way he sometimes had when she was growing up, she relented.

"Of course I do." She hugged both of them. "You could have just called me and saved yourselves a long trip."

"Well, yes, but I finally looked this place up online and had to book a room immediately. I just had to come see it." Her mother kept her arm around her.

"So did we," Lila said as she emerged from the bedroom. "Jake and I told the hospital we needed to leave town for a family emergency."

Her sister was wearing a simple long, red dress, which stood out against her natural beauty.

"Gorgeous!" Millie said. "I can't believe you lied to your work."

Jake came out of the room in a black suit, waving his hand. "Eh, doesn't matter. We both needed a break after all the double shifts we've been doing."

"We're staying for three nights," Mom said. "Want to extend your trip instead of leaving tomorrow? We're heading back Christmas Eve morning. Your father and I can have some much-needed family time with you girls—and Jake, of course."

"Sounds like a plan!" Millie stood and picked up her camera. "Go on. Get yourselves ready and then I'll introduce you to Alpine Ridge."

———

ASHLEY WAS WAITING FOR HER BY THE FIREPLACE when they all got to the lobby, and her face lit up when she saw Millie's relaxed expression.

"My parents and sister and her fiancé are attending with us. Has it started?" Millie asked.

"I hear the DJ, so I'd say that's a yes." Ashley looked at

Millie's family. "So happy you are all joining us. Right this way to the ballroom."

"A ballroom in a ski resort?" Her dad raised his brows. "How fancy."

"Well, it was added in 1997 after couples kept asking to get married here. We throw lots of parties too," Ashley explained.

They walked down a long hallway until they reached double doors, the music blasting through the wall. Millie pushed open the doors, and her eyes widened at how the room had been transformed into a festive, icy haven. With her camera in hand, she didn't even know where to start.

The soft glow of twinkling blue lights set the tone for an unforgettable night and anniversary celebration. Towering white Christmas trees, their lights sparkling like icicles, lined the walls, drooping over as if to hug the room. The ceiling was draped in soft, frosty-blue material, creating a sense of depth that added an elegant feel. The air was filled with the sweet scents of pine and peppermint, evoking the crisp, refreshing air of a winter's day on the slopes. Floor-to-ceiling windows made the whole ballroom appear as if it were floating on the mountain, and Millie made a mental note to come back during the day to check out the view in sunlight.

Ashley led Millie's parents to the bar, while Millie adjusted the settings on her camera for the darker lighting, trying to find the right one when a tap on her shoulder pulled her attention away.

"Care for a dance?" Luke said, holding out his hand.

"Now?" Millie looked at the empty dance floor. "No one is dancing."

"Then let's start the trend." Without another word, Luke took her camera, walked to where Ashley was waiting by the bar, and handed it to her. "Millie needs some pictures of herself for once, especially with how beautiful she is tonight."

"On it!" Ashley took the camera and followed as Luke led Millie to the dance floor.

The loud hum of jazz music floated through the air, mingling with the sounds of laughter and chatter. The lights cast a hypnotic glow over the dance floor as he circled her around.

They began to sway, and she giggled when he dipped her low, while Ashley took as many pictures as she could from the side.

"Smile," he said, and they both turned to Ashley.

When he moved her again, it was slow, and she wrapped her arms around his neck.

"My parents are here." As if that would stop him. "So are my sister and her fiancé. They are probably all watching."

"Then I better meet them after I do this."

Luke slowed her to a full stop, and she stared deeply into his eyes, the same blue as the magical lighting. His lips found hers in a tender yet fiery kiss that left them both breathless. The music swirled around them, a lively beat that seemed to match the rhythm of her heart. The blue ceiling twinkled like diamonds when they finally parted.

"I'm falling for you, Millie Rowan. I don't think I can let you go back to South Carolina." His tone was teasing, but it was clear he still meant what he'd said.

They continued to sway a little longer, lost in their own world amid the icy winter wonderland. When they were done, he led her off the dance floor as half the town watched them in delight.

Irene came over and threw her arms around both of them. "I knew it!"

Millie laughed as her parents approached them, eyeing Luke with curiosity. "Mom, Dad, meet Luke Thayer."

"Well, hello there," her mom said, and her eyes popped when she snuck a glance at Millie, mouthing, "*Wow.*"

"Come on. Let's go have a drink and we can get to know this new friend of yours," her dad said, and they made their way to the bar where Lila and Jake stood waiting to meet the mystery man too.

"Millie Rowan?" a male voice behind her said.

"Yes?" Millie turned around.

"My name is Scott Campbell. I'm the senior editor for *The Vermont Heritage*."

"Hello," Millie said, shaking his hand as Luke continued to the bar with her parents.

"I'm a friend of Bruce's, the owner of Green Mountain Photo. I'd like to talk to you about a job opening we have for a photographer. Bruce showed me some of your work, and we're very interested."

Millie couldn't believe it and glanced at Luke, who came back and handed her a glass of wine, beaming.

"I'd love to talk to you."

Scott pulled out his phone. "I'll store your number and give you a call Monday."

"Sounds great." Millie rattled off her number as the music quieted, and Dylan and Joyce came to the middle of the dance floor holding microphones.

"Thank you, everyone, for attending tonight's special event, Alpine Ski Resort's eighty-fifth anniversary celebration!" Dylan said as the room clapped and cheered. "I could go on and on about this amazing town, but you already know that, right?"

The crowd applauded again.

"Let's just have a little recap anyway, shall we? Millie, where are you?" Dylan scanned the crowd.

Luke gently nudged her forward. "She's hiding over here!" he called.

"Come on over here, Millie!" Joyce waved her over. "You, too, Ashley." The two women made their way to the Clarkes.

"All of you know this special lady by now." Dylan pointed to Millie. "She's been taking photos in town for three weeks and to say she's talented is an understatement. How about we all watch her work on screen in this slide show that my incredible marketing director, Ashley, and her team, put together with Millie's pictures and videos."

Ashley took the microphone from Dylan. "Enjoy, everyone! Millie brought this town alive, and we wanted you all to have a chance to appreciate her work. We present to you *Alpine Ridge: Christmas in Focus*." She looked at Millie and lowered the microphone. "See? The presentation didn't go to waste."

Everyone grew silent and for the next ten minutes they watched as the screen moved through the photos and played Ashley's voice-over, describing the images with Millie's words. Her videos were intertwined and timed perfectly, some making the crowd laugh, especially the footage showing how cold Millie was outside during her first shoot by the slopes. By the end, there was not a dry eye in the room.

Dylan took the microphone again. "And that is the Alpine Ridge we all know and love. Alpine Ski Resort would not be what it is without this town and all of you. Which is why I'm happy to announce that while Joyce and I are still moving to take time for ourselves, we are not selling our house."

More cheers went up around the ballroom as Millie glanced at Ashley, who seemed just as surprised as she was at this information.

"Brandon, come on up," Dylan called.

Mr. Thayer made his way over and shook Dylan's hand, then leaned into the mic. "Good evening, everyone."

Dylan grinned at the audience. "Instead, our house will be turned into a museum. The details are still being worked out by"—he pointed to Brandon—"the Thayer family, who will have much to share soon with their new involvement with the resort. Yes, everyone . . . the feud is officially over."

A trickle of laughter filled the room, followed by an eruption of more cheering and whistling, indicating that the residents were clearly happy with this news.

Dylan smiled. "So let's all celebrate this night together!"

Ashley turned to Millie and leaned in, whispering, "The gift," before walking over to the men. "Now wait just a minute," Ashley interrupted, nodding to a staff member near the dance floor who then disappeared into the back. "We're not done yet, Dylan."

"We're not?" Dylan asked.

"Nope. Millie, care to explain?"

Millie took the mic. "Before we all continue with this wonderful evening, I wanted to extend my thanks for being chosen to do this job."

The employee came back out holding one of the prints, followed by Bruce holding another, and two others on staff holding the rest. When they presented the four framed photos, gasps sounded from some of the audience that were closest.

Joyce, who had been in the front of the crowd, cupped her face, getting closer to the pictures as she joined everyone in the center of the dancefloor. "Millie, you didn't."

"I did. Since you're moving out of the estate, I figured you could take some of it with you to your new home."

The Clarkes hugged Millie, followed by more applause. The music started again, and Luke came over and scooped her up.

"Congratulations on a possible job here in Vermont!" He held her tight. "Looks like I don't have to kidnap you after all."

"I can't believe it!" She laughed as he spun her. "I was seriously considering dropping everything in Charleston and moving into a tent up here."

Luke gave her a playful look. "Oh, I'd have at least found a camper somewhere for you."

They stopped spinning and she gazed up at him, then he gently kissed her forehead. Once again, with Millie's camera in hand, Ashley captured the tender moment.

The camera that was once a barrier between Millie and her emotions had become the lens of a raw and candid picture of her opened heart radiating confidence for her next shot at whatever life brought her.

EPILOGUE
CHRISTMAS EVE, TWO YEARS LATER

"That was my third time photographing around Stowe, and it's still like I'm seeing it for the first time. It's so beautiful up there," Millie said when she plopped herself on the couch after the long drive back to Alpine Ridge.

For the first year after *The Vermont Heritage* offered her a full-time position as one of their travel photographers for the state, Millie had moved into Ashley's apartment. However, the previous Christmas, Luke had asked her to move into his estate with him after his parents officially handed it down . . . and their relationship grew more serious.

"That's more times in Stowe than me," Luke said. "I've only been there once, and I don't blame you. I still remember how stunning and picturesque that town was."

"It is, but it's not much different from Alpine Ridge in that sense." Millie had lived in town for almost two years and still loved the small-town's charm—and the food.

"That's true. I'll be right back." Luke disappeared into their bedroom.

Millie yawned. "I'll just be here . . . trying not to fall

asleep." The magazine had sent her to cover holiday events the past week, and it was now time to celebrate curled up with Luke, watching Christmas movies and relaxing.

Lila and Jake had their wedding the year before, and after delivering hundreds of babies over the past five years, her sister finally delivered her own right before Halloween—a precious baby boy. Millie and Luke went down to be with her family over Thanksgiving, and her parents informed her that they'd be staying with Lila and the baby for Christmas along with Jake's parents. Since Millie had already traveled to three locations in December alone, and Luke's parents were still in Europe, a nice quiet and cozy Christmas with just the two of them was exactly what she needed.

The past two years had been a whirlwind after she landed the job with the magazine. Millie had gotten to experience every corner of Vermont, multiple times, as she covered various events, happy moments, breathtaking scenery and met so many people. As her talent was shown off with each job, her name had begun to spread, and she was even asked the previous June to take pictures for a piece for *New England Today*, covering the region's most famous summer foods.

She was finally in her element, doing what she loved, and some days it still felt surreal. Her family missed her and it was especially hard being away from Lila now her nephew had been born, but her relationship with Luke had grown deeper as the months passed, filling her with hope and excitement over what was to come for their future together.

"Are you already lying down?" he asked, coming into the living room again.

"Don't tell me you want to go out for dinner. I know it's Christmas Eve, but I'm exhausted," she said when she realized he looked much too dressed up to be on the couch for the evening.

"Too tired to eat?"

"I can always eat, but can't we just order in? I don't want to get back in the car at all for about a week." She was complaining, but it was the holidays, which meant the magazine had so much more to cover that month and had sent her to more locations than usual. Even though the traveling got hard at times, it was what she'd always wanted to do, but it wasn't without a physical cost.

"How about just once more in the car, but it's not far, and then we will come back after and cozy up on the couch."

"After?" Millie sighed. "Okay, I surrender. Where are you taking me?" His wide grin meant he had something up his sleeves. "Actually the better question is, what are you planning?"

"Get up and go put on layers and a big coat. Nothing fancy."

Reluctantly standing, her phone lit up on the table. She saw it was Ashley and took it to the bedroom.

"Do you happen to know what Luke is up to?" Millie asked her when she answered. "I just got home from Stowe and he's making me put on layers."

"Layers?" Ashley tried to sound innocent in her tone, but it wasn't working.

"Just tell me. Does it involve the whole town?" Millie loved the closeness of the community, but tonight she just wanted it to be her and Luke.

"Kind of." Millie groaned. "But! You won't need to put on makeup. Honest!"

"Good because the resort's New Year's Eve celebration will be enough dressing up for this holiday break."

The first year after finding the missing surveyor's report included a lot of lawyers and sorting out of legal matters behind learning that the Thayers did, in fact, own part of Alpine Mountain where the slopes were. Even though Luke and his parents had never interfered with Alpine Ski Resort, the confusion was finally laid to rest. For centuries, the two families sat with questions and rumors over what had happened and what was true, and because the land dispute had gone on for so long over so many generations, there were still some unanswered questions. Like, how exactly did Leroy Foster get away with fraud? The flood of 1927 had wiped away so much of Alpine Ridge that it was the only explanation the lawyers could agree on, and the Clarkes and the Thayers were happy to let those mysteries go. Leroy Foster was long gone, and his illegal actions had been done well before the present day, leaving them just one decision: how to move forward.

After months of preparing new documents, sorting out back taxes, profit and loss over eighty-five years, costs to buy out, and so on, it was finally over one gorgeous fall day nearly a year later in the mediation room. Dylan and Joyce had since moved upstate, but their legacy lived on with the museum. Millie had gone to work helping to take more of the photos from the albums she'd discovered in the library and have Bruce enlarge them to display all over the museum— along with the other prints she'd gifted them during her first visit.

Artifacts, including the old grandfather clock, had been donated by the Clarkes so people could learn all about their beginnings and centuries of history in that house and on the land they shared alongside the Thayers.

Millie and Luke kept in contact with them, hoping one day they'd come back and see all the changes and updates the Thayers had done and still planned to do with the resort. It had been increasing in revenue since the Thayers took over, leaving Luke primarily to run it since his term as chairman was over, and bringing the Clarkes so much happiness to know it was thriving. And while their beloved Riley had long been laid to rest, they left Alpine Ridge with full hearts knowing their story never would be.

"Oh, quit moaning and go with your man," Ashley said. "And call me after."

Millie dressed in layers, throwing on a thick sweater over her long-sleeved shirt and then grabbed her gloves and heavy coat from the front-hall closet and got in the car with Luke. The short drive gave her just enough time to figure out he was taking her toward the town hall.

"Are we going for a stroll or something and grabbing a quick bite in town?" she asked.

But all her reasoning ceased when they got closer to the town hall. Just ahead, the wagon she'd seen on her first full day in Alpine Ridge was completely lit up, like it had been since the parade right before she left for Stowe, but now there was a small table in front of it with a big bouquet of red roses on top, waiting for her.

Next to the wagon was an outdoor screen, turned on and ready for a movie. After parking the car, they got out, and when she got to the roses, she picked them up and brought them to her nose, inhaling their heady fragrance.

"I know, the flowers are quite the cheesy touch, but how could I not with this presentation?"

Millie looked at him. "And what presentation is that?"

"You spend your days capturing the most gorgeous landscapes and unforgettable moments." Luke took her hand and led her up onto the wagon, where they sat before he pulled a thick blanket over them. "But now it's time to turn the lens onto our story." He held up a remote and pressed play before glancing at her again. "Right here, where we first met."

Tears stung her eyes as she remembered that first day when she fell in the snow and he found her by the wagon. He put his arm around her as music began and images of them from the past two years slid by on the screen, along with so many familiar faces of Alpine Ridge. Some were pictures she'd taken, and some were taken by him, but all were special. Each memory frozen on screen, their journey unfolding before them.

Finally, it was over, and the screen went blank for a few seconds, and just as Millie was about to turn to Luke, words appeared.

Millie Rowan, will you be my wife?

The tears that had pooled in her eyes began to fall down her cheeks as Luke slid off the seat and got on his knee, right there in the wagon, and held up a ring.

She could barely speak as she tried to stifle a sob, and quickly nodded before she whispered, "Yes."

When he slid on the ring, she looked up just as his lips met hers. After they broke apart, she cast her eyes down at the ring that shone bright alongside the twinkling lights of the wagon.

"I wish—"

"That someone caught that moment?" Luke turned her chin and there was Ashley, waving at her from behind a camera.

Millie excitedly glanced back at Luke.

"Done. It's your turn to be in full focus," he said.

She gazed into his eyes and reached for his face. "As we capture the rest of our lives . . . together."

Acknowledgments

To all my readers, as always, a heartfelt thank you to each and every one of you. Your enthusiasm and support mean everything to me. From all of your reviews and messages, you keep me going . . . writing well into the late-night hours. I am honored to be a part of your reading journey and have such a wonderful community behind me.

I am forever grateful to Jenny Hale and the team at Harpeth Road Press for their unwavering dedication and continuing to pave the way for my career. Their expertise and tireless efforts have once again brought my work to life and out into the world for all my readers to enjoy.

To my editors: To Elizabeth Mazer for weaving the past and present once again in yet, another heartwarming dual timeline. To Jodi Hughes and Lauren Finger for their meticulous attention to details and finding the plot holes. And finally, to Charlotte Hayes-Clemens for ensuring the story was polished to perfection.

As always, to Kristen Ingebretson for pulling it all together on another visual masterpiece!

A very special thank you to Melinda Elliot of the Historical Society in Southbury, Connecticut. For your exceptional expertise and support by providing me with a wealth of information on the history of Vermont. I am so grateful for not only your insight which has helped me enrich this storyline— but to from someone I've known my entire life.

To my husband Jason, my rock through it all once again.

Your love, as always, fueling the creative spark behind my writing. And reminding me of the very first ski trip we ever took . . . and you tumbling down the mountain on your first try—and how you never gave up. Cheering me on to do the same through the challenges of author life.

A Note from Lindsay

Hello!

Thank you so much for picking up my novel, *Christmas in Focus*. May the spirit of this Vermont Christmas story fill your heart with joy, hope, and a renewed sense of purpose, reminding you that your dreams are always within reach.

If you'd like to know when my next book is out, you can sign up for new Harpeth Road release alerts for my novels here:

www.harpethroad.com/lindsay-gibson-newsletter-signup

I won't share your information with anyone else, and I'll only email you a quick message whenever new books come out or go on sale.

If you did enjoy *Christmas in Focus*, I'd be so thankful if you'd write a review online. Getting feedback from readers helps persuade others to pick up my book for the first time. It's one of the biggest gifts you could give me.

Until next time,
Lindsay

www.ingramcontent.com/pod-product-compliance
Lightning Source LLC
Chambersburg PA
CBHW021235310726
48971CB00006B/1828